MOON CUSSERS

JB Lawrence

Faction
Book
Publishers

ISBN 978-0-9882247-4-2

Published and distributed by
Faction Book Publishers

This may very well be a work of fiction.

The strength of a family,
like the strength of an army,
lies in its loyalty to each other.
– *Mario Puzo*

CHECK IN AT FORT MILES

When the intake office door slammed in Franklin's face before he could even ask for clarity, he wanted to kick it in and show Captain O'Dea a thing or two. Instead he stepped backwards down the two steps, boots crunching on the gravel, and decided that he had been treated worse since joining the Army.

All the same, not exactly how I was told things would pan out for an officer.

After graduating with a bachelor's degree in electrical engineering, Franklin found himself caught in the middle of a difficult situation. The economy was in the tank and jobs were scarce, even for college graduates. His father had long passed away, so as the only child in his family, he was left with the responsibility of not only finding gainful employment but also paying the family bills. With the looming wars around the world, Franklin would never have considered joining the military, but he was too aware of how difficult simple things in life were when all one could think about was eating. Luckily for him, the United States had recently declared war on more of the world than he was familiar with, and, at least for the time being, the Army was a great place for a steady paycheck and three meals a day.

Well, maybe the guys on the front lines are hungry. What with supply chains and all the fighting. But I've got a college education. They wouldn't send me to the front, would they?

Within minutes of his first assignment upon leaving Officer Candidate School, as he stood at the bottom of the intake office steps, he found himself sweating in the direct sunlight. This was a different heat than he had felt amidst the buildings of his home city of Baltimore. Different even than the few times he had visited the small beaches along the Chesapeake Bay. Here, on the coast, the sun seemed hotter and came with a brutal humidity. Nearly noon, the sun was inescapable and hung at the perfect angle to torture any side of him that faced south.

Geez! It's almost like Colonel Carp purposely built his office this way 'cause he knew it would be the most uncomfortable.

The only door to Colonel Carp's office had no awning, and there was no other nearby building or tree that offered any shade. Franklin pulled his hat closer to his eyes and extended the visor's-worth of shade with his hand, surveying as much of Fort Miles as he could. Gulls glided in the distant breezes, over low buildings and treetops that descended a slope, away from the ridgeline of the fort. Franklin knew that at the bottom of that small stretch of trees was the beach.

At least no German or Japanese bombs are blowing up around here. He turned to let the left side of his body and face cool off. *How much can I actually complain? Can't forget J.D. assigned to Europe. Samson in the Philippines. For Chrissake, where the hell is the Philippines?*

Just as he had hoped, instead of being sent to any frontline operation, Franklin had been assigned to a less dangerous job in a small metal-detection and sonar technology laboratory at an ocean-side fort in Southern Delaware, called Fort Miles. His assignment was to research and upgrade electrical sensors in metal detectors, and to test his improvements in field exercises on the beaches and dunes. When he received his orders, he was not disappointed.

2

By the time the intake office door opened, his entire shirt was soaked. Captain O'Dea stuck his head out.

"Make it snappy, second lieutenant."

Franklin stepped into the office. It was a long rectangle of open space, with an emaciated pine desk sitting in the middle of the room. Its legs looked too thin to hold up the decrepit piece of furniture, as if it had been found in an old turn of the century military storage room. Along the back wall, behind the desk, was a stretch of file cabinets. When the door closed behind him, a wave of frigid air chilled him in his sweat soaked shirt.

"Goddamn!" He exclaimed, surprised by the extreme temperature change.

Captain O'Dea sat behind the desk, and looked up. He motioned for Franklin to approach. On top of the desk was a bin that held a neat pile of papers and manila folders, a typewriter, a rolodex, a phone, and an intercom. A few loose papers also lay about the desktop. Franklin caught a quick glimpse of his name on the top paper. Captain O'Dea put an arm over them, and said, "You can wait for Colonel Carp over there." He pointed to the wall next to the office door.

Franklin walked the three steps back to the wall, then turned. There was nothing else in the room.

O'Dea's arm was still extended. He said, "Your travel orders, second lieutenant?" Franklin stepped back to the desk and handed the appropriate papers to O'Dea, who then waved him back to the wall.

Franklin crossed his arms for warmth and stepped away from the desk. "Why is it so cold in here?" he asked.

Captain O'Dea did not acknowledge the question.

The two men were only a few feet away from each other. Franklin, freezing in his soaked shirt, asked again, "Excuse me sir—"

O'Dea looked up from his work and shifted his eyes to the left, toward the end of the room. The building was a long double-wide trailer, and split down the middle with a panel wall that separated the front room from Colonel Carp's office. Franklin looked towards the end of the room, where an air conditioner sat in the framing of a window. The AC unit took up the entire bottom half of the opening, and above it was a small section of glass filled with blue sky. It made a consistent humming sound, interrupted by the occasional heavier clank. All the while, drips of water randomly fell out of the bottom into a bucket.

Franklin's skin tightened with gooseflesh. He had not grown up with the luxury of an air conditioner, though some of the offices at his college had them. Captain O'Dea turned back to his work and began to type. Finally, his intercom buzzed. A gravelly voice instructed him to send in the new second lieutenant. O'Dea knew Franklin had to have heard the order, and only looked up to make sure he was right.

When Franklin entered Colonel Carp's office the air was not any warmer. He cursed his luck, and stepped forward to the colonel's desk. He stood at attention, eyes up, and tried to scan as much of the desktop as possible through his peripheral vision. All he could make out were stacks of papers and manila folders. Colonel Carp sat reading at his desk and said nothing.

Franklin stood waiting. Captain O'Dea buzzed through the intercom. "Is there anything else you need, sir?"

"Yes, Captain. Grab me my pistol from the closet," Carp said, rifling through Franklin's files. "I've finally lost my will to live."

O'Dea replied, "Coming right up sir." The intercom clicked off.

Franklin found himself caught off guard. The officers' inside joke only increased his desire to see what the colonel was reading.

Colonel Carp finally addressed Franklin. "Damn, second lieutenant, I see you're one'a them college boys." His eyes sized Franklin up, then looked back down at the papers on his desk. "Says here you got a bit of a criminal record as well. You here on a plea deal, second lieutenant?"

"No sir. My misdemeanors occurred almost a decade ago, when I was a teenager. Just stupid teenage stuff, you know."

"Oh, I know, Second Lieutenant Boone. You don't need to explain your delinquent past to me." Carp continued scrutinizing the files on his desk. "Seems like those charges were expunged, on account of you joining this fine Army of mine. Then you got yourself a goddammed college education. Towson State College? Where the hell is Towson State College?"

"Baltimore, sir."

"Baltimore," repeated Colonel Carp.

Franklin felt like he might have actually caught the colonel off-guard. "Yessir. Baltimore, sir."

Carp leaned back in his chair, and put his hands behind his head. "So, after graduating with," he scanned the papers, "an electrical engineering degree, you decided to join the Army? What the hell'd you want to do that for, a learned city boy like you?"

"Well sir, I want to do my part for the country, and prefer to do it as an officer. Plus, I was told all those charges would be dropped."

"I'll be damned, I got myself a regular threefer over here don't I?"

"Sir?"

"A threefer. A city boy, a college boy, and a goddammed felon. All wrapped up into one pencil-necked engineer." Colonel Carp stared up at Franklin with a complete I-don't-give-a shit smile, not allowing him to

5

stand at ease and loving every minute of it.

Carp's gaze moved back to his desk. He tortured Franklin by taking his time, reading every word in his files. With his eyes down the colonel said, "I was wondering when Brotsky's replacement was going to get here. I just didn't expect him to be such a bundle of talent." He looked back up. "I gotta admit, you've got some impressive entry scores here, Boone, for a felon."

"Thank you sir, but as I'm sure you can see there, I am not a fel—"

Carp raised his hand, stopping Franklin mid-sentence, then leaned back again with his hands behind his head. "You know why I like city boys, Boone?"

"No sir."

"'Cause they're sharp. They're used to keeping an eye out in all directions when walking home late at night. Never knowing what vagabond is gonna try and pull something forces a man to stay sharp. People from the city have a thicker skin for the sounds and sights of war. Not much, but a little bit. Of course, that didn't help your predecessor." Carp's gaze turned to his office window, which had the best view of the beach from any building on Fort Miles—which was to say the only direct view, since his office blocked the only opening in the beach brush that grew up over the ridge on which the fort was built.

Carp continued, "That's not to bash the country boy."

"Yessir."

"You see, the country boy's benefit is that he's most likely already savvy with a rifle, and knows how to sleep in the out-of-doors." The colonel looked back down at the files on his desk. "Before you joined the Army, you ever go camping, Lieutenant Boone?"

"No sir. I hate the woods sir."

"Well Boone, how the hell did you make it to this point? Was your officer school in a dance studio?"

"No sir. Fort Benning."

Carp grumbled about the condition of the young troops under his command. "I know, second lieutenant. That was a rhetorical question, goddammit. Alright, so you're with my metal detection research unit. That's good, 'cause we gotta replace Brotsky, and I guess your city-slicker ass is better than nothing. I gotta tell you, I'm not sure if there's less space in my heart or at this fort for another freeloading R&D jockey. And I cannot believe they sent me an ex-jailbird."

"Again, sir, I never actually spent any time in—"

"Stop," demanded Carp. "You are driving me insane with your bullshit, second lieutenant. You may have a fancy college degree, but I earned my rank in Tunisia. And I know for a fact that a college education doesn't change a man's nature. You got criminal written all over you. I saw that the minute you walked in this room. And no matter what scores you got here, your nature is still your nature. A man doesn't change just 'cause he's an officer."

Franklin stood silent. He wanted to explain again that he had never received an actual felony conviction, but he decided any kind of response would be considered just the first in a long list of mistakes.

"Is there nothing you have to say to that, second lieutenant?"

"No sir, I'm just following my orders."

"Well, then at least you learned something at your OCS. That said, you are aware of who gives the orders here at Fort Miles, yes?"

"Yessir, that would be you."

"That's right, Second Lieutenant Boone. I assume you saw the portrait of our good Admiral Phillips out in the waiting room? He is in charge

7

of all harbor defense, I report directly to him, and he gives me a very comfortable distance here at the fort. And all the engineers here report to me. He raised his hand in the air, "Admiral Phillips is up here, then comes me, then comes everyone else who steps foot on this fort. The first thing you need to remember is that you report to me. I'm not only in charge of your research unit, but the management of all base construction and fortifications as well. So I'm busy, and the last thing I need is to have to babysit another engineer who thinks he knows more than he does."

Franklin dared not change the angle of his gaze. He had learned in OCS that the best way to deal with vindictive officers was to just agree with them and wait until they dismissed him. "Yessir. I understand."

"Just remember that, second lieutenant. And don't mistake the calm goings on of this fort for an easy ride through this war."

"No sir."

"We protect one of the most important waterways on the East Coast, and this base is a well-oiled machine. Thank you very much. At times the work may seem mundane or boring, but we are on full alert status. I don't need to tell you about the five U-boat attacks in the past two years off of Cape May, do I?"

"No sir."

"Good. Those U-boats, by the way, were lucky. They got away. Shit, if I was in charge then they'd be feeding the fish right now."

"Yessir."

Carp sensed a hint of sarcasm in Franklin's reply, though he couldn't be certain.

A loud bang came through the wall from the front office air condi-tioner, as it rumbled to a halt. The noise startled both Carp and Franklin. "Goddammit," exclaimed Carp, then he continued. "At reveille you stand

8

in the last row, behind the 113th." Carp glanced at the files on his desk, then sat back in his chair. "Listen, it's not that I think what you do is not beneficial to the safety of our men, but my last metal detection engineer was a goof, and apparently you are a criminal."

There he goes with the criminal angle again.

"That being said, I accept the fact that in addition to the hundreds of men and countless civilian-contractor-know-it-alls that I have to manage here at Fort Miles, I now, because of your predecessor's inability to stay alive while swimming in the ocean, also have to babysit you. But I will not accept you pulling any bullshit under my watch. I've got your records right here," Carp pushed his index finger down on the files. "I know all about who you are, and I'm gonna be watching you. I promise you boy, you slow down the cogs in the wheels of my fort, and you'll be peeling potatoes with your asshole for the rest of your lackluster military service. Is that clear?"

"Yessir."

"You ever swim in the ocean?"

"No sir."

"Great, Boone. Not that I give a damn, because no matter how well you swim, you gotta watch out for the currents on these beaches. They're strong—weird, actually. So, don't get cocky with your time off. Is that clear?"

"Yessir."

"Good. You're dismissed." Colonel Carp leaned over and pushed a button on his office intercom, and said, "Captain O'Dea, Second Lieutenant Boone's gonna need you to point him in the direction of Barracks Five."

Franklin left the room, and stood in front of Captain O'Dea's desk.

9

O'Dea was busy stapling together a series of papers. He pushed them into a manila folder and handed it to Franklin. He then took a quick glance at Franklin's travel papers, and said, "You're a lucky man. Barracks Five is the best barracks on base. Lots of leg room, and a common area as well."

O'Dea's tone led Franklin to believe he was softening his hardline first impression, and he asked, "Common area? Do we have our own rooms in there?"

Captain O'Dea replied with a tired stare. "Yes Second Lieutenant Boone, everyone has their own rooms, their own personal shower, and every night we bus in some local moms to come over and tuck you in."

O'Dea dismissed him and Franklin stepped back out into the midday heat.

INTRODUCTIONS

Like most of the buildings at Fort Miles, Barracks Five was a cinder block rectangle. The roof was a wooden post-and-beam framed structure covered in cheap asphalt shingles. Four two-by-three-foot windows lined the sides of the barracks. They had screens inset, and each was covered by a wooden shutter that was pulled up, via a rope, from inside the building. Franklin found the front door to Barracks Five wide open, supported by a wedge under the bottom. He stepped over the threshold and was standing in a wide-open space. In front of him was the apparent common area Captain O'Dea had mentioned. The space was cordoned off by way of a small rug that designated it different from the bunk areas, and set up with four semi-comfortably cushioned chairs sitting around a small wood-burning stove. Between two of the chairs was a table constructed from upturned milk crates with a small piece of sanded plywood for its top. Classical music played on a radio somewhere close, and a few GIs sat reading in the lounge.

On both sides of the common area were the bunks; ten bunks a side, each with its own desk and separated from the others by wooden folding room dividers, with white sheets hanging inside the frames. One of the bunks, in the far back corner of the room, was un-made. Its room divider was folded up and tucked between the desk and metal bed frame. The mattress was bare besides a tight-folded pile of white Army linens sitting on it. Franklin assumed that would be his bunk, and was impressed. At

Barracks Five he was going to have more legroom than he had had in his childhood bedroom.

"Trust me—" The voice startled him. Franklin turned to see one of the GIs sitting in the common area place the magazine he was reading on the coffee table. "We've got it good here. All the other barracks have twice the men in them. I don't know how he did it, or why, really, but Carp manages to keep us engineers set up real nice." He stood up and said, "Second Lieutenant Art Thurber," and stuck out his hand.

Franklin shook Thurber's hand and was relieved to find someone who smiled and seemed to know the basics of etiquette. "Second Lieutenant Franklin Boone. Nice to meet you."

Thurber continued, "Nice to meet you as well. Allow me to give you the nickel tour. As you've no doubt already noticed, that bunk in the back corner is yours. And that one, next to yours, is my zone. We all have one bunk, one desk, one trash bin, and a foot locker." He turned and swept his arm across the immediate area. "And this is our lounge. We've got two old recliners, and a few other less comfortable chairs, the community coffee table, and the wood-burning stove. But don't be fooled, it heats the place up real nice in the winter." He pointed past the stove, towards the opposite wall. "Over there we have our sink and our coffee station." Franklin saw a rectangular metal bin sitting on an Army-issue wooden crate. A black hose ran from the bin and disappeared into a low hole in the wall. Next to the metal sink, on its own Army-issue crate, was a field stove, two coffee percolators, and various other jars and coffee-making tools.

"And over there," Thurber pointed to their left, at a GI lounging on his bunk, "is First Lieutenant Ben Craigs. He's in the construction design field, and is also the brains behind the room dividers you see between

Artillery Railway, and a detachment of the 113th Infantry Regiment was kept at the ready in case any Germans tried to come ashore. In addition to the men of these particular regiments, there were hundreds of other men who represented everything from the military police, Army Corps of Engineers, other research units, and countless military contractors who paid daily visits.

Fort Miles was a small, self-sufficient community contained within a perimeter fence that ran from Cape Henlopen, in a horseshoe-like fashion, to the northern edge of the walking dunes and the front face of the pine forest. The oblong-shaped footprint covered about eighteen square miles of land. Along the coastal edge of the fort were ten batteries, each with different firepower and range capabilities, and all securely hidden amongst the dunes. Each gun was seated in a concrete bunker with walls thick enough to withstand anything in the German arsenal. And jutting out from the beach, at the point where bay water met ocean, was a 1,700-foot mine wharf. The wharf was built to allow mine techs easier access to the hundreds of mines that floated around the mouth of the bay, but also as a pier for the yawls and smaller boats operated by Fort Miles.

For the first part of his tour, Second Lieutenant Thurber drove Franklin around the northern half of the fort, where most of the office, barracks, and recreational buildings stood. Franklin was already somewhat familiar with this area since Colonel Carp's office was on the northernmost ridge, but he now had a better idea of his barrack's location in relation to the other buildings. Thurber moved the jeep in a haphazard, jerky fashion. He hit the gas in short bursts, from one landmark to another, while slamming on the brakes as if he was trying to avoid hitting some unseen person or animal. They came to a quick halt in front of a section of perimeter fence that faced the north-western horizon, with a direct view of a long pier.

15

Thurber pointed to the pier. "That there's the mine wharf. The bomb techs use it, but if you're feeling salty, you can also access the occasional boat that's heading over to Cape May for a little R&R." He looked at Franklin and said with a smile, "Despite all the mines they've got floating around here, lots of us take the boats over. Nothing's happened yet."

Thurber slammed the gear shift into reverse, and the jeep jerked backwards. They drove south along the base's main thoroughfare, turned west towards the front gates, then south again and into the parking lot shared by a rail switchyard and the Fort Miles brig. The road continued through the rail yard and into the southern half of the fort, where it snaked around the armory, the weapons training pavilions, and finally ended at a large stretch of level surface called the South Field. Along the outside edge of the field, and parallel to the perimeter fence, was a gravel fire road, from which many small footpaths started then ended either on the beach or in the surrounding forest.

They stopped in the rail yard, where Second Lieutenant Thurber could orient Franklin to the southern areas of the fort. "This here," he said, pointing to the various railroad tracks that wound their way onto, and then almost immediately back out of, the base's grounds, "is the heart of Fort Miles. We intake deliveries and ordinance here, as well as ship out anything from prisoners to machines to leftover debris."

"Debris from what?" Franklin asked.

Thurber leaned to his right and pointed ahead, towards the South Field. They could not see the whole field from their position, but they could see a fleet of dump trucks and front-end loaders sitting on the grass, right behind the back side of the rail depot. "From offloading things like those trucks," said Thurber. "They seem to always be digging a hole somewhere on this base." He pushed the gas pedal, and turned sharply

16

in the rail yard. "And lastly, right there is the fort's brig. Nothing you're going to want to get familiar with. The MPs around here love tightening the screws on us officers."

As they sped up the slight incline from the South Field, Franklin looked back over his shoulder. He got a better look at the one hundred yards or so of field that separated the fort from the pine forest. Being summer, the field outside the perimeter fence was an unkempt scramble of thorny brambles, swaths of wild flowers, and dirt patches that ran up to the foot of the pine forest. Inside the fence, on official Fort Miles ground, the South Field was a groomed area of mowed lawn. The pine forest loomed in the distance. Something about the dark cluster of trees sent a chill up Franklin's spine.

THE 625G

Every day Franklin reported to the electrical engineering lab in another drab cinder block building with insufficient lighting and overcrowded with desks and men. He often hurried through any work that required him to be in the claustrophobic lab, and made his way to the beaches to test his ideas. Indeed, almost daily the fresh air, the sounds of the waves, and the lack of bombs blowing up reminded Franklin of how fortunate he was.

His job was to help design and test the latest ideas in metal detectors, battery packs, and electronic sensory systems. He had a long list of ideas that he wanted to design for the metal detectors, such as establishing a better method of copper coiling for the sensors and an electronic system that would emit higher or lower pitches depending on the density of the metal object. Franklin also hoped to design a system that could sense smaller objects at deeper depths.

The latest model metal detector that he was assigned to test was the SCR-625G. The 625G was a variation of the current commercial designs, backed by a seemingly endless budget for technical upgrades. The 625G changed its power supply every few months to the latest idea coming out of the lab. Franklin found that with each new battery the detector was usually lighter and more efficient. No matter how little it weighed, though, the 625G was always heavy after hours of walking up and down the beach. Franklin found that easy to accept, especially when the sun was shining and he could make a day of it and pack his lunch.

BROTSKY

In about a week's time Franklin had a good working knowledge of his new home, Fort Miles, and had settled into a productive daily routine. Within a few days, he knew all the men who lived in Barracks Five, and soon enough the entire fort had the feel of an extended family.

During lunch the first week, Franklin overheard First Lieutenant Craigs mention his predecessor, Ron Brotsky. He asked his lunch mates, "What's going on with this Brotsky fella?"

The table hushed. Some men continued to eat, while others looked at each other like members of a secret club. To Franklin's relief, the other engineers didn't hide anything from him.

Thurber shook his head and spoke first. "Ronnie Brotsky was a strange bird. Smart as a whip, and as far as I can tell, he was a good guy." A few other of the men mumbled agreements through their mashed potatoes. Thurber continued, "But none of us really got to know him. And whenever he did open up, he was always a bit of a complainer. He didn't like the climate here at Fort Miles, and was always whining about the bugs and the locals."

Craigs added, "Brotsky was a recluse. That's all."

Franklin asked, "Okay, but why do you guys seem to whisper when you talk about him?"

Thurber looked at the other men at the table. They all avoided eye contact. "It's just weird how he went, ya know."

"Didn't he drown?" Franklin asked.

"Well, that's what the brass is trying to sell us, but you know, it was the local police who discovered the body, and—" Thurber hesitated. "Well, ya know, on account of him being found completely naked, no one knew he was a GI, and so the local papers were called before anyone here on base knew about it."

"What's the big deal with that?"

"The papers all say that Brotsky was found jammed up against the rock wall in the inlet. He'd been slammed against the rocks so hard that he had sustained major blunt force trauma to his chest." Thurber leaned over, a little closer to Franklin. "Well, I heard this from a pal who works in the fort hospital. Cause, ya know, after the Army went and picked up the body, he was processed back here at the fort's morgue. And my friend took a peek. Apparently Ol' Brotsky'd been picked at by crabs and seagulls. He had a hole eaten right through him. Which is not what Carp is telling people." Thurber looked around to make sure the colonel or any of his executive officers were not lurking nearby.

Franklin asked, "So, what's Carp telling people?"

Craigs leaned in. "It wasn't so much what he was telling us, as much as how he tried to not tell us anything." The other men mumbled agreements.

Craigs continued, "It was just weird, 'cause despite none of us really knowing Brotsky, we all were certain he'd be the last guy on base to take a private dip in the ocean. Especially in the springtime. There's no reason to be swimming in the ocean in April."

The fact that Franklin was filling the slot of a dead man made him to want to see the situation from every angle. He didn't want to unnecessarily assume any correlations between the work he was to be doing and it being possibly life threatening. He was enjoying his Army life here at Fort Miles too much for the work to be dangerous. He asked, "Well, maybe Brotsky did just go for a swim? I mean, if you guys say you didn't really know him and all–"

Craigs snorted. "Yeah, we knew him at least that well."

Thurber added, "Yeah, Boone. Not only that, but I'm pretty sure seagulls and crabs don't eat right through a body. I think they just peck at your eyes and tongue and things like that."

Craigs said, "Well, crabs on the other hand, they might just start eating anywhere on ya."

Thurber gave Franklin a less-than-reassuring raise of an eyebrow and said, "Well, whatever was peckin' at Brotsky did a real number on him."

THE DUNES

After his first month or so at Fort Miles Franklin didn't think much about his predecessor, Ron Brotsky, and no one else at the fort brought up the subject either. He enjoyed his life in the Army. The Army controlled his schedule; when he would eat, when he would exercise, when he would work. He was never hungry, and was given weekly leave to go into town, or see the countryside. Ironically, Franklin found that the time in his day when he had most say in his decisions was when he was working. Sure, the Army was clear about what they wanted from him, but how he achieved those goals was left to his own ingenuity. And whenever possible, Franklin chose to make the beach his laboratory.

For most of the year the shoreline around the base was nearly devoid of human activity. Besides the training exercises, the daily horseback beach patrols, and a few vacationing families in the summer, nothing much happened on the beaches between Cape Henlopen and the Rehoboth boardwalk. The dunes were a paradise of calm and beauty.

Though non-sentient, the dunes of Southern Delaware moved and breathed as much as any living creature. The constant changes to the more desolate stretches of the grounds were enough to confuse Franklin. He could only imagine how fluid and shifting the dunes must have been before the fort was built, when there was nothing but pine forest for miles in all directions. It had been a time without tarmacs or batteries to obstruct the dunes' changes, and when only the Lewes Beacon and the Cape Henlopen Lighthouse stood vigil over them.

Within a few months of his assignment, Franklin learned as much about the coastal weather patterns as he did about metal detection technology. Often his daily assignment required him to work in the wet sand, just in front of the ankle-deep ocean froth. It was imperative that he know when the tides would be high or low. Franklin also learned to understand how different weather patterns affected the tides, and therefore, the dunes. The stronger a storm, the larger the waves, and the further inland the water's edge would affect the natural berm that the dunes created. But even during a stretch of calm days—when there was no coastal activity strong enough to dramatically shift the dunes—slight changes could be seen by the experienced eye. Some days as Franklin hiked out to the training field, he found himself scaling hills that had not been there the last time he made the trip. It was not uncommon for him to get to a particular area only to find it reshaped.

Franklin enjoyed working in the strange dunes and the hours he got to spend sweeping his metal detectors over the beach. Even the time he spent in the research lab was always better than the front lines. In fact, the most uncomfortable aspect to his life at Fort Miles was continuous scrutiny from Colonel Carp. Despite Franklin being part of a research and development unit, Carp made it a point to include him on as many infantry field-training exercises as possible.

Carp told Franklin, "Shit, Boone, you're not going be living the good life here at the beach forever. At some point you're gonna need to know how those detectors fit into the goings on of the larger unit. And since your college ass has somehow become an officer in my Army, you'll most likely be the one training the soldiers who will ultimately be stuck with the job of digging up those Kraut ankle-poppers. Trust me,

Boone, when the men you train come home each night, you'll thank your old Colonel Carp for keeping your edge sharp."

Franklin initially discovered the mysterious nature of the dunes during a field exercise with a squad from the 113th. The air was hot, humid, and full of mosquitos, which made an otherwise routine bivouac miserable. As a result, protocol was loose, and the men cooked their meals on the open beach while enjoying liquor smuggled in their backpacks. Others swam among the breakers with the reflection of the moon as it made its nightly pass over the Atlantic. By midnight, a light drizzling doused their campfires and sent the men to their tents. All the men retired, and no night-watch schedule was practiced, so no one bore witness to the slow but consistent shift of the sand right under their bedrolls. Rain continued throughout the night, and the next morning the entire encampment woke up to find their sleeping bags almost entirely covered in sand. The GIs' groggy minds took a while to understand what had happened. The A-frame tents sat smaller, like shrunken version of themselves, and sand was piled a foot higher around their poles.

Franklin woke with a start, confused as to why it was so hard to move his arms and legs. Cursing and kicking, he hurried out of the sleeping bag. He stepped out of his tent, and sunk past his ankles in the wet earth. Other men around him were tripping out of their tents and complaining, all of them surprised by how last evening's firm dune-scape had been softened and soaked. As Franklin struggled to get his bearings, he looked back at his bedroll. His sleeping bag was tossed off the ground cover, revealing the rounded outline of his where his body had lay sleeping. The sand had gathered into and around every nook of his frame, and it looked like an eerie sarcophagus that had been exhumed by an archeologist.

News of the incident spread fast throughout the barracks of Fort Miles, and soon the dunes took on a mystical and foreboding nature amongst the men.

CALLING HOME

Since joining the Army, Franklin had made it a point to call his mother, Edith, at least once a week. However, in his opinion, one of the worst elements to living at Fort Miles was the pay phones. If a GI wanted to make a phone call, he had to use the phones at the base recreation center, which were too public for Franklin, or a pay phone at a bank of phones near the front gates. There was a pavilion covering the phones, but other than that, they were out in the open elements. Franklin always used the front gate phone bank because it was used less than the rec-center phones, and he preferred privacy over protection from the weather.

Edith's voice rode on a sigh of relief. "Franky, so good to hear from you." She was not as happy about her son's new MOS as Franklin thought she should be. Indeed, Edith worried that she might lose the only remaining man in her life.

"It's okay Ma," he consoled her. "I'm not going to Europe. I've got a good gig over here. Did you get the money I sent home last week?"

"Yes, but that's how it is now. What happens when you're all done and they have nothing left for you to study, and then they send you off to the fighting?"

"Well, I guess I'll just have to go. Hitler's on the run, anyway. So, if I play my cards right, I won't have to go to Europe."

"I don't know. That's not good enough for me, what with those nasty Japanese waiting over—well—wherever they are."

"I know Ma, but don't worry. If I go to any war zone, if nothing else, they'll pay me a bit more for the frontline station."

"I assume you are just trying to drive me to an early grave?"

"No. Please, there's nothing to worry about. I'm at the beach for Chrissakes—"

"Franky, don't talk like that—"

"Sorry. My point is, that I may be working for the Army, but just today, while testing my new detector, I found a silver ring on the beach, and it had a gem in it. The guys tell me it's an emerald, but I'm not so sure yet. I'll send it home, and maybe you'll know."

"Well, that's exciting isn't it?"

"Yeah, I think so. Who knows, maybe soon I'll find an old pirate's treasure chest and we'll never have to want for anything again."

"That would be nice, Franky. Just be careful. Even if you're not in Europe, it's dangerous being around all those guns and bombs."

"I know, Ma. I know."

THE ANXIETY OF GOLD

After finding the silver ring, Franklin stumbled into what would become his new favorite pastime: treasure hunting. He was a relatively well-read youth from the streets of East Baltimore, so the only pirate or shipwreck treasures he had ever come across were within the pages of books like *The Count of Monte Cristo* and *Treasure Island*. He remembered most the scenes in which the treasure chests were discovered, and re-read those passages while dreaming of overflowing piles of gold, silver, and jewels. It was his accidental and repeated discovery of metal artifacts on the beaches in front of Fort Miles that solidified Franklin's resolve to conduct as much research out in the field as possible.

Before coming to Fort Miles, the thought of exciting finds under the sand of the gray and smoking shorelines of the industrialized Delaware Bay never occurred to Franklin. But for centuries the bay had been travelled by merchant ships, pirates, and now military vessels. The mouth was tight with strong enough currents—and close enough to the Hen and Chickens Shoal—to cause thousands of shipwrecks. Within his first week of treasure hunting, Franklin discovered his first silver coin. He was unsure of its provenance, but according to his research at the local Rehoboth library, he learned it was a Spanish *real*.

After discovering the *real*, Franklin found it difficult to concentrate on anything besides treasure hunting. That night he lay in bed and stared at the ceiling. His heart raced as he realized the potential that waited for him. Centuries of shipwrecks equaled centuries of debris. Metal debris. Valuable metals like gold and silver. And he was the one man in Delaware in the best position to find it.

The thought exploded into his head.

He bolted upright in his bunk, and sat in the dark room, breathing heavy like he had been ripped out of a nightmare. He looked across the room at the lumps of his sleeping bunkmates. *Dammit. Did I say something in my sleep?*

He took a few breaths. His mind calmed. Everyone around him was sound asleep. Several of the men snored in unison, so loud that had he blurted anything out, no one would have heard him. *I'm as good as alone. Thank God. I wouldn't want to have to disappear anyone.* The murderous joke jogged his sleepy mind back to his predecessor, Lieutenant Brotsky, and he regretted having such a thought. Franklin rolled onto his right side and pulled his blankets up over his shoulder, and reassured himself that the idea was just a bit of humor, a quip in the midst of other more important revelations. *Nonetheless,* he thought, *no matter what happens, if I'm going to be finding all this stuff, I'll have to figure out a way to keep it hidden.*

Soon, most of Franklin's professional and spare time was spent treasure hunting. His research work was done primarily in the dunes just south of Fort Miles, but no one raised any eyebrows when he wandered further down the beach. And the beaches south of Fort Miles were more than enough land for one man to scour during his weekends.

Franklin's daily assignments were a perfect cover for treasure hunting because there were no rules against picking up a random object he might bump across, and he usually worked alone. Daily, he returned to the base with a bucket full of artifacts of all makes, nationalities, and metals. He dug up silver and copper coins of the Spanish conquest era, tools and instruments from old grounded vessels, and silverware and jewelry long clustered together.

Every day Franklin returned to Barracks Five with his day's booty. At first, his bunkmates were eager to see what he had in his treasure bucket. But newfound treasure rarely looked enticing or shiny, and the men never saw anything more than the crusted outlines of artifacts. Franklin explained how centuries of sitting in the salty ocean turned silver into black clusters that looked like the lowest of any kind of rock. He passed around copper coins that had turned green and calcified onto other objects. Any individual pieces he found were either brittle as dried oak leaves or clustered together into larger clumps. That is, besides the gold pieces.

Within three months of treasure hunting, Franklin had found ten gold Spanish coins. He soon learned that gold was one of the few metals dense enough that salt water did not destroy its luster. No matter how long it spent under the ocean, gold came out looking not too different from the day it sank.

As he acquired more and more artifacts, he tried to keep his gold discoveries far from his fellow soldiers' attention, though the close quarters of Barracks Five made it difficult to keep his treasures completely hidden from prying eyes. If pressed by a fellow GI to see his latest discoveries, Franklin used decoy treasure items, like silver or copper pieces, to distract his audience and sate their curiosity.

As he understood the 625G more, and learned what different encrusted metals looked like after spending decades or centuries under the sand, Franklin became more wary of how he dealt with his finds. Most he kept for himself. For the really special pieces, he opened a safety deposit box at a bank in Georgetown. However, he found enough treasure that he was able to sell an occasional piece to some of the few GIs whom he trusted. He always asked the purchaser to keep the transaction secret. He didn't want Colonel Carp finding out and potentially ruining his treasure-hunting racket. And after selling off his first few silver pieces, it dawned on him that he had more beach to himself than he could ever excavate in his lifetime, which meant a never-ending stock potential which he could easily use to make more and more money.

THE BEACH PATROL

Despite the seclusion that his field work provided, Franklin still had to remain alert as beach patrols rode horseback from Fort Miles all the way south to the Indian River Inlet. The patrols were a twenty-four-hour continuous detail that both the infantry guys and the MPs handled. While they were primarily looking for enemy activity, other oddities that might affect the goings on at Fort Miles also piqued their interest. The last thing Franklin wanted was to be noticed by the patrols.

Franklin had just pulled up a gold coin from the sand when he heard the neighing of a horse. Clenching the coin, he stood up and looked for the source of the sound. It was the end of the morning beach patrol, and for some reason, the two patrols were riding down near the water, close to where Franklin was working, as opposed to their usual high ground in front of the pine forest. Franklin kept his coin discreet, and struggled to appear relaxed. He had been so wrapped up in his new gold piece that he failed to pay attention to his surroundings.

As the men approached, Franklin saw that they were MPs. They rode slowly, as if the heat was heavy on their shoulders. The first man came abreast of Franklin. In his short time at Fort Miles, Franklin had not met this MP. He was a staff sergeant, and the name tag on his shirt said Wilkins. His helmet and rifle were strapped to the saddlebags behind him. Binoculars hung around his neck.

Staff Sergeant Wilkins did not seem concerned with Franklin's presence on the beach, but nodded drearily as he swayed in the saddle. He moved slowly past Franklin, the horse and human both too tired for any long interaction.

When next to Franklin, the second MP stopped. He too looked tired but managed to nod a slight tilt of a greeting. "How you doing, Second Lieutenant Boone?"

Franklin was surprised. He had never met the man before, and was not currently wearing his uniform, so how did this stranger know his name? The man's voice had the accent that Franklin had learned to associate with people from Southern Delaware. It wasn't quite a southern accent, but definitely was not a city sound either.

He read the man's name tag. "Fine. How are you, Sergeant Radish?"

Radish didn't answer. He pulled his horse to a halt and sat looking down at Franklin, who thought he noticed the man's eyes fixed on his closed fist. But his eyes were squinting in the sunlight, and didn't stay in one place for too long. "Up early today, huh?" he asked. "You having any luck with that detector of yours?"

Franklin wasn't sure what Radish was insinuating. Always careful to not reveal how great the treasure on the beaches was, he answered the MP's question with long-winded, scientifically confusing, and technically boring information: "Well, I've wrapped the coils differently, but they seem to be working fine. The tones are diminished a bit, but that might just be the speaker box playing tricks on me. As far as objects found, there's not been too much today. Just the usual encrustations and con-glomerates."

Radish's eyes flicked down to Franklin's hand again. He said, "Just the usual, huh? Encrustations and conglomerates? That's too bad." He looked up the beach. Staff Sergeant Wilkins had just turned onto the

33

path that led behind Battery Herring. Without looking back to Franklin, Sergeant Radish said, "Pretty good gig we've got here, wouldn't you say, lieutenant?"

Sergeant Radish's vagaries tired Franklin, and made him apprehensive about his new secret hobby. But he had to be calm in the Army, especially when dealing with an MP. There were too many rules that dictated the actions and behaviors of the men in uniform—rules that often did not take into account who was right and who was wrong. As a show of strength, Franklin all but ignored the MP and pretended to return to fixing the connection of a wire on the 625G. He slipped his new gold coin into his pocket in the meantime. Without looking up, he answered quietly. "Yes, I'm happy with my assignment."

As he rode away, Radish looked over his shoulder and said, "That's good. Hopefully, you'll last longer than the guy who used to have your position."

Franklin was taken aback. He called out, "What was that?"

"I said, Keep up the good work, second lieutenant. I'll see you back up at the base sometime."

Franklin knew that the MPs enjoyed keeping themselves aloof from the normal functions of the base, and found Radish's last statement odd. He replied with a quick "okay", and then waited as the MP and his horse moved on.

The encounter shook him, and he cursed himself for not being more careful, more covert, but he had no idea how one might be more hidden while working on a beach.

As he prepared himself for getting back to his work, Franklin took one last scan of the dunes. To the north Sergeant Radish was almost back on Fort Miles' grounds. To the south the beach was empty besides a lone man about a hundred yards away. He had not been there before the MPs came by, and was now sliding down the front face of the dune berm. He stopped clumsily at the foot of the dunes, where he regained his balance and brushed sand off his legs. He wore a fedora, a short-sleeved, button-down shirt, khaki slacks, and carried his shoes in his hands. The only clear feature of his face was a black mustache. He stopped and sat down, making no effort to conceal his steady gaze north. The man unnerved Franklin, and he decided that the stranger's presence was a good reason to stop his treasure hunting for the day.

HUNTING WITH CARP

Franklin sat at his desk cleaning and cataloging his latest treasures, unconcerned about the other men in Barracks Five noticing the crusted old pins and nails with which he busied himself. Outside and up the coast, dark storm clouds covered the horizon, but the winds had yet to reach Cape Henlopen. Franklin noted the storm clouds and waited eagerly for the next morning. He knew the beaches would be churned up and ripe for the picking.

The entrance door to Barracks Five opened and slammed shut. All the men but Captain Bryant leapt from their bunks, and stood at attention. Captain O'Dea stood in the doorway. Franklin shot to his feet.

O'Dea said nothing. He was a short Irish man who, because of his height, his nationality, and adjutant detail, was the butt of unfettered jokes and taunts from the lower-ranking officers. They teased him because they knew he was Colonel Carp's right-hand man, and called O'Dea such things as "Ol' Day Any Day," and more specific epithets such as "Carps' personal beach bitch." O'Dea knew his position and could have reported the lower-ranking men for insubordination, but he was proficient at ignoring people he looked down on. No matter how anyone treated him, he and Carp were inseparable. His assignment gave him a certain invulnerability that freed him from worry about any bullying from the men, and an air of condescension when dealing with anyone besides Carp.

O'Dea saw Franklin standing in front of his bunk. "Second Lieutenant Boone. Colonel Carp wants to see you in his office. Stat."

The captain turned and stepped out the door.

At Carp's office, a steady rattle came from the air conditioner, and the bucket underneath it was almost full. Franklin shivered as he stood at attention. He was cold and nervous, but Colonel Carp did not waste time. Carp made it clear that he was aware of Franklin's discoveries on the beach. "Of course, Second Lieutenant Boone, I'm certain that anything you're finding is discovered off the Army's clock."

The colonel's mood was calm and not accusatory, which only served to confuse Franklin. He didn't want Carp to know that he was treasure hunting while he was conducting his research, so he lied, "Yes, Colonel."

Carp noticed that Franklin was still at attention and said, "At ease, Boone. I'm not gonna kick you in the balls." The colonel pulled something out of his pocket and held it up for Franklin to see. It was one of the Spanish reales Franklin had found, cleaned, then sold to one of his fellow soldiers.

He assumed the colonel was going to reprimand him for unauthorized use of Army property, or perhaps for the selling of his treasures to other soldiers. He stammered, "Sir, I can explain—"

"Shut up, Boone. I don't care what you're about to say. I just have a few questions."

"Yessir."

"Is this a coin you found?"

Franklin studied the coin, and felt confident that it was one that he had recently sold. "Yessir."

"Is this a pure silver coin?"

"Yessir. Well, it's not a hundred percent, but nothing ever is."

Carp listened, still holding up the coin. "Mm-hmm," he said. "And

37

you found this on the beaches around here?"

"Yessir. But I can explain, it wasn't interfering with my work, and—"

"For the last time, Boone, quit your damn babbling. I know every time you're out there conducting research, and when you're out there borrowing your detector for personal reasons. After the brass stuck it to me over the Brotsky situation, you don't think I have my eyes on you?"

This information embarrassed Franklin. He couldn't fathom how Carp might be able to know his whereabouts at all times. Hopefully the colonel was simply trying to intimidate him. He kept his mouth shut.

"So, I'll ask you again, this is a coin that you found on our beach, and cleaned in our barracks, yes?"

"Yessir. I don't remember exactly where I found that particular coin, but it was definitely somewhere just south of the fort."

"Don't remember, huh. You finding that much stuff out there, Boone?"

Franklin was leery of revealing information, and tried to downplay as much of the truth as possible. "Well, when I can, I get out there and find a few trinkets a week. There's always something out there, especially after a good storm, you don't even need the metal detector to find—"

Colonel Carp held up his hand.

Thank God he shut me up. Why am I telling Carp when the best times to treasure hunt are?

"Excellent news, Boone. As I'm sure you know, we currently have a storm brewing up off the coast of New Jersey?"

"Yessir. I am aware of that."

"It doesn't look like a big one, though, does it?"

"No sir."

"But still big enough to make tomorrow morning a smart time to

38

scour the beach, right?"

Franklin tried a smoke screen to deflate the colonel's enthusiasm, and spoke with as little grace as possible. "Well, um, actually, sir, around here, um, any time's a good time to—"

Carp cut Franklin off again, saying, "Goddammit, Boone. Where the hell did you learn English?" He stood up and walked over to his window, staring down at the beach. "Don't answer that." He turned his gaze back over his shoulder, and started a new subject. "You ever find anything more than silver?"

"More than silver, sir?"

"Yes, Boone. You know what I'm talking about."

Now Franklin lied with abandon. He was going to do everything in his power to keep his gold finds to himself. "Oh, gold. Well, I've found the occasional old wedding ring, but I have yet to find anything more exciting than that."

Colonel Carp said, "Mm-hmm. Listen. At some point in your stay here at Fort Miles, you're going to have to stop assuming I'm an idiot." He walked up to face Franklin, standing close, and whispered. "I know, the history of these waters, so I know what's out there. I know there's plenty more than just silver and lost wedding rings. And, Lord knows, I'm not going to sit around and let you grab up all the gold from here to the inlet. So, tomorrow morning you and I are hittin' the beach. Once this storm has broke, and the sun's up, we're going on our own little private mission."

Franklin's heart sunk. Carp stood not a foot away, while Franklin's mind raced to come up with a way out of Carp's proposed 'private mission'.

Carp continued, "Consider this your payment to me. The more good stuff I come back with, the less likely I'll be to stop you from any future treasure hunting. You get me?"

Now Franklin understood. He answered with a low, "Yessir."

Carp was about to address Franklin's unenthusiastic response when Captain O'Dea stepped into the room. Carp turned and looked at O'Dea, his body asking the appropriate question, *What is it?*

Captain O'Dea approached the colonel and whispered something in his ear. While standing and waiting, Franklin had a full view out to Captain O'Dea's office. There in front of the desk stood his roommate, Captain Bryant. His shirt was covered in dirt and sand, and a hard hat was tucked under his arm. He shifted from foot to foot, and seemed agitated. Franklin and Bryant made eye contact, but Bryant immediately turned his eyes away.

Franklin looked back to Carp. He and O'Dea were having a discussion at a low volume, and he could not make out any clear phrases. Carp seemed to not understand what he was being told. He squinted and surveyed his executive officer as if in disbelief. O'Dea shook his head. Carp's talking was temporarily halted, then after one last comment, he finished with O'Dea nodding his head and saying, "Yes."

Carp pushed past his assistant, and was about to leave the room when he remembered that Franklin had not yet been dismissed. He looked at O'Dea, and tilted his head towards the door. O'Dea stepped out. Carp leaned in close to Franklin and whispered, "I'll see you before sunup. You are excused from reveille, and will meet me at the—where exactly should we meet for our expedition?"

"I guess we can meet here, then head—"

"No Boone. I don't need every soldier this side of the Atlantic knowing that I'm walking up and down the beach with you. Pick another place

40

to meet."

"How about behind Battery Herring? On one of those paths that—"

"Perfect, Boone. I'll see you an hour before sun-up. Now get the hell out'a here." Carp practically pushed Franklin out the door, then closed and locked it, then hurried out the front door of the office with Captain Bryant.

Franklin looked down. Captain O'Dea was sitting at his desk, looking at Franklin as if to ask, *Why are you still here?*

Franklin didn't need to hear the question, and left.

•

After the evening meal, as the majority of the personnel at Fort Miles began to settle down for the night, Franklin lounged on his bunk. He was studying an old, crusted piece of silver that he had yet to clean and catalogue. But really his attention was stuck on what exactly Captain Bryant was doing in Carp's office. He knew Bryant was the point man on the construction and excavation of Fort Miles, and therefore close to Carp, but something didn't feel right. The quick glimpse he'd gotten of Bryant was curious. And Carp was so quick to order all of them out of his office.

Maybe I was the stressed one, and that made me see things wrong.

Captain Bryant did not return to Barracks Five until almost midnight. All the other engineers in the barracks were asleep when the door clapped shut and roused Franklin. Captain Bryant moved to his bunk without any care for how much noise he made. Franklin lay still, letting the darkness conceal his open eyes as he watched the captain. Bryant hurried about his bunk area, and seemed to be packing clothes in a rucksack. While he did so, he was mumbling under his breath. Franklin could only make out a few of the words, most of which were curses.

Soon his rucksack was full, and Bryant turned back towards the barracks door. Franklin sat up, propping himself up on his elbows. He whisper-yelled across the room, "Captain Bryant—"

The sound of his voice startled the captain. Bryant stopped as if someone had jumped out of the shadows. "Dammit! What the hell do you want Boone?"

Franklin sat up further and said, "Nothing sir. Just wondering what's going on?"

Bryant was a silhouette, but his voice revealed his frustration. "What the hell are you talking about?"

Franklin was unsure of how to breach the subject, and started, "Well, I saw you in Carp's office earlier–"

Bryant was quick to interrupt, "So what?"

The abrupt nature of the captain's reply further derailed Franklin's attempt at conversation. He knew that everyone in Barracks Five was privy to his treasure hunting, and he had also already sold a few silver coins to Captain Bryant, so he used that as his way into the conversation. "Carp was harassing me about treasure hunting, almost blackmailing me about any gold coins I might find."

"What did you just say?" Captain Bryant's voice was suddenly angrier.

Franklin stammered, "I said, Carp was bothering me to bring him along on a treasure hunting beach trip tomorrow morning, when you came in and I was just wondering–"

Bryant pulled his rucksack up onto his shoulder and said, "Well don't wonder too hard, Boone. I don't think the colonel is going to be too worried about poking around the beach with you anytime soon."

Franklin was about to ask for clarification when Bryant pushed the door open and left the barracks.

Franklin was left amongst the snoring GIs. He reclined in his bunk and as he dozed, he pondered why Captain Bryant seemed so flustered, and where he might possibly be going at this hour of the night.

•

The next morning, Franklin woke up early from too short of a sleep. Captain Bryant's bunk was empty, and showed no signs of being used the previous night. He tried to clear his head with a mug of coffee, then gathered his gear for his impending treasure hunting expedition with Colonel Carp. As he walked in the direction of Battery Herring, passing random soldiers, and finally weaving his way through the buildings on the eastern edge of the fort, Franklin couldn't shake the nervous feeling in his gut. The previous night's interaction with Captain Bryant and his distrust of Carp, added to his foggy, un-rested state of mind. He wanted to determine how he might keep any good treasure out of Carp's hands, but decided that, for the sake of his nerves, he was just going to not get attached to anything he found on this trip.

Maybe we'll become friends, and Carp will stop harassing me all the time.

The darkened backside of Battery Herring loomed in the distance.

Yeah, and maybe pigs will fly soon too.

Franklin wandered down to the trail that was on the south side of Battery Herring. Carp was already there.

"Jesus, Boone. What took you so long?"

Franklin did not realize he was late. "Sorry sir. I didn't sleep well last night, what with all the commotion."

Carp lifted his chin, examining Franklin. "What sort of commotion?"

Franklin attempted a subtle dig at Colonel Carp. He hoped to draw out some sort of reaction that might be a clue as to what was going on with Captain Bryant. He answered, "One of the guys in my barracks was making a ruckus around midnight. Not sure, but I think it was Captain Bryant."

Carp squinted, examining Franklin, then said, "Alright, well, I need you to focus on the here and now."

"Yessir."

The two men turned and made their way out to the beach just off the Hen and Chickens Shoal. The trail wound down the front of the ridge on which the fort was built. Behind them, and up on the hill, swallowing most of Fort Miles' footprint, was the front side of the pine forest. It was a black-green wall in the early morning sun. This was the forest that shrouded Fort Miles from the west, and hid the batteries and buildings from any ocean-borne surveillance. It was the last natural barrier for any waves, or enemies, that made it over the dunes.

The sun was not completely up, and fog sat like a shallow blanket that hid the source of the lapping noises from the ankle-deep edges of the surf. The sand under their boots was dense, and saturated with the previous evening's rain. In the morning light the short peaks of the dunes rose above the fog like a miniature mountain chain that rolled right up to the base of the pine forest. They walked out onto the open beach. Franklin wore a backpack full of gear and carried with him a sand sifter, a shovel for the deeper finds, and the 625G. Carp walked beside him, with a folding chair tucked under one arm and the empty treasure collection bucket in his other hand.

Franklin noted how little Carp was helping with the heavy lifting. He also seemed to be distracted or bothered by something not related to the current treasure hunt. Carp was new to beachcombing, Franklin figured. Perhaps he hadn't realized how much more time it took to walk, lug gear, and dig worthless holes compared to making actual discoveries.

For most of the morning, they hunted a small fifty-foot stretch of beach directly in front of the Hen & Chickens Shoal. Not long into the hunt Carp had practically given up. In fact, the colonel turned out to be a terrible treasure hunting partner. He lacked patience, offered little assistance, and confiscated what few items Franklin found.

Franklin honed in on Carp's impatience, and tried a number of tactics that he felt might bore the colonel so much that he would not ask to come on any future treasure hunting trips. First, he feigned signals from the 625G, and dug decoy holes that revealed nothing but wet sand. *Maybe I can bore him so much that he gives up and leaves me alone.* But the fake signals only made Carp angry and sent him into short tirades that questioned the validity of the engineers working at his fort. Next Franklin tried turning down the volume on his detector speaker so Carp might not hear the signs of any treasure. But with the dune winds and the wave noise, it was difficult for him to hear his 625G speak, despite being so close to it. So he turned the volume up, and remembered his resolve to not get attached to anything he found that morning.

The beach was selfish for the better half of their hunting, but towards late morning, Franklin found an area where a lot of debris had settled. With the sudden barrage of beeps and chirps from the 625G, Colonel Carp hovered closer. The most frustrating part for Franklin was that Carp seldom had any idea about the treasures they found. If it had no signs of antiquity or economy, the colonel didn't seem to care about the artifact. He would scoff at Franklin for putting any tar and rock-like conglomerates in the treasure bucket. Franklin knew, because the 625G told him, that inside the encrustations waited something with interesting potential. However, if the artifact had any semblance of shine or shape to it, Carp

45

would bring it back to his folding chair, where he would sit and study the piece as if nothing else in the world existed. But most artifacts were not dug up looking museum ready, and took hours of painstaking cleaning to determine if they were worth anything. Carp's greedy impatience helped settle Franklin's worried heart, and with each breath he took, with each scoop of the sifter into the sand, he became more and more determined to never again go hunting with his commanding officer.

By noon, when the sun was scorching the sand to an uncomfortable heat, the two men decided to finish combing the beach. They had been out for almost six hours and were tired and sunburned. Despite finding a good amount of small artifacts, they did not find anything fancy enough to invigorate their dehydrated hunting spirits. They agreed to call it quits. Franklin couldn't have been happier, and was glad that they had not found anything worth keeping. The heat, and having to guard any treasure from Carp, had worn him out to the point that he was no longer worried who saw him. And since they were packing up, Franklin felt relieved that he wasn't going to lose anything to Carp's greedy hands.

Carp picked up the bucket, now laden with many minor treasures, and his chair, while Franklin carried the rest of the tools. They walked north. Out of habit, as was his custom, Franklin walked the long trek back with the detector power switched on, and dragged the machine behind him. He felt if there was any battery charge remaining, he should use it, and there was no better time than during the walk home.

Both men walked in silence, but the 625G wasn't finished with the treasure hunt. A familiar beep sounded. Franklin froze in his tracks. Carp also stopped. Franklin knelt down and shoved his sifter into the sand. *Please don't be gold. Please don't be gold.* He didn't want to share his booty with the colonel, who now stood over him like a sentry. Franklin scooped up the debris and let it sift out and collect into a side pile. With each scoop of sand, he tried to be ahead of Carp and cover anything that looked important before his commanding officer noticed. As he repeated this a few times, he finally saw the coin. It was covered in wet sand, but the luster of the gold was clear.

Carp grabbed the coin from the debris pile. "Holy shit, Boone. Is that what I think it is?" Franklin felt a surge of anger well up in his chest at the sight of the colonel handling the gold coin. That was Franklin's job, to drool over the shiny ancient piece of metal, and the colonel had snatched it out from under him. *Perhaps I can knock him over the head with my shovel, then just float him out to sea. No one knows he's with me. Well, maybe O'Dea does. I would have to disappear O'Dea too. It might just work.* The plot came and went, as Franklin gathered his senses and choked down his anger. *Maybe if I let Carp have this one piece it will be enough to sate his desire to treasure hunt.* But Franklin also knew that when he'd held his first piece of gold, he could think of nothing else but acquiring more.

Franklin considered his best options for getting the gold coin back, and looked at the shovel in his hand. The thought of bludgeoning the colonel to death came into his head again just as the Fort Miles warning alarms were raised. The siren broke Franklin's train of thought, surprising him and making him drop his shovel. His face flushed with heat. *What the—how did they know what I was going to do?* For a brief moment Franklin believed he was going to be charged with attempted murder, but just as quickly he realized the alarms had nothing to do with him.

Colonel Carp was equally startled by the alarms. He shoved the gold coin into his pant pocket, and turned to face north. "What the hell?"

Franklin said, "Maybe it's an emergency drill?"

"No, I don't remember any drills planned."

Franklin was about to ask if he could take a look at the new gold coin, but his attention was interrupted. "Holy shit!" he said, and pointed up towards the mouth of the bay. The commotion of the alarm was soon matched by the clatter of a helicopter flying overhead. The helicopter circled around the point off of Cape May. Then two of Fort Miles' yawls came around the point. They moved into view and stopped at different locations to block any other vessels that were entering or leaving the bay.

As Franklin and Carp watched the helicopter and boats, their attention was drawn towards the closed-off beaches in front of Fort Miles. Groups of GIs gathered on the shore, pointing out towards the hazy silhouette of the Cape May shoreline around which came a surrendered German U-boat. Franklin watched as the yawls and U-boat made their way to the mine wharf. The yawls were loaded down with passengers who wore the colors of the German Kriegsmarine. Meanwhile, a Navy sub-chaser sat out on the horizon like a patient shark. Even further out were several other members of the Navy flotilla.

Carp cursed, "Shit! Looks like everyone knew about this but me. How long have we been out here today, Boone?"

Franklin began to speak. However, as usual, he didn't know if the colonel's question was one that really demanded an answer. Carp didn't wait. Without another word (or mention of the gold coin he had just confiscated) he started up the shore, leaving behind the treasure bucket and folding chair.

Franklin was happy to be rid of the colonel, and was used to carrying all the equipment. As curious as he was about the sudden appearance of the U-boat, he still took his time getting back to the fort. The entire walk north, he cursed Carp's name for pocketing his gold piece.

The vessels were tied to the mine wharf, with the yawls in their usual place and the U-boat taking up most of the southern side. The scene wasn't too strange as military boats were in the water all the time escorting merchant ships through the bay. The U-boat, however, added a surreal element. Even from Franklin's distance, the German sub sat huge and ominous above the smaller crafts, with the Iron Cross and the numbers U-856 painted right above the water line. As Franklin watched and walked, the commotion on the wharf increased, as soldiers with rifles met the boats, and other men milled about, doing things he could not determine. He shaded his eyes as he stood and stared in amazement, and the surrendered submarine sat dappled by the reflection of the sunlight off the surrounding waves.

THE U-BOAT AND OTHER DISTRACTIONS

Much to Franklin's relief, the U-boat was a huge distraction for Colonel Carp. The crew of the U-boat would be housed in the Fort Miles stockade until the brass in Washington figured out how best to use them. After days of interrogations, little was gleaned from the prisoners that the Army didn't already know, and it was assumed that they would be transported north to Fort Dupont, the Mid-Atlantic holding grounds for German POWs.

Meanwhile, the U-boat sat moored to the mine wharf like a broken-down trophy. A memo was released instructing the men of Fort Miles not to mention or discuss the incident with anyone, because Uncle Sam didn't want the public privy to how close the Germans were still getting to the East Coast. The blaring sirens hadn't drawn attention because although audible all the way down to the boardwalk, the sirens were used so often during drills that local civilians no longer raised eyebrows when they heard them. Of course the American public was well aware of the U-boat attacks that had already occurred since Hitler declared war on the US.

With Carp otherwise occupied, Franklin went on with his research work and his personal treasure hunting. Not a week after the arrival of the U-boat, Franklin found his twelfth gold coin near where he and the colonel had discovered their small treasure. He felt as if an invisible scale had been balanced, elated that he was going to be able to put another gold piece in his safety deposit box without Carp knowing about it.

Franklin's excitement, however, caused him to let his guard down. Back on base, he found Barracks Five empty of all occupants. He sat hunched over his desk squinting through a magnifying glass at the markings on the flat piece of gold, leaving some other valuable pieces out in the open. The smell of salt water and brine distracted him, and he did not notice the front door open and close or the boots thumping a few steps into the barracks.

A familiar voice asked, "Second Lieutenant Boone?"

The sound broke his concentration, and he jumped in his seat. "What the hell?"

The MP, Sergeant Radish, approached Franklin's desk. "Why so skittish?"

Franklin covered the coin with his hands and pushed the treasure down into his lap. His attempt at concealment was obvious, and his nerves were on edge so he gave a hurried answer. "Just cleaning a coin I found." He immediately realized the weight of his mistake and hoped that Radish would assume the coin was copper or silver.

As he walked over to Franklin's bunk, Radish said, "You find a gold coin, Boone?"

Franklin brought his hands back up to the desk. He conceded and opened up his closed hands. He said, "Oh well, sergeant, there it is. My first gold coin."

Radish came closer to the desk and said, "Well, aren't you something. You're a regular Robinson Cer-ru-so."

Franklin tried to minimize the significance of the coin. "It's just a small piece. Nothing to lose your head over." He held the coin up so that Radish might take a closer look. The ounce of gold glimmered in the

51

overhead lighting of the room clearly displaying the Pillars of Hercules pressed into one side and the eighteenth-century royal Spanish insignia on the other.

"Are you gonna arrest me now?"

Radish stood over Franklin's outstretched hand and stared at his face—as if waiting for some sign of deceit—and never once looked at the coin. He finally stepped away from the desk and sat down on the edge of Franklin's bunk. "I don't give a shit about your gold coins, Boone."

"What do you mean, coins?"

Radish laughed and said, "Coins, Boone. Like, multiple coins. You think I don't know about the other ones you've found? Relax! I promise, I'm not here to harass you about your treasure hunting."

Franklin was relieved, but directed the conversation away from the topic of gold and to the events surrounding the U-boat.

"So, Sergeant Radish, what do you think about that U-boat crew? They seem to have taken all the beds over at the brig."

Radish leaned forward, elbows on knees, and replied, "All I know is that they're going to be here for a little bit. Washington doesn't know what they want to do with 'em. So we give 'em the shittiest jobs possible, like cleaning the latrines and the stables." He mocked and said in his best German accent, "Sometimes those Krauts complain and say, Ve did not join ze Kriegsmarine to spend our time cleaning up American scheisse! That's when I tell them, then don't surrender next time your scheisse U-boat stops working."

Franklin laughed. "Wow. They've really got some nerve."

"Shit, Boone. That's not the half of it. We're instructed to allow those Krauts an hour of exercise a day. So not only are they living and sleeping in better conditions than our boys overseas, but they're exercising on our beach and eating our food. I can't tell you how many times I've wanted to spit in one of those Krauts' faces. Bringing that damn U-boat all this way to sink our ships. Then breaking down and surrendering like a bunch of amateurs. Then, by God, having the audacity to tell me they ain't going to eat the potatoes we feed 'em, and the chicken was too tough. It just burns me to think of that shit."

They talked long enough that Franklin forgot to be wary of Radish's intentions, and to Franklin's surprise, he found that the sergeant wasn't such a bad guy after all. Though, throughout the half hour of chitchat Franklin couldn't help but wonder why the MP had made the trip to Barracks Five.

As if sensing Franklin's curiosity, Sergeant Radish asked, "So Boone, looks like the treasure hunting is going well for you?"

Franklin's mind raced in search of any possible direction in which Radish was heading. Radish was an MP, and he didn't seem to be too bad of a fellow, so Franklin didn't think he would resort to blackmail to get to any of his loot. A lot of MPs on base used their position to bully other GIs. But the only close-to-illegal thing Franklin had done was walk the 625G up and down the beach. He spoke up, "Carp knows what I'm doing, Radish."

"Calm down, Boone. I don't really care what Carp knows or doesn't know. I ain't here to arrest you. Though you know I could make a good case for you being written up. Seems you're using that detector of yours for more than just research."

Franklin knew Radish had no real grounds for any harassment, but he could make his freelance treasure hunting more difficult. He asked, "What do you want Radish?"

Radish replied, "I was thinking about all that loot you're finding out on the beach." He watched Franklin's expression, like he enjoyed making him squirm, and continued, "All those gold coins you've found."

My gold! A river of anxiety flooded Franklin's mind. *How many times has Radish seen me treasure hunting? And how much of my treasure does he know about?*

"What exactly are you getting at?"

"My point is, Boone, how you're finding those gold coins."

Franklin studied Radish's face. "Again, Sergeant, what do you want?"

"Jeez, don't get so worked up. Actually, I ain't the one who wants to talk with you."

Franklin's curiosity was piqued. What with so much gold laying around the Delaware beaches, he didn't like having strangers asking about his activities. "Who wants to see me?"

"A friend of mine. His name is Israel Mouzellas."

Franklin found it strange that Sergeant Radish had a local friend. "You've made friends off the base?"

"I'm actually from around here. My hometown is close enough that I can go home on the weekends, should I need a break from this dump of a fort."

"Aha, a backyard soldier, are you?"

"I guess so, Boone. Whatever that means. Listen, I just need you to figure out a good time that you can meet me an' Israel."

Franklin sized up the situation. If Radish was from a nearby town, then he had to be from farm country. Franklin, however, was a city boy, and all the dark forest and swampland around the base made him nervous. Therefore, simply by geographical association, any of Radish's local friends also made him nervous. He asked, "Why should I care

54

about meeting any friend of yours?"

"Come on Boone, don't be so wishy-washy. Israel just wants to talk with you about that metal detector of yours."

"Well, you can tell this Israel fellow where to find me."

"No, Boone." He continued, "Israel wants to meet you at a bar in Rehoboth, not on base. He has a job he thinks you'd be interested in. What day can I tell him you'll meet him?"

Franklin wasn't about to be pressured, but his curiosity was stirred. He asked, "A bar in Rehoboth? Why would I agree to meet anyone at one of those places?"

Radish shook his head and leaned back as he shoved his hand into his hip pocket. He pulled out a small leather pouch, with a pull-string tie keeping the opening shut, and tossed it at Franklin. "Well, he can pay you in these."

Franklin caught the pouch. It landed against his palm with a dull, metallic sound. He recognized it, but because it came to him from some strange leather pouch in the seclusion of Barracks Five he did not at first place the tone. He dumped the contents onto his artifact ledger. Five Spanish gold pieces fell out. They were all their own unique shape, as Franklin knew an authentic doubloon should be; the result of each ounce of gold being pounded and printed at the hands of an aboriginal slave in a lead-smoke-filled factory under the whip of a Spanish conquistador. Each coin had the same markings as the ones that Franklin had already found.

ISRAEL MOUZELLAS

Franklin agreed to meet Israel Mouzellas at the Swordfish Cantina, a local Rehoboth watering hole. Radish would arrive with his friend, and Franklin would meet them at the venue. Franklin, however, didn't have a car, so he had to call a cab. On his way to the pay phones near the front gates of Fort Miles, he found two of his fellow GIs already waiting for their own cab, and he was able to split the fare. The two men were MPs; one was Staff Sergeant Wilkins, whom he had met on the beach a few weeks earlier, and the other was Master Sergeant Marteen. The MPs were not great company, but the cab ride was short, and saving a few pennies never hurt.

Like all cabbies in the Rehoboth area, their driver was more than amenable to his servicemen passengers. He told them right away that their money was no good in his cab. However, once the driver was informed of their destination, the Swordfish Cantina, he became cold and joined any conversation with nothing more than grunted answers. The cab pulled up outside the cantina with a hard brake. When the three GIs opened the door, the cabby turned around and told them that their fare was going to be two dollars. The soldiers looked at the weathered and paint-stripped old building that was the Swordfish, then back to the cabbie and couldn't figure out what they had done to deserve their driver's ire. He grabbed the money from Franklin's hand, and without another word drove off.

Marteen and Wilkins' intention for the trip was to peruse the boardwalk, drink copious amounts of beer, and meet as many women as possible. They had no particular destination in mind, and decided they would stick close to Franklin. Franklin, however, told them that he was there for a personal business meeting unrelated to anything he was doing for the Army, and that he would not be able to sit with them.

Marteen said, "Business meeting, huh?"

Wilkins laughed and said, "Come on, Boone, we had our hearts set on cuddlin' with you all day."

Marteen continued, "Yeah, Boone. We know about Rehoboth Beach. We know what kind of business meetings happen around here."

Franklin knew that Rehoboth Beach was open to all walks of life, and was worried about the MPs spreading rumors back on the fort. Fort Miles was a very small and intimate community with a short grapevine. Information, true or not, spread fast and had the potential to morph into countless unforeseen fabrications.

Wilkins said, "Remember, Boone. We were coming down here before your scrawny ass showed up."

Franklin wasn't sure how much of Marteen and Wilkins' slights were jokes. He hoped that any real contempt might compel the two men to patronize another bar, but they knew Radish well. Marteen said, "I'll come over to your table when I damn well want to."

Franklin, already nervous about meeting Radish's strange, gold-coin-collecting friend at an all-inclusive Rehoboth cantina, took a deep breath. He wanted to be sharp for the meeting and not distracted with having to babysit two annoying MPs. Mostly, what Franklin wanted was for Marteen and Wilkins not to hear anything about the gold coins.

The Swordfish was more rustic on the inside than on the outside. Sitting at the bar were soldiers from Fort Miles as well as a few old locals who looked like they had more salt water in their veins than blood and more barnacles than teeth in their heads. To Franklin, the older locals from Rehoboth Beach were always a rough looking bunch. The women looked as weather-worn as the men, and even in the winter months their skin was tanned leather from years of coastal sunshine.

Though the middle of the day, the bar room was dark from little overhead lighting, foggy stained windows, and the dark, salt-aged mahogany benches and tables. Marteen and Wilkins were noticeably put off by the dark ambience of the room, and moved to two open seats near the door. Through the dim lighting, Franklin found Radish at the back of the room, sitting at a booth right outside the kitchen. A pint of lager sat in front of him, and he wore a white t-shirt and light canvas pants; nothing that spoke of his Army job. He sat across from an eccentric-looking man who wore sandals, canvas pants, and a black leather vest over a dirty, loose linen shirt. He sat bolt upright in the middle of his bench seat, with an opened liquor flask on the table in front of him. Israel's hair was a huge mop of dense brush. He had attempted to part the hair down the side, but the combed roots were overrun by the unruly ends. Franklin wasn't sure, and didn't want to stare, but Israel seemed to have a slight dent in his forehead. His hairline gave away the divot, just like the grasses on the dunes defined the slopes of the different hills. From certain angles, Israel's eyes seemed to be set wide in his skull, and Franklin couldn't tell if that was a result of a blow to his head, or just the natural cranium he was dealt. He was also impressed by Israel's beard, above which curled a mustache that he thought should be reserved for a circus conductor. It grew five or six inches off Israel's lips and was waxed to tight curls on the ends that looked like they would break if bent in any other direction.

When he introduced himself, Franklin was unsure on which side of the table to sit, but then he noticed an overstuffed, leather rucksack on the seat next to Israel, and he looked at Radish. Radish shifted towards the wall and Franklin sat down. Franklin's initial impression was that Israel was a bit stuffy. He tried to break the ice, "Interesting place. You guys come here a lot?"

Israel answered, "You're young, Franklin, but, if you're lucky, soon you will find that in places like this you can hide as easily as in any dune or woods."

Franklin turned to formally greet Radish, who returned a relatively genial shrug of his shoulders as he sipped his lager. He then replied, "Well Mr. Mouzellas, I'm not sure what you're talking about but, it's nice to meet you, and I could sure use a beer."

Israel looked towards the bar, raised his hand, and yelled to the bartender, "Oliver, another pint," then turned back to Franklin. "Good to finally make your acquaintance as well," he said. "So Franklin, Jameson tells me that you're pretty savvy with that metal detector of yours?"

Franklin had yet to hear Radish addressed by his first name. He replied, "That I am. It's not difficult. The more you use it, the more you learn how it speaks. If you know what I mean?"

Oliver sat a tray with two pints of beer on the edge of their table. He moved the beers in front of Radish and Franklin.

"Thank you Oliver," said Israel as he placed three dollar bills on the tray. Oliver walked away and Israel raised his flask to his lips. He sipped, then said, "I believe I do, Franklin. I believe I know exactly what you mean."

As the introductions continued, Israel said that he had grown up in the coastal regions of Southern Delaware and was as comfortable in the walking dunes as anywhere else in the world. He cursed the US Army for building Fort Miles where they did, and said he'd been working those dunes his entire life and now he couldn't walk among them without being arrested for trespassing on government property.

Franklin did not say a word for forty-five minutes.

THE *JACINTA*
AND SAMUEL SHAMFT

Israel explained that he did not want to talk with Franklin about finding gold coins. His interest was in finding a boat called the *Jacinta*. According to Israel, the *Jacinta* was a sixty-five-foot, blue-water cruiser, with a beam of about sixteen feet. His recounting was wishy-washy, and when Franklin asked him any question about the boat and its last trip, Israel answered with vague references that didn't seem to get at the exact question. Almost in passing, Israel mentioned that the *Jacinta* was a boat that his father had been interested in, but had never found.

"All I know about the boat is what my father told me. It was originally owned by some swell down in South Carolina, and floated to the Bahamas every year. But when the Kaiser started sendin' U-boats across the Atlantic, apparently pleasure cruisin' came to a halt, and the boat then spent the next five years or so on-the-hard. Which is considered bad luck for any boat." Israel took a sip from his flask. "For me, that makes for a cursed boat. But the details were not certain, and any superstitious curse didn't mean much to my father. Either way, that boat oughta just been scrapped. But it wasn't. Instead it was bought and repaired by a cheap, two-bit rumrunner from Charleston, South Carolina, named Samuel Shamft."

Radish shifted in his seat and sipped his beer.

Israel continued, "Before his death in 1923, Samuel Shamft was a big fish in the small pond of criminals in Charleston, and with the help of his son Randal, was the head of South Carolina's coastal syndicate for the state's illegal liquor trade. On the surface, they were pig farmers, but all the local businessmen and police knew that the livestock was just for show, occasionally for intimidation, and not so much to turn a profit. Of course, I'm sure you know Franklin, that the definition of 'profit' changes with the man sayin' it."

•

Samuel Shamft was smart enough to know that the one smuggling route filled with holes the size of an entire coastline started in the Gulf Stream. He also knew that he was no sailor and was never going to be a savvy waterman. So he immersed his seventeen-year-old son, Randal, in as many maritime activities and sailing lessons as the teenager could tolerate. Having established connections at most of the ports along the East Coast, it was not difficult for the elder Shamft to find a captain and crew that would join him in his liquor running, and hopefully teach his son all he needed to know about working on the water. He assumed that by the time Randal was done with his primary schooling, the maritime liquor routes would be well established, and the boy would be ready to join the family business full-time.

Unbeknownst to Samuel Shamft, Randal did not absorb his lessons well, as he had already established a strong penchant for booze. Samuel Shamft presented his first solo job to Randal like it was a rite of passage, and in May of 1919, Randal was tasked with captaining the *Jacinta* from Charleston to their primary offloading area, just north of the Rehoboth Beach boardwalk. But the beam of Randal's ego was wider than the biggest sailing yachts, and to crew his first ship he hired two drinking buddies. Young, stupid men who thought more of drinking booze than

62

they did of selling it.

Israel told Franklin, "So, Samuel Shamft took care of as many partic-
ulars as he could in preparin' his son for the *Jacinta* command, but what
he failed to account for was hurricane season, that the boat was so full of
rum it sat well below its safe draft line, and of course, mooncussers. The
cargo was bound for Philadelphia, where a group of customers waited for
the rum, and—" Israel looked Franklin in the eyes "—a case full of gold
bars that were stolen from a Charleston antiquity dealer's cargo."

Franklin finally heard something that he cared about.

"But you see, the *Jacinta* had to stop up here around Rehoboth.
Prohibition laws were strict and authorities had tightened their hold over
all the Delaware Bay ports and marinas, so transportation of any contraband had to move to dry land south of the bay. And this is what made the
thought of plunderin' that boat so temptin' for my father. Randal Shamft
knew little about sea travel. I've met plenty of runners like him. Men who
believe all they have to do is make it to the Gulf Stream and keep the
coast off their port side.

"My father knew from experience that any booze runnin' comin' into
Delaware stopped south of the bay. So he assumed that Randal Shamft's
plans were to head north until he saw the light from the Lewes Beacon.
Randal would have been told that the light would be visible by the time
he was outside of the boardwalk. After which he would continue for
another couple miles, to link up with his Delaware connections—local
Rehoboth men, Ethan and Jonathan Stoccaccio. He would turn in towards
land for the night. No more than a hundred yards offshore. There, he
would have dropped anchor, set up some sort of signal, and waited for
the offloadin'. At some point durin' the night, the Stoccaccios' crew were
supposed to motor out in their fishin' boats and off-load the cargo, which

would then be brought ashore and loaded into trucks bound for Wilmington."

Israel sipped from his flask, and continued his explanation of the *Jacinta's* last voyage, like someone who had pondered the situation for way too many hours. "The ship must have entered Maryland waters in the late afternoon, but it wasn't outside of the boardwalk until after dusk. I imagine that crew was exhausted from what had to have been over a week at sea. Which was another element that made it an easy target. As I'm sure you know, Franklin, fatigue can make a man impatient. So, my father hoped to exploit that possibility and lure Randal into makin' poor decisions. When we knew he was just north of the boardwalk we set our plan into action. Our crew-mate, Smitty Smithsenson, worked the Lewes Beacon, so he was tasked with turnin' it off. At which time our false beacon was turned on. We lit a kerosene lantern and hung it on a post in front of a large, concave reflectin' glass. The shape of the mirror expanded the lantern's light, and created the illusion that the device was actually the beacon light. But bein' smaller than the beacon light, any captain at sea would assume his safe anchorage was farther away than it really was. So, naturally, the captain would continue north, then turn inland when he found himself directly offshore from the light. But, bein' closer than he thought, he would soon find himself runnin' aground. And once he was stuck on the shoals... well... that's when the plunderin' would begin." Israel took another sip, then said, "This was the trap that we set up that night, about a mile south of the real Lewes Beacon, and directly ashore of the Hen and Chickens Shoal. You know anythin' about the Hen and Chickens Shoal, Franklin?"

"Not much. Just that it's the best place around here to find treasure."

"That's right. But as well as that, the currents there are some of the most dangerous on the Eastern Shore. And underneath those waves, there's hundreds of years of shipwrecks. Which is why the treasure huntin' is so good around there. I'm sure you've seen a ship's beam or two stickin' out of the water every now and again. But Randal Shamft wouldn't'a known anythin' about that, even with those Stoccaccios workin' with him. And that's why we always set up off the shoals. My dad liked to use those natural elements to his advantage.

"So we loaded our cart with all the usual gear, includin' an upturned lifeboat we used to shield the tools and gun powder from the rain. The cart and boat were pulled to the beach behind Smitty's truck. Like I said, Smitty was tasked with turnin' off the beacon light, so once we were at the beachhead he unhitched the cart and then drove north. Then the rest of us pushed the cart and boat to our designated spot on the beach. It was above the dunes, on the forest berm, where we knew the lantern light would project the best. My mother and sister worked the lantern, while the rest of us readied the other gear.

"My father was certain Randal Shamft would be an easy target, and I gotta admit, after we turned on the lantern, he bit like a hungry fish. Unfortunately, he turned towards land just as the first blast of thunder sounded off the top of the bay. In a single moment the skies blew up, the *Jacinta* ran aground, and my father ordered me to light the Lyle gun. Of course I asked him, 'If we fire too early, won't they know we've been waitin' for 'em?' But time was not on our side, and we had to fire the canon before the powder got wet. I recall, as the weight shot over the boat's deck, the *Jacinta* was pushed forward by a wave that ground it deeper into the shoals, and then the second thunderclap opened up the sky.

"It was the most difficult job I had done up to that time in my life. I

65

could see waves breakin' far out from shore, and I got no relief as I rowed the lifeboat. Even with my father and Buster Rolfe guiding the boat via the hawser line that the *Jacinta's* crew had attached to their grounded boat's mast, rowin' was near impossible. Finally, though, we made it close enough for Buster to lash the bow and stern of the lifeboat to the side rails of the *Jacinta*. My father and Buster then disappeared over the rail. I heard gunfire but struggled with my balance so I couldn't easily get to my feet. The winds pounded my boat into the side of the yacht, and screeched through the riggin'. I saw shadows of men on the deck, then the mast of the *Jacinta* was snapped in half, and the hawser line to my lifeboat was attached to was cut. Another wave came on and crashed my boat against the side of the yacht, and I was thrown down under the benches and knocked unconscious. I awoke the next day underneath the lifeboat. It was stuck in the side of the forest berm, completely over the dunes. After diggin' myself out, I searched the rest of that day, up and down the beach, and found no trace of that damned sailboat."

A SCUFFLE

Israel's story was interrupted by an argument at the bar. The uproar involved Marteen and Wilkins. Since arriving they had consumed enough beer that they spoke to each other as if they were having a conversation from different sides of the room. Their voices carried enough to get on the nerves of the patrons sitting next to them. And when they were asked to speak in a lower volume, the MPs became cross. The commotion did not last long, as Oliver moved to their end of the bar and reminded the MPs that this was his place and he didn't care if they were in the Army or not, and that he would personally see to their forceful removal should they continue with any obnoxious behavior. Marteen and Wilkins did not leave. Instead they sat back at their bar stools, scowling and talking between themselves.

Israel looked across the room then turned his eyes back to Franklin as if to ask why he would want to associate with such riffraff. He also made note of the MP's repeated glances towards his table. Franklin could see the agitation in Israel's face.

"Those your friends, Franklin?"

"Not particularly. Acquaintances, really. More friends with Radish."

Israel looked at Radish. "Hmm. I should'a known."

Israel had not given Radish much attention during the meeting, and Radish had not said a word since Franklin greeted him.

For the next hour, the topics at the table ranged between Franklin's metal detector upgrades, and the large clusters of metal that might be buried with the *Jacinta*, like the keel, or, as Franklin hoped, the gold. Israel didn't know much about the origins of the gold bars, but said they were from some wealthy philanthropist who had found piles of Spanish gold, silver, and jewels up and down the coasts of Florida. The man had apparently melted the precious metals and reconstituted them into 10 ounce bars and was planning on shipping all of it to Switzerland via steamer.

"But he was paranoid," explained Israel, "He hired too many guards to watch over his loot, and Samuel Shamft had too many people in his employ, especially around the ports of South Carolina. I don't know what exactly happened, but Shamft's guys ended up with the gold, and there was no mention of it at the port, or in the papers, because no one knew about the shipment in the first place. But Smitty Smithsenson knew. Somehow that rotten old waste of air knew that on the *Jacinta* there would be a collection of those gold bars."

Franklin latched on to every word in Israel's story. He needed to know as much as possible before deciding what to believe. But the thought of this mysterious collection of gold bars made the hairs on his neck stand up. Without knowing what a reconstituted gold bar might look like, he thought of all he had learned as a result of his recent treasure hunting hobby. He had purchased a purity kit that had the necessary chemicals and steps to determine the karat value of a precious metal, and he knew that the more pure silver or gold was, the more it shines.

These gold bars must be amazing. Adding a few of them to my collection would certainly be nice.

Israel brought up a topic that was something of a surprise for Franklin. "You strike me as an educated man."

Franklin joked, "I've read a few books."

"I'm sure you have," Israel said. "I'm curious if you have ever come across Homer's *Odyssey*?"

Radish scoffed.

Franklin had read the epic poem once while in a Classic Literature class at college. His mind raced to remember specifics from the story. He answered, "Of course. Why do you ask?"

"It's a great maritime tale, isn't it?"

"I suppose it is."

"Do you remember the Sirens?"

Franklin thought back to the section of the poem in which Odysseus is lashed to the mast of his ship so he can witness the dangerously hypnotizing song of the Sirens without jumping overboard in an attempt to find the sweet singers. Meanwhile, Odysseus had his crew fill their ears with beeswax so they won't hear the song and therefore be able to continue to man the ship. "Yeah, I know that story. What about it?"

"In your opinion, do you think Odysseus was successful?"

"Yes, for the most part, I believe he was. He seemed to never be able to get on Poseidon's good side, but after all was said and done, things seem to work out pretty well for him."

Israel agreed and said, "But do you know why he is so successful?"

Franklin had no answer.

Israel said, "Because he has a good crew on his side. That's right, Odysseus would never have achieved what he does without his crew. As a result of their sacrifice, he is able to complete his journey."

Franklin tried to remember the whole poem. "I'm not sure it's all his crew's doing, I recall something about a woman named Calypso, a witch who allows him safe travels back home—"

"I'm not talking about Calypso. I'm tryin' to impress upon you the value of a trustworthy crew." He waited, staring at Franklin. "I'm wonderin' what the word means to you?"

"Well, I guess—"

"No guessin'! I want to know right now if you value the sanctity of a good crew."

"Sanctity?"

"Yes. The benefits of a group of men workin' towards the same goal. None greater than the sum of their collective parts."

"You mean like an Army platoon."

"Or like a pirate crew."

Radish snorted out a quick laugh. Israel cracked a smile.

Franklin tensed in anticipation of being the butt of an inside joke. "A pirate crew, huh?"

"Yes, Franklin. Don't knock the notion of a pirate crew. They were just outlaws who operated on the water, and were more organized than you might think. Like any trustworthy crew, any successful group of pirates had rules and policies to which they adhered."

While Israel proceeded to instruct Franklin on the merits of working with a trustworthy crew, Franklin appreciated the similarities between a pirate crew and an Army platoon. There was a common mission; members were organized into a rank and file; everyone was assigned a specific task or job; and no one worked solely for themselves as much as for the success of the entire group. The allure of being on a crew was strong for most men. There was great emotional benefit in knowing that a group of good men trusted your brains and talent enough to let you run with a task, naturally compelling one to want to work harder, or suffer the price of compromising the crews' goals, and therefore being ostracized, or worse.

Franklin finished the conversation with an answer to Israel's initial question. "Yes, Israel, I understand the value in a trustworthy crew. I wouldn't be where I am today if I felt any different."

Israel was about to speak, but the conversation was again stumped by another verbal altercation at the bar. Marteen and Wilkins were now more drunk, and had gotten up to confront two other men. The sudden outburst startled Israel, and in a knee-jerk fashion he slammed his fist onto the table and yelled across the room, "Oliver, what's the problem?"

At the sound of Israel's voice, the entire room, including Marteen and Wilkins, crashed into silence.

Oliver raised his hands and tilted his head at the MPs, not sure if he wanted to escalate their drunken emotions. Franklin was wary of hanging around with MPs, especially because one never knew when they might try and pull rank, and these two didn't strike him as the most rational of men. His main worry was the treasure hunt. If Israel associated Franklin with the two drunks at the bar, then Israel might not want to work with him. Franklin hoped Marteen and Wilkins would shut up and leave. But they didn't shut up. They gulped down what remained of their beers and slammed the glasses onto the bar. Oliver told them to get out of his cantina. They ignored the order, and walked over to Franklin's table, clattering any chair out of their way.

Standing at the head of the table, Marteen said, "Do you have something you want to say, old man?"

Franklin interjected, "Wait a minute you guys–" but was cut off by Wilkins.

"Shut up, Boone. You'd rather associate with this poofer instead of us. Well you can kiss my ass."

Under the table Franklin clenched his fists, despite knowing that fighting an MP never ended well for a GI.

Radish tried to speak. "Okay Wilkins, this is—" But Marteen out-ranked Radish, both in his Army position and in his current level of ine-briation. Marteen ordered him to shut up, and Radish did as he was told.

Marteen then turned back to Israel, who sat upright and unmoved, while the MP leaned closer and slurred, "I assed you a question, old man…"

Israel ignored the MP, despite Marteen's beer-breath being so close to his face, and looked at Radish. He shook his head in disgrace at his tablemate and said, "You're going to let these idiots treat you like that, Jameson? Is this the kind of coward that the US Army produces these days?"

Israel's challenge made Radish shift in his seat, but it also angered the two drunk MPs. They demanded the undistracted attention of every-one at the table.

Israel looked across the table, and said, "You see Franklin, this is my biggest problem with the Army. As often as not, you have to take orders from people who have nothin' over you other than a few more stripes on their shoulders." He pointed his thumb at Marteen. "Like these two—"

Finally getting the attention that he wanted, Marteen snarled, "Hey, old man," and grabbed at Israel's thumb. At the first sense of the MPs hand on his own, Israel reacted with uncanny speed and managed to twist his hand free, and then, like a magician's sleight of hand, had Marteen's own fingers under his control. In one fluid movement Israel snapped Marteen's index finger backwards by pushing Marteen's hand up into his face. Marteen's fingers crumpled willy-nilly across his mouth and nose, poking eyes and pulling nostrils, and he looked like a marionette chas-ing a bothersome fly. Marteen stumbled backwards, but Israel did not let go. Instead, he stood up, then slipped his foot behind Marteen. Marteen tripped, and Israel gave his hand one last push. The MP fell into another table, slamming his head against the edge.

Seeing his friend in peril, Wilkins turned to help. He took a swing at Israel and connected square in the back of his head. Wilkins cursed at the pain in his fist. Franklin was certain that Israel was done, but he hardly budged. The punch seemed to only fuel Israel's contempt for the MPs. He turned around to find Wilkins cocking his arm back for another strike. Israel did not try to dodge, but rather sacrificed his unprotected head in order to lure his opponent's arm in close. Wilkins swung, but Israel moved forward, rending the punch ineffective. He had his hands around Wilkins' throat before he could evade them. Wilkins tried to unhinge Israel's fingers, but he found himself unbalanced and being pushed back against the chairs at a neighboring table.

Radish yelled, "No!" He pushed past Franklin, and jumped between Wilkins and Israel. "Come on Israel, don't do this again. Think about where you are." Israel did not stop squeezing. Wilkins' face turned purple and he choked out spit across Israel's hands.

Radish continued, "Israel, let him go. This isn't the old days. These are US soldiers. Do yourself a favor and let this one go."

Israel released his grip, and Wilkins fell to the ground gasping. Radish turned to him and yelled, "Wilkins, you know getting in fights with civilians is a one way ticket to the brig. You'll never leave base again. You guys have already done enough, so you and Marteen get the hell out of here."

Wilkins got to his feet. Pain and adrenaline sobered him enough to see he was in no shape to continue challenging Israel. Wilkins slapped Radish's hands out of his way and bent down to help Marteen, who cursed as he stood up, cradling his distorted fist like one might carry a full glass of piping hot water.

Israel stepped back to the table, looked at Franklin, and before sitting down he motioned to Oliver for another round of drinks. As if none of the fighting had just occurred, and while Marteen and Wilkins were still trying to get their bearings, Israel began a new subject. "Franklin, I am a strict leader. I believe that nothin' is too difficult to achieve. Yes, a harder task may be time-consumin'. But success requires discipline and patience. I believe that I can do anythin' I put my mind to."

Franklin waited for Israel to say more as he watched the MPs collect themselves. Israel went on, "I like your savvy nature, your wirin' up-grades, and your drive to find treasure." The new round of drinks arrived. The conversation stalled for a few seconds. Everyone took a breath and finally relaxed as Marteen and Wilkins stumbled out the door. Israel changed the subject again. "I think of myself as somethin' of an Odysseus, and you and Jameson here will be my crew." Israel looked from Radish back to Franklin. "Of course on my crew those who work hard will have more value."

Franklin remembered more of the *Odyssey* and asked, "Yeah, but if I recall correctly, don't all of Odysseus' crew die?"

Israel grabbed his flask and before putting it to his lips he said, "Yes, but that's neither here nor there."

MOONCUSSING

After some silent moments while the three of them sipped their drinks, Israel followed up on an earlier topic. "Franklin, you ever hear of the term mooncusser?"

"No."

"They're a certain kind of pirate. A mooncusser works from land, and only durin' the darkest nights, as opposed to your standard, run-of-the-mill pirate who works any time of the month, and will know as much about sailin' as he does about killin'. Believe me, since the first European asshole put his foot on the coast of this land, there have been hundreds of thousands of ships driftin' into the Delaware Bay. Easy pickin's for anyone who's not afraid to test his mettle on the waves."

•

Mooncussers looked forward to the days of the month around the new moon when there would be little light in the sky, and the darkness of night was just as confusing to a sailor as the whiteout of a thick fog. Under the shroud of a moonless night, a smart mooncusser had many options at his fingertips for luring ocean-going vessels to their demise: from setting bonfires, to walking donkeys with lanterns around their necks back and forth on the highest dune, to using the lantern-and-reflective-glass-panel method. In order to then plunder the newly-grounded ship, a mooncusser then had to leave land. This was a task performed by way of rowboat and a small crew of men. Rafael Mouzellas, Israel's father, had improved upon this when he stole equipment from the local Life Saving Station. Rafael Mouzellas assumed that no sailor would expect a pirate crew to have access to a Lyle gun and use the same tools that the Life Saving Service used.

To save the crew of a vessel that had run aground was no small feat, and before 1915, when the US Coast Guard Service was instituted, the vigil over the North American Eastern Seaboard was kept by what was called the National Life Saving Service. From Maine to Florida, life saving houses were built. Most of the houses were set up in the more desolate areas of the coastline, as areas around major ports already had long established lookouts and infrastructure that could locate and launch a rescue. In the southern, warmer areas a life saving house was more of a "refuge house." These buildings were usually watched over by one man and a lifeboat; the thought was that the warm water was less of a threat and sailors could successfully swim to safety. Whereas in the colder and more deadly waters off the northern shoreline a house might be manned by twenty or more trained men, and equipped with all the necessary tools for saving sailors in need.

In the more desolate areas of the coast, such as Southern Delaware, the life saving houses were built close enough to each other that the men could cover the distance between houses on foot as they patrolled the shoreline. Of course, the distance between the station houses was not made too wide because in the event of an emergency, the life saving men had to manually push or carry all their equipment potentially miles up the beach.

In times of emergency, not only did the life saving men have to haul their gear, but once at the best location for action, they had to set up the equipment. The task was daunting because more often than not, they were working during a storm. Ships didn't usually run aground in calm weather. But the men were thoroughly trained, and once the best location on the beach was established, the crew could have their equipment set up within minutes.

The life saving equipment consisted of many unique tools that were used in no other trade. First, two tarred, wooden beams called the crotch posts were secured in the sand, near the froth, with their topmost points crossed like an X. Over the center of the X, the *hawser* line was run and then anchored two feet into the sand by way of a heavy weight or large stone. Between the end of the hawser and the ground were a series of pulleys and a *hauling lever* that was used to adjust tension on the hawser line once it was secured on the sinking vessel's mast. One man's job was to watch over the hauling lever and be constantly ready to adjust the tension, as a grounded vessel was most likely pushed back and forth by the waves and stormy currents.

But before the hawser was attached to the ship's mast, it had to be delivered. This was accomplished by way of a small cannon called a *lyle gun*. The lyle gun was loaded with a twenty pound threaded weight that could be shot upwards of 700 yards. The rope threaded through the shot weight was called the *shot line*. These ropes were hundreds of yards long and were woven around pegs in a *faking box*. This was a large wooden box inside of which was a flat platform with long pegs sticking out of it, not unlike a weaving loom. How the shot line was woven around the pegs in the box and then how the box was set up on shore was critical for any successful life saving operation. If woven incorrectly, the shot line could snap when the weight was fired, or might tangle so quickly that the rescue operation was hampered.

The ignition of the lyle gun heated up the shot weight so much that it glowed bright red, and was visible during the darkest of nights. Sailors of the time were trained in emergency management, and would look for the glowing weight. The weight would fly high over the ship, pulling the shot line behind it, until finally falling into the water.

Once the shot line was fired, and retrieved by the stranded crew, it was then used to pull out the hawser line. Once in the hands of the crew, the hawser was then lashed as high as possible to the mast. Along with the hawser came two other ropes that were set up by way of pulleys, and were used to move the breeches buoy out to the ship for human retrieval, and then back to the safety of shore. The hawser was no common rope. It was at least two inches thick, and able to support the weight of the breeches buoy and one to three humans who were most likely soaking wet. The breeches buoy was a canvas "seat" that was hung from a pulley on the hawser line. It had leg holes through which a man could sit, and be pulled to shore. In times of dire need, two or three men could straddle the edges of the breeches buoy. But this was not ideal, since the more weight in the buoy, the more likely the people being saved would be dragged to shore through the water.

Of course, rescue crews were equipped with all other tools necessary for setting up their life saving gear, and for comforting wet, freezing sailors.

•

As far back as Israel could remember, the men in his family had worked the shoreline of Southern Delaware. His grandfather was a surfman at the Indian River Life Saving Station. It was a time when regulations were loose, and for as many lives that were saved, an equal number were left to perish and have their possessions plundered.

Israel's father, Rafael, was also a surfman until 1915, when the Life

Saving department was combined with the Revenue Cutter Service and the US Coast Guard was created. But with the advent of such a regulated federal institution came an entrance exam that all new recruits and experienced surfmen had to pass. Rafael, and many other surfmen who either were not educated enough or didn't believe that some desk jockey in Washington ought to tell them how to do their work, soon found themselves jobless. This was what pushed Israel's father towards a side of his skill set that was very much effective, although under the table and not by the book.

Israel explained, "My father's trick, you see, was to exploit the emotional state of his victims and lead 'em to believe that the rope they just tied to their mast was there to save 'em. Any seasoned captain or crew knew about the Life Savin' Service, and even though all of my father's illegal use of those tools was after the service was disbanded, most grounded sailors rarely thought not to attach a rope that was shot their way. Likewise, no crew was going to just wait for a Coast Guard rescue that may or may not ever show up. It was a safe bet that they would tie first, and worry about everythin' else later. My father loved it if the crew were really scared, because they were easier to give orders to. If they were scared enough, all my father had to do was hand 'em the breeches buoy ropes and they would hop to it. Then he could grab ahold of any random rigging and wait."

Franklin interrupted, "He would wait on a sinking ship?"

"Yes. Just because a ship has run aground, doesn't mean it's necessarily sinkin' fast. It's a lot more frightenin' when you're the crew on a grounded boat. If you've caused the groundin', as my father did, then control of your emotions is easier, and imperative." Israel continued, "Once the buoy ropes were tied, the crew would ride the breeches to shore. And when they reached the shallow waves, the sailors would be overtaken by Buster Rolfe, or whoever was on beach duty. If the sailors had any fight to 'em, they'd have their throats slit, but usually they were so tired they could barely get out of the breeches. Those ones would be held down in the waves 'til they stopped kickin'. And any corpses left layin' around just looked like they floated ashore from the wreck.

"Then came the plunderin'. You ever try to plunder a boat while it's grounded in a current like the Hen and Chickens Shoal?"

Franklin assumed Israel was joking. Like most people, he had little boat plundering experience. He shrugged and sipped his lager. But he was impressed by the sheer guts it would have taken to not just coerce a ship into running aground, but to then row out to the broken vessel, kill its crew, and finally plunder the boat as it slowly sank. Rafael Mouzellas had successfully done this countless times, and failed only once. Israel relayed this information as if apologetic, but finished with a shrug of his shoulders and said, "After so many successful plunderin's you're only pressin' your luck anyway."

1921

When Israel regained consciousness the morning after the botched *Jacinta* plundering, it took him close to an hour to hobble down the berm, over the dunes, and back to the beach. He could not stop himself from intermittently passing out. His entire body was in pain, and he could not clear his vision. Eventually, he was picked up by a fisherman who had been out casting all morning, and the good samaritan drove him home. Sumi-Sun and Lulu-Pine tended to his wounds, and it was not long before Smitty Smithsenson made a house call.

Sumi-Sun stood on the porch with her arms crossed. Her eyes scoured Smitty. She too had not yet recovered from having to flee the previous night's hurricane, and was certain that she was a widow. She knew it wasn't Smitty's fault—he did not control the weather—but he had been the one to bring the fateful caper to her husband's attention.

Israel lay convalescing, aching and covered in bandages made from ripped up pants that were of questionable cleanliness. Every breath came with a tight, stab to his side, and allowed him no rest.

Smitty entered the bedroom and couldn't help but say, 'Dear Jesus!' as he approached Israel's bed. He didn't know which swollen eye to look into when he spoke.

Israel could only see a thin haze of a man standing next to his bed, but he knew it was Smitty because of the smell of salt and whiskey that followed him everywhere. It was nearly impossible for Israel to speak. He lifted a hand to let Smitty know he was aware of his presence. The pauses between Smitty's sentences and the rattle to his voice made it clear that he was afraid. The effort of listening and trying to speak made Israel more delirious. Smitty started the conversation with, 'I don't suppose you've seen your father?' Then there was a long period of his voice echoing in the back of Israel's head.

•

Smitty had done his job. He'd made it to the beacon and turned the light off, and from the top of the beacon tower saw the lantern come on about a mile down the beach. Then all he had to do was watch the horizon. The sky was an early dark grey, broken only by the blazing fire that Sumi-Sun and Lulu-Pine had ignited. It was a small pit in which the fire was lit, but it sat in front of a mirror that magnified the light. To the left, close to the breaking waves, he saw the dark figures of his crew. They had finished setting up the equipment and were waiting and watching the distant ship. Smitty followed their obvious gaze, out to the faint silhouette of the *Jacinta*. It moved due north, then turned hard to port, in towards land. But something about the image confused Smitty. It was as if the dark boat suddenly became lost in the sky behind it. Smitty turned to look north, past the tip of Cape May, New Jersey, where the horizon was engulfed in a leviathan of clouds. The storm was distant, but moving fast towards the shore. Lightning blinked and the thunder rolled by seconds later. This was no ordinary rainstorm.

Smitty grabbed the pull-chain that triggered the Beacon's foghorn. He and Rafael had long established an emergency signal system, in case Smitty observed something pressing enough that a job should be immediately canceled. Three consecutive blasts of the horn was the shut-down signal. But Smitty held his hand still and considered the impending storm.

He looked back through the monocular at his friends on the shore, when the next clap of thunder reached the shoals. The clouds were closer now, and when every inch of sky was shrouded in darkness, Smitty let go of the pull-chain.

In the few conversations that Smitty Smithsenson would later have regarding the hurricane of 1921, he described how the winds pushed against the beacon tower, shaking it like it was a mere blade of grass in the dunes. He said the tower leaned under the stress of the wind right before he made a dash to the keeper's house, which was about fifty yards inland. Sand and dirt filled the air and stung his face as he stumbled to the house.

At the keeper's house, Smitty found shelter in the cellar, where he waited out the storm. But the last thing he told Israel on that visit was, "Izzy, I swear there weren't nothin' I could'a done to help you down 'nere on the beach, but I think we might've a bit of a chance to—"

Israel raised his hand again, not sure if he was trying to hurry Smitty or shut him up. But the old man kept talking. "I swear, when'd I was runnin' to the house, with the wind and sand piercin' every inch of my body, I was movin' on instinc', as a man who don't need his eyes to git where he's goin'. But, you know, a man's natural tendency is to try an' open his eyes despite what might be blowin' outside his lids. Like a fool I done that once as I run across't the beacon yard, once before the sting of the rain forced 'em shut agin. And in that very secont a burst of lightnen' opened up the sky, and from where I was I could see all the way across't the dunes, and there was that boat push't right up on the beach. And that was the last I saw of anythin' on account of my eyes bein' blinded by the weather."

After Rafael Mouzellas disappeared, Smitty became more distant from the Mouzellas family. Once or twice, out of guilt, he brought a few dollars or scraps of food by the house. Sometimes he would help Israel hunt for the *Jacinta* wreckage, but those trips were scattered and he wasn't much of a help.

Israel spent almost every day for the next two years searching and digging around the dunes. At first, he just picked a spot and began digging north, and when he didn't find anything in that direction, he turned around and dug south. And when he found nothing in that direction, he searched north again. But it was useless. That hurricane could have pushed the *Jacinta* anywhere up, down, inland, or back out to sea.

AN INVITATION

❝ After two years of searchin', I had just about given up hope.
I was tired and had no new strategy for diggin' any deeper than
my intuition, two arms, and a shovel might allow," Israel said. "Smitty
was also at the end of his rope. It was our mutual belief that the boat had
become mixed in with all the other shipwrecks that covered the shoal.
That was, until I overheard the Henlopen Lighthouse keeper—I don't
remember his name, as the lighthouse guys were more tightly wound than
us locals, due to their allegiance to their government jobs."

Franklin was trying to understand all the characters in Israel's tale.
He interrupted, "You mean the beacon operator?"

"No. Before the hurricane of 1921 there was the Lewes Beacon, and
the larger lighthouse about a mile north, up on the cape, called the Cape
Henlopen Lighthouse. Due to the nature of the shoals, the powers that be
built the beacon to supplement the lighthouse. Apparently, the two lights
made navigatin' the Delaware Bay's mouth less threatenin'. Locals like
Smitty worked the beacon, and the feds worked the lighthouse. That is,
before both lights fell into the ocean.

"Turns out, the lighthouse guys were no friends of my father. They
weren't sons of any locals, so my father had always kept his distance, as
they were sure to not be obliged to join him in any plunderin' operations.
Smitty and I had just finished a long stint on the beach, and were about to
have a rum. He got up from the bar to hit the jakes, and I had a moment

of quiet to collect my thoughts, when I overheard their conversation a few seats down the bar. Apparently the lighthouse man was retirin' and was havin' a drink with his replacement. They were recountin' their most harrowin' tales of the sea, when the operator brought up a tale of a hurricane he had to sit through a few years earlier. Knowin' that the last storm to hit Rehoboth Beach was the hurricane that killed my father, I was interested in hearin' what he had to say.

"The operator raised his right hand as if it made his tale more true, and said, 'Now I might have been boozed up that night. That I will not deny, though it was certainly not any worse than any previous night in the tower. But I swear I saw a boat sittin' up in the dunes.' The new recruit didn't seem too phased by the story. That is, until he was told the end. 'I swear,' said the old operator, 'there was a ship in the damn dunes. It looked like a small sailin' vessel, but without the mast, and its stern was crushed. And in the time it took me to grab a lookin' glass and focus back down the shoreline, there was not a trace of boat remainin'.'"

Israel described the lighthouse keeper's conversation, claiming, "That decrepit slob laughed at how, as soon as he retired, he was goin' to spend some quality time diggin' that boat up." He shook his head and continued, "I tell you what, Franklin, I could barely contain myself. All that information sent my mind reelin' and filled it with new hope. Apparently the hurricane had moved the *Jacinta* up-shore about half a mile before tossin' it onto the dunes. This meant that I could use the location of the Lewes Beacon—where Smitty saw the boat on shore—and triangulate it with a general idea of where the boat might have been seen from the lighthouse, and come up with a more accurate location to search. Needless to say, this news couldn't have come at a better time. My will to keep searchin' needed a shot in the arm. Of course, I told Smitty nothin' of

86

what I had just heard, as I was losin' my faith in him. But that discovery fueled me for the next couple years. That is, until I had to leave town."

The conversation lasted another half hour. As he got up from the table, Israel said, "If Uncle Sam doesn't need you this Sunday, why don't you pay me a visit for supper? You and Jameson can drive out to the farmhouse together. I'm goin' to need to see that detector of yours sooner or later."

Franklin felt like he was about to be asked to join in on an adventure the scale of which he had yet to take part. It was a treasure hunt that was questionably legal in its ownership by Israel, though definitely illegal in its presence on US military land.

THE PINE FOREST

For the rest of the week, whenever he had a moment to think about anything other than his research, Franklin stewed over Israel's dinner invitation. Israel had asked him to bring the 625G, reminding him that this was his ticket onto the crew. Israel came across as a man who had experience with mechanical things, and Franklin knew that his metal detector was not something that took a lot of studying to operate. Of all the parts, the copper coil was the most technically difficult element of the 625G, and, Franklin assumed, his knowledge of this was the best avenue through which he could prove his value.

By Sunday, Franklin had decided that he would have dinner with Israel and hear what he had to say. So, that afternoon, he packed the 625G in its travel duffel and waited outside the lab for Sergeant Radish. He was dismayed to see that the guard working the exit gates that night was Master Sergeant Marteen. He'd been taken off his beach patrol duties and relegated to the front gate detail due to his broken fingers. Despite it being a temporary assignment, he was not happy about his current job. Since his drunken dismantling the previous week at the Swordfish, anytime they bumped into each other, Marteen had been just short of threatening to Franklin, and even standoffish with his fellow MP, Sergeant Radish.

It would be next to impossible for Franklin to get the 625G past the front gates without being scrutinized. Radish was driving one of the fort's many jeeps, and it had no enclosed trunk. The 625G's duffel was not small, would be in plain view, and Marteen would surely give Franklin a hard time about it.

They turned onto the road that headed towards the front gates.

"Stop," said Franklin.

Radish pushed the brakes.

Franklin asked, "Aren't you worried about trying to get the detector past Marteen?"

Radish stared from behind the steering wheel. "Dammit," he mumbled, and pushed the gas. Before the traffic control area at the mouth of the gate was the stockyard road that led to the southern half of Fort Miles. Radish turned a hard left. His barracks were on the left, and the train switch station on the right.

Franklin asked, "What the hell are you doing?"

"I have an idea," replied Radish.

He drove out to the fire road that ran past the South Field and the shooting range. Several empty dump trucks sat along the backside of the field, blocking a small section of the perimeter fence. Radish stopped in front of a locked gate, and hopped out of the driver's seat. He hurried around the jeep and unlocked the padlock with a key from a cluster that hung off his belt. He pulled the gate open and turned to Franklin. "Grab your duffel, and take that path there." He pointed to the path that led from the gate to a bend that turned south, on the top edge of the dune berm, and paralleled the pine forest. "About a half mile after that bend you'll find a deer trail that turns into the forest. You can't miss it. Just keep walking in the same direction that the deer trail takes you and you will get to Route 9 in about thirty minutes. The trail may veer south at some point, but you gotta keep goin' straight towards the road, or west—I guess. It ain't hard, Boone. You got this far in life, navigating those woods won't be the hardest thing you ever do. "

Franklin wasn't sure if Radish was joking. The evening sun was low and on the other side of the forest from where Franklin stood. He surveyed the path. After the bend, the path moved into the long shadow of the forest. It might as well have gone straight into the woods for all he was concerned. "What the hell are you trying to pull here Radish?"

"Nothing, Boone. If you have a better idea, you can tell me. I don't give a damn if we have dinner at Israel's. But he sure seems to want to meet that detector of yours as much as he wants to talk with you. So, give me a better idea. You could hike to the boardwalk on the open beach, but that's over four miles, and every local this side of the bay will see you. Or you could hike a mile through the woods. Jesus, Boone, if you somehow get lost, just follow the pink of the sun. It's setting, so you know it's in the west. Or, just keep the damn ocean to your back." Radish waited a few seconds for a response, then drove off saying, "I'll pick you up on the other side."

Franklin was not happy with the plan. The hike out to Route 9 was close to a mile on the dune berm path, then another mile through the pine forest, and that was assuming he didn't get lost. For Franklin, hiking that distance was easy, as he had done it countless times in his training. But moving through a dense forest was difficult at best, and now he would be carrying his duffel with the 625G and all its components, at dusk, and alone.

On the other side of the gate, the terrain continued to be flat for another hundred yards before dropping down into the dunes. This was the dune berm, or the wall that rose up to create the ridge on which Fort Miles and the pine forest sat. And immediately to the right of the perimeter fence was a long, flat stretch of low shrubs, milkweed, grasses, and small trees that reached all the way around to the train tracks and road just outside of Fort Miles' front gates.

Franklin pulled the duffel over his shoulder and followed the path from the fence. He skirted along the top of the dune ridgeline. The bend was a slow southern turn, and brought him right up against the ocean-side face of the pine forest. The low sun, however, shone little light on the path, and Franklin wondered if he would miss the deer trail. A cacophony of birds sang from the dark innards of the woods, as all the treetops swayed and hissed in the ocean breeze. The smell of the forest was close and heavy.

After walking for what he considered a mile, Franklin decided he had missed the deer trail. He stopped and looked at the trees. He knew it was not a long hike from where he was to the edge of Route 9, but stood frozen. Besides in a few picture books, he had never seen a forest before joining the Army, and did not like being in them by himself. The pine trees stood too close, and had thousands of low, dead branches that protruded in every direction like a wall of bayonets. He looked up, searching for any trace of the sun. At the very top of the trees, the pine needles floated colorless amongst the waning daylight.

Stepping into the forest, his fears were compounded by the darkness. Immediately the branches dragged against his duffel bag, making it seem heavier. It may have been early dusk, but any remaining sunlight was blocked once he went under the pine canopy. He moved slowly, twisting around branches and stumbling over fallen limbs. As he hiked, he cursed Radish, Israel Mouzellas, and all the gold buried on the Delaware shores.

In addition to the crunching of his feet on the loamy bed of pine needles, Franklin thought he heard a twig snap. He stopped to listen, turning his head left and right to try and catch any new sounds.

Another snap came from somewhere behind him. Franklin swung his whole body, his duffel swiping and getting caught on the branches. He could see a faint line of white moonlight on the edge of the ocean's horizon, but that light source did nothing to help him make out any details within the trunks of the forest. He waited a few more long seconds for any strange sounds, then continued toward Route 9.

Once he was again facing west, Franklin noticed something odd about a particular large tree trunk in front of him. He couldn't make out for sure what it was, so he walked over to the tree and leaned in close, wishing he had thought to bring a flashlight. The bark on the trunk was the distinct style of the beach pines, but on one side of the tree was a strange, unnatural pattern. The bark was blackened, as if something extremely hot had hit it. He moved, observing. Another tree had the same burned striations, while yet others were riddled with scratch marks and round holes. *That's a shotgun blast*, he thought, and followed the direction that the blast pattern moved. Not ten feet away was a tree with a large chunk of its bark removed, and was peppered with holes that only buckshot could make. *Maybe just some hunters.*

Another snapping noise in the dark.

Franklin hurried off, glancing over his shoulders until he saw a slight break in the density of tree branches ahead. The thick smell of pine, which reminded him of his Christmas holidays in Baltimore, was turning into a more open, breezy air, and he knew he had to be close to the road. By this time his duffel bag had become cumbersome and he shifted it to another shoulder. At last, he crunched over the last clump of pine needles, and not twenty yards ahead, up a small slope, was Route 9. A quick strobe of lights from a handheld flashlight grabbed Franklin's attention. Radish was there, signaling from his jeep on the edge of the road. "Goddammit, Boone," he yelled from his seat. "What the hell took you so long?"

Franklin's adrenaline from hurrying through the pine forest had yet to dissipate, so he ignored Radish's comment, and dropped his duffel onto the back seat of the jeep. The young evening was already dark, and overcast. Due to the wartime light restrictions, Radish drove along Route 9 at a cautious pace with his headlights off. The first big intersection was Route 1. After that, they entered an inland network of roads that cut through farm and forest alike.

Soon enough, Franklin's heart slowed to its normal pace, and he returned his thoughts to the current trip. Since meeting at the Swordfish, the ride out to Israel's was their first opportunity to talk. Franklin had a million questions for Radish.

Radish answered Franklin's questions with dismissive and short accounts. As he dodged more and more, and seemed to be agitated, Franklin cared less about how he was bothering Radish. He remembered something his father used to say: 'Never be afraid to ask a question. And remember, no answer is one of the clearest answers.' Unfortunately, Radish's mumbled responses did more to confuse Franklin than clear anything up.

Franklin's frustration compelled him to raise his voice when he asked, "So why did Israel have to leave town?"

Radish looked at him with such surprise that the jeep swerved in the same direction as his gaze. He jerked the wheel to the left and the jeep regained its place in the middle of the lane. Radish's features were shadowed but his emotional state was discernible in his voice. "I only know a little bit about it." He stopped, as if to think, and when he continued his words seemed distressed. "I was born the same year that all this happened, and all I know is what the old folks from my hometown had to say. Israel's told me a little–not enough for me to know the finer details–but I'm certain it was for murder."

THE MASSACRE

They rode in the dark. The hum of the jeep's wheels trailed Franklin's thoughts. He tried reasoning with Radish. "Look, I just want to know more about who I'm dealing with."

Radish turned to face Franklin as if he wanted to say something but changed his mind. Finally, he spoke. "According to Israel, he had just come home from searching the beach. It had only been a week or so since he heard the story from that old lighthouse keeper and he was going at the search for the *Jacinta* with a new hope. Apparently, his friend Smitty Smithsenson was with him, and dropped him off. About halfway down his driveway he saw a strange car parked right next to his porch. He knew no one that owned such a car, and the sight caused him to stop in his tracks. That's when he heard the first scream. It was his sister, Lulu-Pine. Then there was his mother's voice. He ran down the driveway and saw a man standing on the porch. He said this was Ethan Stoccaccio. Well, they got to scrappin' and somehow Israel killed the guy. Israel then ran around to the back of the house and slipped in the back door." Radish held up his hands to symbolize two rooms next to each other. The jeep swerved. "You'll see for yourself when you're at the farmhouse. From the back room, or pantry, you can see into the dining room and kitchen." He grabbed the wheel again and continued. "There, on the other side of the dinning room, was Samuel Shamft lying on top of his sister." He paused, as if trying to recollect the next few details.

Franklin could not understand why Israel would have told this story to Radish. Perhaps it was just another way for Israel to brag about himself, or scare someone into keeping their mouth shut. Franklin remembered he was getting involved with admitted criminals, and actually entertained the notion that perhaps Radish's story was just the beginning of an elaborate set-up scheme in which Franklin and his metal detector were the mark.

After a silent minute, Radish spoke, "The kitchen—as you'll see—is not big and in two steps any grown man can be across it. Israel said he snuck up on Shamft and before he could take another breath, had him by the throat. He strangled him right there on top of his sister. When he finished with Shamft, he remembered his mother. That's when he saw the other Stoccaccio coming down the steps, zipping up his pants and breathing heavy. When Stoccaccio saw Israel he ran out the front door. Israel pursued him onto the porch, but by the time he was there, Stoccaccio was halfway to his car. I believe he then grabbed a brick and threw it at the guy, hitting him square in the side of his head. After which Israel had no problem pounding another brick into him. Again, I wasn't born yet, so I really don't know what to believe. But the answer to your question as to why Israel had to leave town wasn't just for his killing of those three men, but rather, as he tells it, because the mayor of Rehoboth told him to leave."

Franklin asked, "Why would the mayor tell Israel to leave town for killing three crooks in his house? That sounds like self defense to me."

"Because the mayor was in on some deals with those Stoccaccios for some heavy shit, and without Rafael Mouzellas around to keep them in line, they were becoming a nuisance. The mayor probably saw their deaths as a big weight off his shoulders, so he didn't feel any malice towards Israel. The only problem was, the mayor wasn't the only criminal working with the Stoccaccios. The murders occurred on a Friday afternoon. Those three corpses sat in that Cadillac, on the side of the road, for the entire weekend before someone passed by and reported the scene to the authorities. Israel had just drove them up his driveway and parked the car on the shoulder across from the entrance to his farm. This was 1923, and that section of road was less travelled than it is now."

"Wait a minute," Franklin interrupted. "Why would Israel leave three corpses on the side of the road, in front of his farmhouse?"

"You won't ask that after you get to know Israel."

"What's that supposed to mean?"

"Well, Boone, I have only my opinion. Which is, I believe Israel snapped. Or maybe he was trying to regain the foothold that his father once had in Southern Delaware? I don't know. There's no logical answer that I can think of."

Radish continued, "So, after the Cadillac was discovered and word was brought back to the local authorities, the police arrived. The Stoccaccios had deals with crooked authorities and politicians from Rehoboth Beach to as far away as Wilmington, and officers from most of the local districts came out to investigate the scene. More worried about their own asses, I imagine, than any honest investigation. After the deceased were finally zipped up and taken away, the detectives gathered at the head of Israel's driveway. Most of them knew the Mouzellas family, so they didn't rush into anything hasty. They were probably just worried about whether or not any covers were blown, and discussed what their next steps should be. I imagine they couldn't understand how a lone teenager had single-handedly killed three seasoned thugs. Meanwhile, I'm sure Israel was watching them the whole time. He told me he had his father's

12-gauge—something he brought back with him from the war—with a sixteen-inch bayonet fixed to the barrel.

"I'm not sure who was luckier, the police or Israel. I have yet to hear of any Mouzellas man being bested by anything other than the forces of nature. Israel claims there were ten officers waiting on the road. I'm sure he would have taken out a few of them before himself being killed, but again, it was the arrival of the mayor that calmed them down. I think his name was Whilliger, or something like that. This Whilliger fellow probably knew that if there was a shoot-out at the Mouzellas farmhouse, all the local surfmen would hear about it. His career was on the line, and he already had to manage a gang of crooked police officers, and probably had no desire to raise the attention of any local pirates. Whilliger asked the men to let him straighten out the mess. Most likely he assured them that the responsible party was not in any position to name names."

THE FARMHOUSE

Radish finished talking and Franklin thought about Israel Mouzellas. Israel had been seventeen in 1923. He might have had a few inches left to grow, but a few shy of six-foot-seven was still tall. So his seventeen-year-old hands would not have been much smaller than those Franklin saw wrapped around Wilkins' neck back at the Swordfish.

"He came back twenty years later," said Radish. "At least, that's what I'm told. I hadn't met him until last year. He recruited me, so to speak, just like I recruited you. He liked that I was a local and thought since I was an MP, I could easily look the other way when he wanted to snoop around the dunes, or the base."

Franklin was surprised by that admission. He remembered that he was considering working with a man who was not worried about trespassing on US government property. But he was more curious than worried about any of Israel Mouzellas' inclinations. "So, Israel believes that the *Jacinta* is buried somewhere under Fort Miles?"

"I don't know, Boone, Israel is the one to talk to about that."

The trip out to the farmhouse was as eerie as the dunes under a thick night-time fog. They arrived in a small town called Milford, through back roads that were dark, moonless, and starless tunnels of trees. No road looked any different from the next, and if it weren't for the random light in some farmhouse window, Franklin would have had no distinguishing landmarks to remind him that he was still attached to the earth.

After thirty minutes, the jeep slowed down and turned onto an un-paved surface. The tires crunched gravel, but it was too dark for Franklin to see where they were headed. As they rounded a long bend, the dim lights of a farmhouse came into view.

At the house, the porch and indoor lights shone bright enough to give a musty, amber-hued picture of their surroundings. The scene was a dilapidated mess. Franklin couldn't see any details of the roof or siding. There was, however, enough light for Franklin to see that the porch had several floorboards missing while others were warped into uselessness. In the mothy light that surrounded the front door were piles of objects the likes of which Franklin had never seen. Stacked about were old farm tools, tires, boxes, piles of warped two-by-fours, and several rusted bicycles. To the left of the door, the pile of junk was so high that half the front window was blocked, creating a dusty dark corner. And on the right side was more of the same. Only on that side, a porch swing hung amidst the surrounding junk in such a way that whoever stacked the debris there had simply worked around the swing as if it had been too much trouble to remove it first.

The walk from the steps to the front door contradicted the rest of the porch. The area was swept and relatively clean. The floor was also un-warped and partially covered by a long runner with a dirty floral pattern. However, once standing on the runner, Franklin saw that it was there only to conceal a piece of plywood haphazardly nailed to two joists. Where there should have been the tongue & groove slats like the rest of the porch was a ramshackle repair job. As Radish and Franklin stepped up to the door the carpet bounced up and down with their weight.

Israel was at the door before they had a chance to knock. He greeted them with a welcoming smile. He stood in the threshold wearing a blue and white striped button-down shirt over a white V-neck t-shirt and black casual smoking pants. In his right hand was an ornately carved shotgun stock with the barrel and other parts removed. He gripped the wooden stock with a white rag stained from previous oil polishings. Israel stepped back to make way for his guests, and Radish moved past him with an abrupt grunt of a greeting. Israel watched him with a scornful eye but Radish did not look back. Shaking his head, Israel turned to face Franklin. He was hesitant to enter the house.

A smile returned to Israel's face. He said, "Nice work. You boys did a fine job," and slapped Franklin on the shoulder that stuck out from under the 625G duffel's canvas strap. As Franklin walked through the door, Israel tilted his head back to get a better look at the duffel, then followed the two men into the front room. He repeated, "Yes indeed, a fine job."

The first floor was divided into three sections but each area was so cluttered with junk that any doors or dividers were meaningless. Debris flowed from one room to the next. The largest area was the living room. It was the first space inside the front door, with a fireplace set into the left-hand wall. Directly across from the entrance was the dining room. To the right, behind a small partition wall, was the kitchen. As Franklin stood for his first time in the farmhouse, he tried not to let any visions from the story Radish had just told him add to the decor.

Israel walked over to a wooden coffee table sitting among a sofa, a matching love seat, and a recliner. The furniture was arranged in a U-shape, with the coffee table in the middle. The open end of the U faced the fireplace, around which were stacked piles of chopped logs. All the furniture looked as weathered as the exterior of the house. Fabric in the arms of the chairs was loose and frayed, with bare wood showing through several holes. The seat cushions were all pressed into valleys that looked like the same ass had been using them since before Israel's father died. In the corner next to the firewood were stacks of magazines, newspapers, and boxes full of countless objects. Narrow paths weaved through the mess from the living room to the dining room; or in the other direction, to the flight of stairs that led to the top floor.

The mantel was cluttered with a menagerie of small mechanical pieces, bookended by dusty candle holders. Above the mantel hung a portrait of a man in a dark blue vest with silver-dollar-sized brown buttons down the chest. The painting's subject had sandy blond hair tightly combed into a coiffure that came down to a low forehead. His eyebrows, thick but otherwise trimmed, sat over eyes that were dark pits with a dab of white to signify the life behind them. An unruly and curling beard belied the man's otherwise neat visage. Franklin's attention was captured by the face. Except for a different style of mustache, he could see a distinct resemblance between the man in the portrait and Israel.

In front of the fireplace, on the edge of the sofa, sat a young boy. He was about the age of twelve, with olive skin and pitch-black hair that flopped loosely over pudgy cheeks. He sat with a straight posture, leaning forward as he pushed a bore brush up and down inside a shotgun barrel. Israel stepped next to the boy, who didn't look up from his work but rather tilted his head just enough to show acknowledgement. Israel whispered something in a language that Franklin did not recognize and placed the shotgun stock on the table next to an organized collection of tools and firearm parts. Also on the coffee table sat a large bowl full of empty shotgun shells, and next to that was the loader press, as well as all the other ingredients needed to make a round. As a trained rifleman, Franklin was familiar with most of what he saw in Israel's living room, but what

101

surprised him was the boy doing the work.

"Please forgive the mess," said Israel, standing up from talking with the boy. He turned to face the love seat directly across from the sofa. Radish reclined in the seat with a .44 caliber pistol in his hands. His feet were up on the edge of the coffee table, all the while flipping the cylinder in and out of the housing, making a repeated clicking and clacking noise. At random intervals, Radish aimed the unloaded weapon at the fireplace and sighted down its barrel like he was a gunslinger from the Wild West. Israel leaned over and swatted Radish's feet to the ground. "This is what happens when you leave your house in the care of miscreants and entitled wastes of air."

Radish sat up as his legs were pushed off the table. The gun clacked against the wooden frame of the love seat as he brought his hands down to support himself. His five-foot-seven frame was dwarfed by Israel, who stood almost a foot taller and whose limbs seemed strong as tree trunks. Israel reached down and grabbed the pistol from Radish with no resistance. Radish's face showed no deference towards his host nor accountability for his rude behavior as a guest. Israel snapped another strange slight in Radish's direction, and said, "Miscreants who involve themselves in matters that are too big for them to handle."

Franklin wondered just how long Israel and Radish had known each other.

Radish slouched, and whispered a low "Fuck you" as he turned his head to feign interest in the empty shotgun cartridges scattered on the table. At the sound of the curse, the boy looked up from his cleaning operation. Israel stopped short as well. He towered above Radish for a long few seconds, but eventually turned his attention away. Radish did not make eye contact with him. In the thick of the tension, the boy returned to pushing the bore brush.

Israel said, "I also apologize for the rude introduction to my home, Franklin. Some people just don't understand manners, no matter how many times they've been in another's house."

The uneasiness in the room was palpable. Franklin had no idea what secret communication, or grudges, the two members of his future crew were trying to keep at bay. He looked at Radish and wondered how he could believe his behavior was acceptable, if not dangerous. While avoiding eye contact with Israel, Radish had no problem looking at Franklin. Radish's eyes were like black coals, daring Franklin to say anything. But soon enough Radish moved on and engaged himself in cleaning the insides of some empty .44 caliber cartridges. Franklin couldn't be certain—because Radish was talking low—but he was surprised to hear Radish speaking to the young boy in the same foreign language that Israel had used. The boy shook his head at random times, but never looked up from his work.

Israel pointed to the boy and said, "Franklin, this is my son Jojo."

Jojo lifted his chin, but not his eyes, and that was his greeting. Israel put his hand on Franklin's shoulder, and said, "Come, let's get a rum, and go out back."

He led Franklin through the dining room, which was, structurally speaking, a mirror image of the living room without the fireplace. The walls and light were as stained and dingy as the rest of the house. However, like an oasis of cleanliness, the long antique table sat pristine with 6 well-set places. The plates, utensils, and glasses sparkled amongst the house's otherwise dusty ambience.

The wall behind the dining table contained two windows, and on the left-hand wall hung an oil painting of a sailboat tossing on a massive

103

wave. Below this portrait, stretching the entire length of the wall, sat a four-foot-high china hutch. The top was clean other than Israel's leather pouch. It sat like a dusty pile of beach debris in an otherwise spotless room. The pouch sat oddly, and was leaning over three small boxes. They were slightly hidden underneath the opened top flap of the pouch, but Franklin recognized them. The lettering on the side of the paper boxes was the familiar faded black print set on an orange-ish paper that he was used to seeing at the shooting range. His eyes moved lower to the glass doors of the hutch. The front glass panels were dark, and mostly blocked by the dining room table, and Franklin could not get a good view of anything that was stored in the cabinet. The most he could see were the front corners of what looked like metal boxes. But the shape of the box edges kept his attention.

"Excuse me, Franklin," said Israel. He stood at the other end of the table with a slight lean so he could look at Franklin below the low-hanging chandelier. He pointed his thumb over his shoulder, into the kitchen. "Franklin, this is my beautiful wife Sueli."

Behind Israel stood two of the tallest women Franklin had ever seen. Sueli was as tall as her husband, and her hair puffed out from under a yellow bandanna, framing her brown-skinned face. Franklin stood silent and unsure, shocked as he was at the thought of a white man and a black woman being married. Initially, he assumed that the white woman at the sink, who did not turn around to say hello, was Israel's wife. But at Israel's introduction, the dark-skinned woman nodded her head. Franklin stammered a pitiful greeting.

Israel continued, "And that other gem is my sister, Lulu-Pine."

Lulu-Pine stood silent and hunched behind Sueli. She barely looked up as she worked at the sink. He noticed a strange quality to Lulu-Pine's face, though it was cast down and difficult to see. It was flushed from the hot work of the kitchen. Franklin could see that despite her reddened cheeks, her skin was also a natural olive tone. Her hair was pulled tight and up under a stained, white bandanna. Below its knot of fabric were a few wispy hairs but Franklin could not determine if they were grey or sandy blonde. She barely acknowledged her guest. Israel smiled and followed with, "Don't be offended, Franklin. She'll warm up to you eventually." He looked back at Lulu-Pine. "Actually, maybe she won't."

The kitchen was tucked behind the partition wall. Like the dinning room, the cooking area was well kept, and any objects were either being used or cleaned. A hedge of base cabinets created an island between the kitchen and dinning room. They stretched three feet from the left-hand wall, creating a short aisle past the cooking area that led to a door, on the other side of which was a pantry that led to the deck.

Israel stepped past the cabinets, and started for the pantry, telling Franklin to follow him as he walked away. He stopped at a screen door. Pushing it open, he turned to Franklin and said, "I don't mean to be a rude host, but I wanted to have a look at your little toy here before we start with the rum."

Franklin stepped past Israel and down onto a small deck. The deck was as cluttered as the front porch. Franklin wondered if Israel was a pack rat, as most of the things he saw lying around were so rusty that he could not figure out why they'd been kept.

Once on the deck, Israel looked up at the black canvas of the night sky, and said, "Nice night, Franklin. No moon to be seen. You know what that means?"

"What's that?"

"It's a good night to do some pirating."

"Of course. How could I forget?"

The way Franklin felt around Israel reminded him of his childhood in Baltimore. He'd been a small child in elementary school, an easy target for the bigger kids who sometimes befriended him only to gain his trust and then make him feel guilty for not handing over the cookies or candies from his lunch bag. And if he didn't give them his dessert, they would punch him in his gut and take the treats. Then the next day, the bullies called Franklin crazy, or a crybaby, as if they had done nothing wrong. *Of course, cookies and candy aren't gold.* Franklin considered his current position in the Army; how it not only helped his mother, but also allowed him to save a little money, and allowed him to treasure hunt. These were all things that he didn't want to stop, and he wasn't sure how much he wanted to be dragged into any adventures by another potential bully.

Israel slapped him on the shoulder and said, "Relax, Franklin. You really gotta relax."

They walked down the steps from the deck to the backyard into what looked like a well-organized outdoor laboratory. Lining the far edge of the yard was a huge stash of firewood. Logs of all sizes lay under a shingled rain-cover. And behind the firewood sat a robust inventory of junk; an old push lawnmower, Army-issue jerry cans, buckets and planters of all sizes, sacks of different seed varieties, garden tools, as well as what looked like marine and auto engine parts.

Workbenches and tables lined the back of the house. The tops of the workbenches were as neat and organized as the labs at Fort Miles. No tool was misplaced, and all working parts were laid out on cloths in their own respective section. The benches were lit under dull, dangling bulbs that sat on the top of pyramids of dusty beams infused with moths all vying for their own potential treasure.

Behind the rows of junk, the backyard stretched into a blackness that sat heavy in front of the darker edge of a forest line. Israel was standing at the side of the house where his workbenches ended. Radish and Jojo stood looking down from the deck. They had slipped out and surprised Franklin, then sat on two nearby stools.

Franklin asked, "So, what are we doing in your backyard?"

Israel held a large metal-halide flashlight in his hand. Franklin recognized it by the specific portable battery pack attached to it, and on its side were the words "Property of the US Army." Israel aimed the beam of light towards a cleared section of bench-top, and motioned for Franklin to put his bag on the bench.

Franklin unzipped the canvas duffel that housed the 625G. Behind him he heard a quick shuffling and soon Radish and Jojo were standing next to Israel, right over Franklin's shoulder. Jojo leaned in the closest and stared at the 625G like an inquisitive child might watch his father sharpen the blade of a hatchet. Franklin felt proud, like he was finally presenting his specialty to an appreciative audience; the reason that he was valued. But Jojo took one look at the 625G and laughed. Even just the slight scoff had a strange accent to it. Franklin's pride was pricked.

Jojo looked at his dad. *É o mesmo que o seu.*

Israel reprimanded his son. *Não seja mau educado! Vai terminar de limpar.*

The boy left with a shrug of his shoulders.

Israel unscrewed his rum flask. He took a sip and said, "So, what exactly do we have here?"

Franklin spread apart the opening of the duffel bag, allowing a clearer view of the disassembled detector. Israel squeezed Franklin's shoulder. His grip was solid and filled with the excitement of innovation. He said,

"This, Franklin, is exactly why I thought of you." He shook his head in deep approval at the sight lying on his workbench. His eyes moved quickly to Radish then back to the workbench before he continued. "Tell me everything about this model. Specifically the sensor disc. I'd like to see how you've got it coiled."

Franklin explained that he wasn't going to take the sensor disc apart. Despite the detector being simple and durable, the sensor disc and all the copper coiling were fragile. He did not want to risk any problems by dissecting it so far away from the fort. Israel didn't press to see the coil, and was happy to focus on what Franklin had to say. He stood with one elbow resting on the opposite crossed arm while he tugged at the ends of his beard.

During one of the natural pauses in Franklin's explanation, Israel interjected, "So you think that what makes this sensor so strong is your copper wrap layout?"

"Yes and no. It's the coiling and—"

With no regard for the answer, Israel continued, "And you claim that this detector can reach depths of over fifteen feet?"

"Well, the bigger the object, the better the chance we would have of detecting it at that depth."

Israel shook his head, silent for a few seconds, then said, "And you claim that the tone this machine makes gets louder, or changes, with the size—or cluster size—of metal?"

"Yes, and no. I'm still trying to figure out how to improve that. Certain metals do seem to create changes in pitch. But I have yet to nail down a solid wiring design that creates a consistent result."

Israel said, "That is amazing, Franklin. That is exactly what I am hoping for. You see, I am not hoping that your detector finds the small cache of gold on the boat, but rather the sheer mass of metals that would have been built into the *Jacinta*. Like the keel, for example."

He turned and paced back and forth, tugging at his mustache. "Indeed, I'm betting on there being enough metal or mineral deposits that your machine will pick up a huge zone of detection, and that will be the direction in which we move forward."

Israel stopped and turned to Franklin. "You know, I've built something of my own metal detection system." He pointed to the carcass of a metal detector on another workbench. Franklin hadn't previously noticed it there because the pole, control box, and homemade sensor disc blended in with the rest of the junk. At the sight of Israel's metal detector, Franklin's gut twisted. He wasn't certain, but the detector looked like it could have been an Army-issue machine. It was practically dissected and torn apart, but what with all the other items that had obviously been stolen from the Army, Franklin was not surprised. But more than that, he felt like he was less of a value to the crew than he originally thought. "So Israel, if you've got your own detector, why do you need me?"

"I'm not as savvy as I'd like to be with intricate wiring of things. My detector has more flaws than I have patience to sort out. If you're up for it, I believe you will be a good addition to the crew. You know how to operate that thing, and we can always use an extra set of hands." He looked back at Radish, and said, "Jameson over here helps me hunt sometimes, but his schedule doesn't let him off that much. So he claims."

Franklin tried to steer the conversation away from Radish, and asked, "Do you have any idea about the size or type of metals that might have been on board?" He didn't really care about the obvious metals that would have been in the construction of such an expensive sailing yacht, but rather an accurate account of what might have been in the covert

109

cargo. He added, "All metals are different and this thing picks up denser metals at greater depths, metals like lead," he tried to throw in something from his training, "—plutonium—" and end with the obvious, "—or gold."

A smile grew under Israel's mustache. He said, "I like you, Franklin. I can see you've got a sense of the importance of having a goal and the capacity to know how to achieve it."

Franklin was glad to hear Israel's positive words, and proceeded to unpack the 625G. As he assembled it he made a point to show Israel how the process went. Franklin was able to take the detector apart and put it back together blindfolded and in any environment. Despite the important nature of the 625G's work, it was sparse in any superfluous gadgetry. It had a side battery pack that weighed several pounds. The pole was about three-and-a-half feet long. Close to the hand grip end of the pole was a control box. Plugged into the box were three cables, one for the battery charge, one went to the speaker (the only other element sitting on the pole), and the other reached all the way down to the twelve-inch sensor disc at the bottom.

Israel watched from over Franklin's shoulder. Meanwhile, Radish stood staring down at the 625G. Franklin had the detector put together in about sixty seconds. Once constructed, he explained how the switches, knobs, and dials functioned. On the control box was a power switch, a frequency dial that moved left or right depending on what type of metal was being received, and a sensitivity knob for adjusting to different envi-ronments. He turned the power switch on and the machine emitted a long sharp beep.

Israel voiced what Franklin was thinking. "It's picking up the various metals around here, on the benches." Franklin agreed and looked at the end of the workbench where engine parts and other junk sat.

Israel stepped back a few feet and said, "Let's move to the yard. I'd like to conduct a few test runs." He turned towards the abyss behind his house. Franklin followed the swinging beam of the flashlight. They crunched over gravel and dirt until the only sign of the farmhouse was the few lights in the back windows and the dull backyard bench lights. Israel stopped walking and searched the ground with his flashlight, sweeping it back and forth until it shone on a short wooden stick standing straight up. It had a yellow piece of cloth tied to one end.

They stood around the stick. Israel said, "All around here, I will not tell you where, I have buried different metal objects. I want you to find them, using this marker stick as your waypoint. So, if you don't find anything in a particular direction, you can come back to here," he pointed down, "and start again in another direction." Meanwhile he pulled out a folded piece of paper on which Franklin caught a glimpse of a crude map laying out several Xs that represented buried objects. "Okay Franklin, show me what you can find."

As he prepared to search the area, Franklin heard the screen door of Israel's farmhouse slam shut. Jojo's small silhouette came out of the house and disappeared down the steps. Franklin swung the battery pack over his shoulder and let it rest against his hip. He adjusted his shoulders and back under its weight while moving the pole down into the proper position for sweeping. He switched the power on. No sound came from the speaker; it was not close enough to the ground to pick up any signals. He turned the sensitivity knob until a steady beep was heard. If the soil was too full of iron ore, or any other natural metal, the sensitivity levels would need to be adjusted down.

Finding the highest sensitivity level possible for Israel's backyard,

Franklin held the sensor disc down at about an inch above the ground and began a steady sweeping rhythm to the left and right. With his back to the marker stick he walked in a direct line away from it. At about twenty feet out the speaker emitted a steady high-pitched tone. Franklin looked up to see that he had almost bumped into an old wooden cart with a small, upturned boat on top. It was a dark and overgrown monolith that sat abandoned on the back edge of Israel's property.

Franklin stepped to his right, then turned and walked back towards the waypoint. Once there he moved a few feet to his left, turned, and began to walk a route parallel to where he had just come. Soon enough, he heard a high-pitched squawk from the speaker. The tone was similar to what he thought a small conglomeration of iron might cause. He stopped and turned back to Israel, standing close behind him. While walking back and forth, Franklin had not kept track of his host's whereabouts and was startled by Israel's proximity. He also noticed that Jojo was standing beside his father.

The detector beeped. Franklin asked, "Do we need a shovel?"

Israel scanned his map and answered, "Don't worry about that. I know what's down there and how deeply it's buried. Any chance you want to take a guess?"

"I believe it's a cluster of something dense, like iron."

Israel was about to reply when Jojo held up a pistol and mumbled a question in their foreign tongue, *Isso tá certo?* The question startled Israel. He was so engrossed in his work that he was unaware of Jojo's presence. He turned and looked down at the gun in Jojo's hands and said something quick and dismissive, pointing out towards the distant swamp's tree line.

Franklin looked back at his control box as if some gadget on it might tell him the depth of the metal cluster that he had just found. "Based on the pitch, and volume of the sound, I'd say the object is no more than a foot below the surface."

Israel searched his map with the Army flashlight and said, "That is correct. That one isn't deep. It's a small handful of sixteen-penny nails."

Franklin was not impressed. He was used to finding objects much more dangerous than a bunch of nails. He started a new search, sweeping the detector on a parallel path back the way he came. Along the way, he was surprised by an explosion near the swamp-line. The 625G's headphones did little to muffle the sound and he almost jumped out of his shoes. He yanked his headset off. "What the hell was that?"

"That's Jojo. He's testin' the .44."

The ringing in Franklin's ears confused him. "The .44?"

Israel said, "Yeah. We're workin' on a new powder mixture. It's got a bit more kick to it, but Jojo can handle it."

"Powder mixture?" Franklin asked, and was startled again when another explosion sounded in the distance. This time he was facing the direction and witnessed a quick burst of flame accompany the explosion. "Goddammit, Israel! What the hell is that?"

Israel took his eye off the map and joined Franklin in watching the dark woods. Jojo was engulfed by the night, until the third blast fired. A quick strobe lit up the field, revealing the boy's struggle to retain his footing while firing such a powerful handgun. Israel answered his question, "That, my friend, sounds like a good mix."

Franklin couldn't help but comment on the foot of flames that shot out of the gun when it was fired, and Israel seemed amused by his guest's shock. Jojo fired his fourth round. Israel smiled in the light of the flashlight, and said, "That's nothin' Franklin. We make all our own ammuni-

113

tion around here."

Israel's recipe for gunpowder was not interesting for Franklin. He was now more concerned with the ringing in his ears and how that might effect his listening for the sounds of his detector. He started his next pass away from the waypoint stick. At the edge of Israel's property, next to a barren field of weeds and corn stalks, the 625G honked out a low tone, and his foot sunk into soft earth. Stepping back, he swept the detector over his footprint. It emitted the same low pitch. Franklin continued sweeping as he adjusted the sensitivity knob to a greater level. He said, "Looks like something under here, but I'm not sure what it is." He continued to adjust the sensor knob.

Israel replied, "That's okay, Franklin. I've seen all that I need to see."

Israel's response made Franklin look up from the control box. He asked, "What is it that you wanted to know?"

"I wanted to get an idea of how strong the coils are on your model. Our efforts here tonight have proven themselves very hopeful for our future hunt. The objects you've found were buried at different depths, and right here was an object buried over ten feet down."

Franklin asked, "What is it?"

"A jeep," said Israel, then swept his flashlight towards the farmhouse. As he walked into the darkness, the glow of his flashlight outlined his tall frame. He continued, "Dinner's probably ready by now." Another blast and flash of muzzle fire from Jojo's direction interrupted him. He turned toward Jojo's direction and blew a sharp whistle across the yard.

DINNER

In the dinning room, Lulu-Pine put the finishing touches on the table while Sueli set the last dish of food on a hot plate. Jojo pushed past his father and Franklin and hurried into his seat. Sueli shot him a raised eyebrow, and he got up equally fast and ran to the kitchen sink to wash his hands. Radish also hurried ahead of the rest of the crew and sat at his place with his hands resting over his fork and knife as if he was at the Fort Miles mess hall and had an entire regiment to contend with for his food. He reached for a serving spoon that was stuck into a piping hot baking dish full of a dark purple mush. Sueli hissed at him, and he removed his hand.

"Please, Franklin," said Israel. He pointed to the chair next to the head of the table. "An honored seat at my table," he said, with a label-less bottle of cloudy rum tucked under his arm. Franklin could not determine the brand of the liquor.

Israel noticed his guest studying the bottle. "Somethin' you'd like to ask?"

"I was just wondering what's your preference?"

Israel replied, "That is a very observant question, Franklin. That being said, I only drink the rum that has no label: homemade." He produced four small glasses and poured a finger of the amber liquid into each one. He handed a glass to Sueli, Radish, Franklin and dropped another dollop into the last glass and held it up for himself. "To a delicious feast made by a goddess. *Saúde!* " He tipped the glass towards Sueli, who sipped and then passed the glass to Jojo. Israel continued his toast, and looked at Franklin. "This isn't your grandpa's rum, Franklin. Take it slow. Ol' Jameson over there has been bested by my rum many a night."

Franklin clinked his glass against Israel's, and tried his best to repeat the words that Israel had said in his initial toast. The smile drained from Israel's face and he looked Franklin dead in the eyes. "Do you know what you just said to my wife?"

Franklin's face blushed a deep red, as if he was hung upside down. He was frozen without a reply. The entire table's eyes were on him. Jojo said something, but Franklin did not understand. Lulu-Pine snorted out a quick laugh, and Sueli's lips curled up into a silent smile that she hid as she served Jojo's plate.

Israel continued, "You just told her that you want to sleep with her in my very own bed."

Franklin was mortified. He turned to Sueli, ready to apologize. She plopped another scoop of food on to the plate next to her, but did not look up at Franklin. He couldn't tell if she was simply standoffish or bored. He began to mumble the beginning of an apology, "Sueli... I—" but was interrupted by a slap on his shoulder and an explosion of laughter from around the table. Israel still held his glass of rum up in toast, and said, "Ha, Franklin, m'boy. You may be observant, but you definitely don't know Portuguese!!!"

Stunned with embarrassment, Franklin realized that he had been the butt of an inside joke. He was a good sport, and knew that Israel's teasing probably meant that he was accepted amongst the house, and then of course, the crew. Sueli and Lulu-Pine shook their heads and finished serving the plates. Jojo rocked back in his seat and hollered a highly charged laugh. Sueli slapped a mound of the potato on his plate with a vehemence that reminded him of his manners. Meanwhile, Radish leaned forward, scooping food into his mouth as if he were late for his guard shift. Franklin knew that most soldiers ate fast—it was a conditioning engrained in them from the first meal in basic training—but he was shocked by Radish's poor etiquette. Israel paid no attention to Radish. Still amused by his teasing of Franklin, Israel tipped his glass toward his sister. His laughter died down and he finished his toast. "And, of course, for her share in the preparation of this meal, here's to my sister, the ever-pleasant Lulu-Pine."

RAFAEL MOUZELLAS

The feast was delicious. Franklin had never tasted anything like the food Sueli prepared. It was a welcome change of pace from his meals at Fort Miles, and made him never want to step foot in the mess hall again. Not long into the meal, Israel began to relate stories of his father, Rafael Mouzellas.

"A brilliant man. A true believer in liberty, and the harder one worked, the more one reaped. Before the war, my father had established himself as the man in charge of everythin' south of the Delaware Bay. At first he saved lives, then when they kicked him off the Lifesavin' Service, he took them. He ran a crew of men, and anythin' floatin' into the Delaware had to go through him. He set the prices for any operation that was movin' product to Wilmington or Philadelphia. Consistent, yet not selfish, he would never take in tolls more than he needed. But sometimes, he had to get his hands dirty, and that's when he plundered. When workin' for himself in such a way, he would take everythin' from his victims. But again, Franklin, my father only plundered if we were really hungry, or maybe for revenge. But revenge is a rotten motivatin' factor.

"Or when one of those swells from the city, like the one you're from, came into town on their private yachts, those were the ones his crew mates preferred. All the old surfmen loved plunderin' politicians' and rich men's boats. The boardin' was easy, and hardly ever had protection because those city boys were usually with their mistresses. And if they didn't pay up, my father would just let his crew have their way, and no one would ever know what happened."

Israel defended his father with a shrug of his shoulders and took a sip of rum. "My point is, he was a genius and that goddamned war changed him. There was not one thing that my father couldn't do. From growin' food, to clammin', to fixin' an engine, to buildin' a better rifle, my dad never looked at anythin' like it was a problem. I wish I had his resilience. But you know, I don't seem to have control over the wheels in my head like my father did his. That is until he came back—" Israel shook his head in disgust, and took a sip of rum.

Israel's eyes drifted over to the living room, to the portrait that hung above the mantel. The tone of his voice sat comfortable on the story he related. "Sometimes, we would sit on the beaches and just watch the darkness out on the horizon, and my father would tell me of his plunderin' days, but also of his life-savin' days. Not really too different, when you think about it."

Franklin wasn't sure what to make of Israel's story. He was enjoying the food too much to want to talk about the ethics of murder.

But Israel was never silent for too long. "Either way, after the war, my father's stories were mostly about that single day. He was with the Sixth Marine Regiment. As far as his time in Europe, all I ever got from him was somethin' about—" Israel searched for some slippery memory "—somethin' called the Belleau Wood, or Woods. I can't remember."

Franklin shook his head. He had heard about the Belleau Wood in his military history class, but was unsure of the exact details.

THE BELLEAU WOOD

It was dawn, the time of morning when the sun was rising yet everything was still grey enough to surprise the enemy. Rafael Mouzellas was in the first wave that moved on the woods. Somewhere in the trees ahead, the Germans were well established. He crouched as he crossed an open field. Virtually unscathed by the previous night's artillery and covered in knee-high wheatgrass. Rafael wished he could drop down and crawl below the dense fronds, but that wasn't what he'd been told to do.

In the distance, the forest trees were blackened and smoldering, thinned by the night's bombardment. Rafael could not see very far into the forest before all details were absorbed in grey. A heavy mist sat over the floor of the wood, shrouding the German trenches. Trunks of broken trees grew from the mist like black streaks of charcoal smeared against a canvas. The natural front edge of the forest used to have a slight drop of a few yards that gradually faded into the field. But now the trees were bordered by a tangled mess of dense brush, barbed wire, wooden pikes, and mortar craters.

Rafael cursed the sunrise. He couldn't remember the last time he decided to kill anything during the day, animal or man. The sun was still not visible in the sky, but the clouds reflected its early glow, as if the sun were ashamed of itself for blowing his cover, but still, it had to shine.

Even a boar wouldn't be stupid enough to do this.

He understood the dangers of moving across an open field. The previous day he had insisted on the assault beginning an hour earlier, when the sun was not up. He believed that he and his fellow Marines could establish themselves in a better attack position if they used the darkness to their advantage. His commanding officer, Second Lieutenant Smalls, agreed with him, but by the time plans for the assault were organized, the sky began to lighten.

The woods gave him no more time to think about his predicament. From hidden bunkers the Germans opened up.

The woods lit up as if powered by their own electrical source. Rounds burst from the trees on his far left flank. Rafael was a smart man, and had prepared for many a fight, but he was not ready for the speed with which his piece of war began. It was nothing like Rafael's training, and it was certainly nothing like his experience in his homeland swamps. He was a man who needed to be in control. And that was the first thing the Germans took away from him.

Instantly, he found himself surrounded by the popping of machine gun fire. It was from this vantage point that his most recurring future nightmare originated. It was a nightmare born from the strobe light of machine-gun fire from the depths of a shadowed woods. Each round was accompanied by a flash that lit up the space between trees and revealed the enemy, with their rounded stahlhelm bobbing up and down behind their entrenchments. They were dark, faceless specters that, at least in his dreams, grew more frightening with each night.

Rafael was an experienced quick thinker, with a penchant for doing his best to stay alive in dangerous situations. He saw the men to his left riddled with bullets, and had just enough time to dive to the ground as two rounds knocked against the top of his helmet then moved on to finish off the man on his right. The rounds whipped the helmet off his head and rolled him a few feet backwards. He lay dazed as more boots hurried past him, kicking dirt into his face.

Another Marine grabbed Rafael by his arm and helped him back up to his feet. It was Second Lieutenant Smalls. Smalls was yelling something in Rafael's face, but his voice was drowned out by explosions of mortars, gunfire, and men screaming. As Rafael readied himself to stand, Smalls pushed him back into the grass. He fell, face up, with the lieutenant lying on top of him, as German rounds flew less than two feet overhead. Rafael rolled the man off of him, then scrambled to find his helmet. He turned back to help the lieutenant up, only to see that the back of his head and shoulders were open pockets of flesh.

As his mind synthesized the surreal visions and sounds of war, he made a short list of priorities; the first being to stay alive, and the second to stop the people who were trying to kill him. The Germans had the drop, but there were plenty of distractions on which they could focus. He found that if he lay flat enough the bullets were more likely to fly overhead looking for easier targets.

The side of his head felt heavy, like an anchor was chained to it, and his helmet sat cockeyed as if it were too small. He poked his head up and down, above the security of wheat grass to try and assess the front line. The first wave of the offensive was greatly reduced. The sun's reflection from the clouds enhanced hidden red shadows in a field strewn with death. Rafael fought to control his head, both mentally and physically. It throbbed with a pain he had never before experienced, but adrenaline kept him moving. He found his shotgun, bayonet fixed, and decided that the only thing to do was move forward. Clarity returned with the act of making a decision. The woods were fifty yards ahead. Behind him, more men were moving into the field, while others crawled on elbow and belly towards the woods. He lifted his head, as far as his sanity would allow, and saw three Marines on their bellies, mustering in the gouges of earth that had been made in a recent mortar barrage. So much artillery had been dropped on the woods that an unnatural berm had been created in front of the tree line. He moved for those ditches.

Snaking through the grass and then mud, Rafael made his way to the tree line. Marines were regrouping in the fresh mortar pockets and craters. He was grateful for the cover of the mortar pits, because he could at least sit up behind the trees. He hated being on his belly. It was no way for a man to stage an attack. He took a few seconds to wipe the mud off the side of his shotgun.

Not twenty yards up the line, four Marines prepped rifles and shotguns for a charge into the woods. Two of the men stood up and lobbed grenades into the trees. One was shot through his neck. As he clutched his throat and squirmed in the mud, the fourth man tried to comfort him, but there was little room to move and not be the next one shot. When the explosions from the grenades thumped, the other three men lunged up and into the trees. They scrambled from one large trunk to another, took or gave cover, then moved into the darkness. Their small arms shot flashes that showed how far they got before being overpowered.

A strange energy coursed up Rafael's spine when he saw his brothers-in-arms disappear into the forest. He believed in the power of a man's brains and brawn, and was inspired by the bravery of his fellow Marines. He motioned at the three men next to him to follow, and crawled towards the enemy's left flank. He made it to the man who had just been shot, and rolled him out of the way. Once past the corpse, he motioned for the last man in his group to grab the deceased's grenades from his ammo bag.

The men moved over yards of debris and craters from mortar explosions, trying to get as far away from where the bursts of enemy rounds were concentrated. They dove from ditch to ditch, and crawled through a loose earth that gave them no traction. Despite being wet, the soil smoldered from an ordinance that didn't care for the laws of nature. Soon, they came to the edge of the mortar pits, and found themselves behind some large tree trunks. The thick trunks had withstood the night's mortar barrage, but were stripped of all their branches.

Rafael and his small crew had not yet been seen by the Germans, which gave them a few extra seconds to check their weapons. Rafael looked at the men with him. All their eyes said the same thing, *No use standing around.* Their eyes also made it clear that Rafael was the point man. That didn't bother him. He preferred to be the leader of whatever crew he might be on.

Rafael looked around the tree between him and the German line, then brought his head back. He signaled for the grenade in the fourth man's hand. The Marine passed it up the line. Rafael slung his shotgun over his shoulder, then pulled the pin of the grenade, keeping his hand tight on the safety lever as he snuck around the backside of their tree cover. The others followed with their bayonets at the ready, steadying their hands and moving into the woods, rifles aimed, leapfrogging from tree to tree. The Germans had still not yet noticed the small band moving far on their flanks. Rafael tossed his grenade between the two closest foxholes, to fool the closest hole into believing the enemy was behind them, then ducked. The explosion was followed by German screams. The two men in the closest hole aimed towards the front lines, where they assumed the enemy would have tossed the grenade. And before they realized their mistake, Rafael was on top of them. His adrenaline empowered him. It blessed him with the ability to think fast when his bayonet got stuck in the ribs of the first German he met; how he had to kick the man's chest in order to release the weapon just in time to turn and slam the butt of his shotgun into the face of the other man who shared the foxhole, and then turn back to the first man and fire a round into his already blood-stained chest. It allowed him to endure the pain from the next German who sprang up from a nearby ditch, took aim at him, and managed to put a round through his shoulder. One of the Marines with him finished the German before he could fire another round. And finally, Rafael's adrenaline numbed his entire body, and graced him with the belief that he no longer cared if he lived or died.

With the right flank now breached, and many of the Germans haphazardly turning their guns in that direction, more Marines were able to get into the woods. And once they were in the woods, the close killing began.

Rafael and his three compatriots were not done. He had become their de-facto leader, and he found himself in the middle of the enemy line. He put his sights on the closest machine gun nest. About twenty-five yards away was a ditch with a German 08. The gun was angled over the open field and had enfilade across the right flank of the Marine's advance. One of the men in the battery had noticed the Americans moving about the trenches with little resistance, but the pit was lined with piles of sandbags, and the Germans couldn't quickly move their machine guns to take aim at Rafael and his small crew. On his command, the three other Marines provided covering fire. Rounds whistled and puffed into the dirt and trees. Rafael moved closer and took aim at the German giving orders. He fired a spray of shot into the man's head, and he disappeared below the sandbags. With the killing of the German officer, any remaining cover was lost. Luckily, for Rafael and his brave three, the front edge of the woods was flooded with charging Marines.

The initial raid on the woods lasted until the early evening. Rafael survived the day by moving within groups of any Marines he could find, but the battle had quickly lost all sense of direction and orderly movement. Officers were killed quicker than the chain of command could keep up. Precision was forgotten, and the tables were turned by a brute force that the Germans could not equal. Rafael was stuck in a maddened state of survival that had him moving forward, hunting. Despite his pounding head and wounded shoulder, he managed to end the lives of three more Germans. By the time the sun began to set, the enemy lines were weakened enough that intermittent skirmishes were all that remained.

In the tenuous calm that followed the initial breaching of the Belleau Wood, a corpsman found Rafael lying in a foxhole. He appeared unconscious and still had one of his hands gripped around the neck of a deceased German. Rafael's helmet was missing and the corpsman saw the swollen mass on his temple, and assumed he was dead. But as the corpsman was about to hurry over to the next Marine who could actually use his help, Rafael's hand twitched. His lips then moved as if he was speaking in a dream.

The corpsman jumped into the ditch and grabbed Rafael by the wounded shoulder that he had not yet noticed. This woke Rafael. Pain surged through his body, and he tried to push the medic away. He rolled over to face whomever was causing such pain, and the corpsman saw the wide-eyed state of his face. He had seen this type of expression before, and knew that what was behind Rafael's eyes may not belong to his body any longer. It was the look most men got when they see too much violence in too short a time. A damage that was deeper than any bullet wound. Rafael went for the corpsman's throat, but his wound wouldn't let him move his arm. The corpsman noticed the bloodstained shoulder and grabbed Rafael's other arm, motioning for him to lay back and be calm. No mortars were exploding in his vicinity, no rounds split the branches around him, so Rafael stopped. His body gave way to the relative silence and relaxed back into the earth. Tension released from his muscles, until finally he lost consciousness.

AT THE TABLE

As Israel bragged about his father's wartime exploits, Franklin couldn't be sure if the details were possible. "That's right," he said. "My father fought that entire day without food or water, and with hardly any ammunition other than the butt and bayonet of his shotgun. He knew better than to stop movin' forward because stoppin' is for dyin'. Turns out he also had a concussion, and a German round had pierced his left shoulder. He told me the last thing he remembered was lookin' at his swollen shoulder and thinkin', *thank God it's not my good arm*. The next thing he knew, he woke up in a hospital surrounded by blood-stained and bandaged soldiers and white-uniformed nurses. That was it for my father's military service. They told him he had shell shock and discharged him. Shipped him home without any recognition for his singlehandedly breakin' the German line in that battle." Israel checked Franklin's face for any signs of disbelief as he took a sip of rum, and continued, "It's funny, Franklin. They spent all that money trainin' him, feedin' him, and shippin' him overseas, when all he did was fight in a single battle for a single day. I guess that's some sort of a thumb in Washington's eye."

Israel kept his gaze on the table, his meal hardly touched. "After he came back he could never use his arm like he used to, and his head was broken beyond repair. His mind, that is. At least as far as any of these country doctors around here could determine. Butchers really. He could barely tie his shoes after comin' home. The same man who could swim a mile in the ocean, row a lifeboat out over the breakers in a storm, skin a buck, snap a man's neck with a single arm." Israel slowed down and gazed at his right hand with a reminiscent look in his eye.

The stories were colorful and over the top. As his host talked, Franklin looked about the table. Sueli and Jojo, used to hearing the stories, minded their own business. Radish, however, snorted a slight breathy laugh when Israel mentioned "snapping a man's neck." At the sound of his exaggerated breath, Lulu-Pine who sat across from him, shot him a look that he could not match for long. He stared and fidgeted with what remained on his plate.

"No, Franklin, after he came back from Europe, nothin' really got better. He could barely figure out his right from his left. That last job, the *Jacinta*, that was his only job since comin' home. Momma guilted him into doin' it because she knew it would bring in enough money to feed us for a long while—or kill him. But my father was a surfman, and it would'a been hard for him to resist this particular job no matter what his mental state. Of course, Momma put the last nail in his coffin when she claimed they had no other choice but for him to do it or we would all starve. I was old enough at the time to remember her tellin' him that. Both of them standin' right there in that kitchen."

"Why would your mom want him dead?"

"Because she was tired of takin' care of her broken husband." No one at the table was ready for Israel's comment. "I asked him a few times not to go through with it, but he never really listened to me. At least that didn't change after he came home. Plus, once he got to thinkin' about that boat, I could see in his face, his eyes, how my old dad was still in there. It was like mooncussin' was such a natural part of him that it had its own brain, or memory." Israel smiled after another sip. "This brought me some relief at the time." But then his smile melted away, and his tone grew more serious. "It is my belief that the government of this country, in cahoots with the government of Germany, killed my father. And now both are payin' the price. I have never forgotten the last time I saw my father. I saw him climb aboard that boat, and a few minutes later I saw him at the rail. He was clutchin' his left shoulder like if he didn't it would fall off, and his face was nothin' but agony. The waves tossed the boat and caused him to have to let go of his wounded limb, and as he was rolled around that mast—well—did its thing. It was that German round that sat lodged in his shoulder while he fought; that goddamned bullet that weakened one of the two strongest arms I had ever seen. And it was the government of the United States that put him there."

Franklin tried to reason, "Yeah but the war had to—"

"Don't feed me that bullshit at my table, Franklin." There was a long pause as Israel brought his eyes to Radish, then his gaze drifted to the center of the table. It was an empty scanning of everything and nothing at all. Franklin had seen it in his father's face when he had consumed too much whiskey. Israel came back to Franklin and said, "I don't give a damn about your patriotic delusions."

Franklin felt like his visit should be coming to an end. He was glad his plate—though delicious—was finished. The energy about the dinner table was slipping into a strange tension, with the ladies and Jojo occasionally talking amongst themselves, and Radish sitting like a child ignoring everything but his fork. Franklin was left to be the sole audience of a drunk Israel. He had only met Israel twice, but could tell that he was a man who preferred to do the talking.

After the meal, Franklin helped clear the table and then proceeded to break down and pack up the 625G. While doing so, Israel approached him in the backyard and said, "Franklin, thank you for comin' out tonight, and bringin' that with you. I look forward to workin' with you on the dig. I really think that detector and you will be great additions to the crew."

Franklin answered, "My detector and I thank you very much." Despite being spoken of as secondary in value to his 625G, Franklin was excited. The thought of using his skills to find gold and other potential shipwreck treasure was enticing, even though the playing field was so close to a US government owned swath of land. Of course, he wasn't sure how well he was going to get along with Israel, but was willing to keep an open mind. *Indeed, all that gold makes it easy enough to keep an open mind for at least a little while.* He asked, "So what's the next step?"

"The next step will be to meet me at the site."

Franklin knew that the site was somewhere in the dunes just south of Fort Miles, but he still asked, "The site?"

"Yes, as I've already told you, based on my calculations, I believe I have found the most logical location at which the ship should be sittin'."

"If I'm hearing you correctly, I believe we will be working on the dunes just south of the fort," Franklin said. "You are aware that that is government property?"

Israel smiled again, happy to make Franklin squirm. "Yes, I am aware of that. And, for the record, do not care. You dig to the boat. It doesn't come to you."

"Well, I work in those dunes all the time. So, no one should suspect anything when they see me out there. I'm not sure how they'll handle you being there, but—"

Israel interrupted him. "Franklin, the last thing I'm worried about is how the US Army will, as you say, *handle*, me. And I know you've worked the dunes before, but I'm certain you haven't worked them the way you will when you start with me."

"Whatever it takes then, Israel. But I gotta tell you, we've got patrols riding up and down those dunes on a regular basis. In fact, I do field training in those dunes every—"

Israel put his hand up and said, "I could care less about any patrols or exercises that you or your little Army buddies will be conductin'. I've been workin' in those dunes since I was a kid, and almost every day since that fort was built." He looked at Franklin and his smile straightened out. "How do you think I knew about you?"

THE RIDE BACK
TO FORT MILES

The drive back from the farmhouse was a half hour, and
Franklin still had to be dropped off on the edge of Route 9,
then walk back to base. He was going to backtrack through the pine
forest, then around the dune berm, and finally through the South Field,
where Radish would be waiting to pick him up. After the heavy dinner
and discussion, and because of the late hour, Franklin knew it was going
to be a long while before he was back in his bunk.

At the top of the driveway, Franklin looked in the side-view mirror.
The farmhouse's dingy lighting was distant, and soft. But Franklin could
not relax until the jeep made its first turn off of Israel's road. As he took
his eyes off the mirror, he thought he saw in the reflection a dark shape
sitting at the top of the driveway. It looked like a vehicle, but it also could
have been the silhouette of the trees behind Israel's land. He checked the
side mirror again. Nothing moved on the road behind them. He settled
back into his seat, and asked, "So, Israel is married to a black woman?"

Radish shook his head and looked over his shoulder as if he was
sitting next to Hitler himself. He said, "She's from Brazil."

Franklin replied, almost thinking out loud, "Brazil?" He had no idea
what someone from Brazil was supposed to look like. "Are people from
Brazil not white?"

Radish laughed. "What planet are you from, Boone?"

Franklin was caught between his contempt for Radish and the fact that this time the man was right. He was not well educated in regards to the different peoples of the world. If one wasn't obviously dark-skinned or Asian, Franklin was not really sure what to call him or her. And in all his education, he had never been asked to give much attention to the country of Brazil other than where it lay on a map. His small high school had no students from Central or South America, and Franklin assumed anyone south of Texas looked like the Mexican outlaws he saw in Western movies. Sueli did not remind Franklin of anyone he had ever met. It made sense to him, however, that Israel would marry a woman of color, since his father had done the same thing.

"So, when Israel returned a couple years ago, did anyone care that he was married to a black girl?"

"I don't know, Boone. I don't know what every farmer this side of the Chesapeake was thinking when Israel showed up with a colored girl on his arm. Especially with that son of his. I would imagine that when Israel Mouzellas came back to town, half the people who knew him couldn't a cared less who he showed up with, and the other half were just smart enough to know not to say anything about it."

Franklin saw this as a perfect gateway into his next question. "Why would people be scared of Israel?"

"Don't give me that shit, Boone. You know Israel has blood on his hands."

Franklin assumed it was true that Israel had killed the Stoccaccios and Samuel Shamft, but he felt like that incident was justifiable self-defense. He also felt like Israel was a bit of an exaggerator; his adventures in the Caribbean and South America were so colorful and full of potentially illegal and murderous accounts, and he told stories of his father's exploits as if he'd been there, despite many of them happening a world away. If the tales were true, then Franklin concluded there could be countless deceased in Israel's wake, and he couldn't help but think of his predecessor, Ron Brotsky. Despite this, he wanted to see what Radish would divulge. He asked, "Blood on his hands?"

"Yeah, Boone. Goddammit."

Franklin thought back to something his dad would often tell him, *Someone quick to anger is your first sign of a low intelligence, and is someone to stay clear of.* Perhaps, if he had just forgotten about the gold, Franklin would have been able to heed his father's words. But he still believed Radish was an important ally on Israel's crew. In the equation in Franklin's mind, his prize of gold banked on him having to deal with Radish on a more regular basis.

In the thick of Radish's short-tempered answers, Franklin considered why he might be growing so defensive. *Radish was just as unpleasant with Israel and the ladies of the house. He hardly said a word during the meal—though one can't blame him for being quiet when Israel controlled the conversation. But Radish's silence didn't feel comfortable. He seemed to be stewing more in his seat than the spices in that pot of mush that Sueli cooked. Perhaps Radish sees me as a threat to his share of the loot? My presence on the crew has reduced his share to a third as opposed to a half.*

Radish was an open sore of emotion and Franklin had no problem sprinkling a little salt. He asked, "So, Radish, remind me where exactly you grew up."

"Delaware, Boone. I told you that."

"Yeah, I know, but where in Delaware?"

He stared at Franklin for longer than someone driving a vehicle should. "Wilmington. Why's it so important for you to know that?"

135

Franklin ignored the question and continued with his train of thought. "And that's the town you go home to every weekend?"

"Where I go when I'm not at the fort is none of your business."

"So remind me how you came to meet Israel?"

"And why is that your business?"

"It's not, really. I just feel like something isn't adding up. You acted like someone way too comfortable to be in the house of a person like Israel. You acted like you've been at that table before."

Radish scowled and finally broke, repeating, "Not that it's your business, but I've been renting a room at the farmhouse since being assigned to Fort Miles." Franklin sat in shocked silence. Radish continued, "I just like having a place to go—" then slammed his open hands on the steering wheel. The jeep jerked to the left. "I'm so sick of that goddamned fort, and all the crap they pass off as food, and all the too-smart-for-their-own-good officers, who assign me shit jobs, and don't know shit about anything."

Franklin said, "Jesus, Radish. You have got to relax, man." He attempted the math in his head. *Radish has been at Fort Miles since its official upgrade in 1941. Israel came back from his twenty-year excursion in 1943. That meant that Radish was at the farmhouse two years before they met.* He felt like he had not been given full disclosure on the exact relationship between the two members of his new crew. He wasn't certain what was happening, so he kept his mouth shut, and tried to keep his questions focused on the hunt. "So, that's how you both joined forces for the *Jacinta* hunt?"

"Yeah, that's how me an' Israel joined forces."

The drop-off point was in the distance. Franklin gave Radish one last question. "So why, after working with you, did Israel want me on the crew?"

No answer, save the hum of the jeep tires and the whistle of the wind. Radish did not say a word until pulling over. "I have no idea, Boone. But I am gettin' really sick of your questions."

Franklin climbed out of the jeep, and as he grabbed his duffel bag from the back, he said, "Don't worry about picking me up. I'll make my own way."

Radish yelled at the back of Franklin's head, "How's that gonna look, you wandering back in the middle of the night with your gear like that?"

"I don't know, Radish. Maybe you'll have to tell your MP buddies to arrest me."

"Fine," growled Radish. "But if anyone hears about you roaming around the dunes like this, like Carp, you know not to mention me when you're being questioned."

"Shut up Radish. Why would Carp bother with such a thing?"

"I don't know, maybe because you and him are such buddies."

Franklin stopped short, and turned back towards the jeep. "What the hell does that mean?"

"Come on Boone, you don't think half the base knows about that little private treasure hunting trip you and Carp took?" Radish sensed that he had struck a nerve and before speeding off, he said, "And you know not to mention Israel's name. That would be a dumb decision."

Franklin turned and walked away from the sound of Radish's voice. His patience had run its course, and he wondered how well they would work together on Israel's crew. His first few steps were down a short slope that ran parallel to the shoulder of Route 9. At the bottom he looked up, and there was the pine forest. A cold chill ran up his spine. The dense-ness of the undergrowth, and the low, needled limbs concerned him that he might not be able to find his way. And the late hour made it impossible for him to make out any sign of a deer trail.

Goddammit! I hope whatever's on that damn boat is worth this shit.

Finding no trailhead, he walked straight into the brambles. His eyes strained amongst the dark trees the same way they did whenever he walked home at night alone along the marinas and alleys of East Baltimore. Only here, the city sounds were substituted with the snapping of branches and the crunching of a dense layer of pine needles; sounds that unnerved him more than anything he'd experienced in the alleys of his hometown. The most comforting difference was that after the pine forest, somewhere not far behind the trees, waited the beach. Though eerie at night, the dunes did not make Franklin feel uneasy, despite having never stepped foot onto a beach any more than he had into a forest. The dunes brought him a sense of calm that helped him sleep at night, and made his days go by as if they were a dream.

After twenty minutes of walking through the trees, Franklin wasn't sure if he was heading in the right direction. He was in the middle of the forest, where the undergrowth wasn't thick, and stopped in a small clearing. The sounds of the ocean were faint, but he saw no backdrop of the night's sky behind the trees in any direction. He could not shake the thought of being lost. He cursed his anxiety. *A grown man who is afraid of so little is having trouble walking through the woods.* He pushed ahead.

The forest showed no signs of ending, and with each step Franklin became more and more hurried, and moved with less care for where he was going. The low pine branches slashed at his shoulders, pulling at the 625G's duffel, and thorny shrubs threatened pant legs and ankles. He found himself again in a dense section of undergrowth with no comfortable place that he could stop and collect his thoughts. He tried to keep

138

his face out of the reach of the branches, covering his eyes and moving so clumsily that he fell past the last line of trees, and slid, hands first, down the dune berm. The duffel bag rolled behind him. At the foot of the slope he collapsed, gasping and spitting sand. When his nerves calmed, he looked back up the berm and at the breadth of the wall of pine trees not twenty feet away. They shook in their own secret breezes, protecting centuries of mysteries perpetrated on the dunes. He stood up and decided to walk north along the beach to get back to Fort Miles. *If I'm going to be covered in darkness, I still prefer to be out in the open.*

DRUNKEN CARP

Franklin did not hear from or see much of Radish until the next Friday evening, when both men had the night off. Their paths crossed at the mess hall, and Franklin asked if he could stop by the MP barracks after eating.

At the MP barracks, the men had fashioned their own version of a sitting area. The space was more crowded than Barracks Five, but still accommodated a few comfortable chairs around the wood-burning stove. After some initial jeers and taunts from the few men in the barracks—directed not only at Franklin for being a no-account officer, but also at Radish for associating with such a person—the two sat down in the lounge. Both men were used to the bullying, and knew it was more of a harmless, brotherly greeting than any type of mean-spirited harassment.

Franklin wanted to break the ice with some minor conversation, so he asked about the German prisoners. He had seen Radish guarding them a few times throughout the week, but Radish quickly shut him down.

"Is that why you wanted to talk with me, Boone? About the damn Germans?"

"No. I was just shooting the breeze, Radish."

"I get it, but I don't want to keep the German situation fresh in your mind. I don't need you slippin' word of it to Israel." Then Radish stood up and said, "Hold on Boone." He walked over to his bunk and opened his footlocker, and pulled out a bottle of whiskey and two bottles of ginger ale. The other MPs in the barracks saw him, and re-ignited their taunts, this time letting Radish know that they'll be right over for their own cocktail. Radish grabbed two Army-issue metal coffee mugs and set them on the wooden crate that sat between Franklin and his own chair. He then looked up and asked the room, "Any chance the ice helmet is filled?"

Another MP replied, "It's over the door, Radish. Be a good boy, and fill it up for everyone."

Radish stood up and scowled. "I'll be right back Boone."

Before leaving for the ice machine, Radish grabbed a field helmet off a hook that was above the door. He leapt down the steps then headed over to the ice machine that was near the latrine building. Meanwhile, Franklin sat, and none of the four other men in the building spoke to him, or even bothered to look up from what they were doing. But Radish did not take long, and returned with the upturned helmet full of ice.

"Here you go, Boone," said Radish. He handed the helmet to Franklin, who then placed a few cubes in both of their glasses.

After two of the other MPs poured their own drinks, and Radish sat down, Franklin continued with the conversation. "Radish, I don't know why it's such a big deal, but I won't mention anything about your post to Israel. I haven't even seen him since dinner last week."

Radish answered, "I get that, Boone. But I need you to understand the magnitude and potential disaster should Israel catch wind of any German prisoners on the Delaware shore."

"What's he going to do, blow up Fort Miles?"

Franklin's off-the-cuff joke did not lighten Radish's mood, but he reassured Radish that he would do his best to forget about the German prisoners. And after a few more whiskeys on the rocks, both men couldn't have cared less about much. Still, they spoke low, and tried to make sure no important information was discernible by the other MPs. Franklin filled the time with questions about treasure hunting on the beaches, how experienced Radish was, and what it was like to work on Israel's crew. Radish was distant and tough to get any clear information out of, but they got along fine, and Franklin began to feel like that they would work well together on the hunt for the *Jacinta*.

While they talked and sipped, the barracks door opened and slammed shut. The other MPs in the barracks jumped up from their bunks and snapped to attention. Franklin turned to see what the excitement was all about and saw Colonel Carp standing in the doorway. The colonel hadn't noticed Franklin until he turned around. "Aha," he said. "I've been look-ing for you, Boone." Then, to the other MPs he said, "At ease."

Franklin thought he heard a drunken edge to Colonel Carp's voice. He had addressed Franklin by his surname, as opposed to his usual "jail-bird," or "lazy-engineer-ass". Ironically this made Franklin more nervous, because it might lead the other MPs to believe he and Carp were more friendly than they were. Somehow they had been seen treasure hunting, and despite an enemy submarine showing up at Fort Miles' doorstep, the entire base knew about Franklin's expedition with Carp within twen-ty-four hours. Radish looked equally surprised by the colonel's demeanor.

Carp was alone. He stepped into the barracks, then turned to the other MPs who were sitting as if they weren't sure what to do. It was not usual for an officer of Carp's rank to visit the barracks, and despite them having a sort of power that only MPs had (they could arrest Colonel Carp for drunken behavior if they wanted) they sat still. Carp growled at them, "You four, beat it."

The MPs looked at each other, like they weren't sure if their individ-ual thoughts were mutual. They didn't budge. Colonel Carp said, "Move your asses. I don't give two shits that you're police, and promise that if any of you wanna arrest me, you're going to have to go through me first."

Franklin looked at Radish. Now they both knew Carp was drunk.

As the four MPs filed out the door, they were compliant and respectful as they passed Carp. Carp then turned back to Franklin and said, "Jesus, what a boring night." He squinted and looked from Franklin to Radish and back, then down at the two drinks sitting on the upturned wooden crate. Carp stepped over and sat down heavily into a metal folding chair. He leaned forward and grabbed the mug of whiskey that Radish had been sipping.

"You boys don't mind sharing this with your old CO?" Carp could see that the two soldiers were unsure of how to comport themselves in his presence. They had no idea what to say. Carp repeated, "Goddammit! I'm not here to harass you two. I wanna see your latest treasures, Boone."

Franklin raced to try and figure out how he was going to get out of Carp's request. He coveted his artifacts, and cringed at the thought of sharing them with anyone, especially Colonel Carp. Luckily they were not in his barracks, where his current finds were waiting to be cleaned and catalogued. He hadn't been too active on the beaches in the past week, though, and had found only minor metal objects. Any of the more important artifacts had already been transferred to a safety-deposit box at the Georgetown Savings & Trust. He asked, "Latest treasures, sir?"

"Yeah Boone. Let's see what you've got. And pour me another round of whatever that was. I have the night off too, and I'm thinking we'd all go out and do some treasure hunting."

Carp finished his drink in two gulps. Franklin and Radish looked at each other, neither of them interested in combing the beach with a drunk CO.

Franklin motioned for Radish to make the colonel another drink, and said, "Treasure hunting, sir? At this hour?"

"Yeah, Boone. What's the problem? I know you've done night drills with that contraption of yours. You scared of the dark? You scared of a moonless night?"

The reference to the moon's phase surprised both Franklin and Radish. They gave each other a quick acknowledging glance. Franklin said, "No sir. I just—It's just, that, hunting at night is not easy, and—"

"Ah, zip it, Boone." Carp waved his hand in the air, and clutched the mug of ice and whiskey. Radish was about to pour the ginger ale into the glass, when Carp stopped him. He tipped it to his lips so quickly that the ice clacked off his teeth.

"Yessir," replied Franklin.

Radish poured himself another drink and said, "Sir, Lieutenant Boone and I had plans to head into town for the night, and we were—"

"Okay great," interrupted the colonel. "Let's get that going."

A quick wave of anxiety surged through Franklin. *If news of our one treasure hunting trip spread so fast around Fort Miles, then being seen in town with him would certainly not spread any slower. That would definitely look questionable amongst the other officers.*

Carp pushed his empty mug forward and said, "Pour me another of those whiskeys."

Plus, he seems like an annoying drunk.

Radish poured Carp's drink. Carp grew more inebriated with each sip. To Franklin's relief, within a few minutes, Carp seemed to forget about heading into town, but he did not seem to be able to control his consumption of booze. He demanded another round, then rambled on about how much he missed his wife and how boring it was at Fort Miles.

144

"You pukes don't get it. You've got it good. You sit around here, playing in the sand, riding horses back and forth, tinkering with your little gadgets. And what do you have to show for your time?"

His drunken speech then turned to how sad he was since being transferred to Fort Miles. "You know, I was almost there. North Africa was lit to pop, and I was at the head of the brigade. We were set to push those Nazi fucks into Tunisia and then to their knees." Carp tipped the whiskey glass up for several seconds, letting the melted ice run into his mouth. "God, but here I am now. Sitting in bum-fuck Delaware drinking with a bunch of jailbirds and coastal miscreants... Goddammit Boone, you better have found some good shit."

Being called jailbird always made Franklin nervous. He looked to Radish to gauge his reaction to the comment, but he did not register the slight. Radish seemed more angered by the coastal miscreant comment than anything else.

Carp sat with the two for twenty minutes, while his ramblings blurred into context-less phrases. When he asked for his next round, Radish said, "Sorry sir but I'm going to need to grab some more ice from the machine."

Carp waved him off, cursing, "Hurry the hell up then, Sergeant." His eyes were heavy and looked nowhere in particular. He no longer seemed to care that the other two were in the room.

Radish said, "Come on Boone. I need your help."

Franklin grabbed the ice-bucket-helmet and followed him out onto the tarmac.

"Jesus!" exclaimed Franklin. "What the hell was that?"

"I don't know, but I am sick of his bullshit. Ever since those Germans got here, Carp's been breaking my balls. Suddenly, 'cause of what they're

145

doing, he's my new CO, or some shit."

"What are you talking about, Radish?"

Radish took a deep breath, and paused to collect his thoughts. "I'm saying, because of the tasks that those Krauts have been assigned, suddenly I am taking orders from Colonel Carp. I'm sick of listening to that no-account drunk, who has nothing over me than a few more strips of fabric on his arm, talking to me that way."

"Watch what you're saying Radish." Franklin looked back at their door.

"So what, he's drunker than shit. Talking to me that way—'hurry the hell up then'—I don't care what his rank is."

Franklin whisper-yelled at Radish, "Well what the hell are you going to do, Radish, arrest him?"

"Oh, I'm gonna do better than that, Boone. Just you watch." Radish finished filling the ice helmet, then motioned for Franklin to follow him into the latrine. He put the helmet on the sink counter, then unzipped his pants and urinated over the ice.

"I'm gonna make the colonel a drink."

Franklin's inebriated mind was impressed with Radish's audacity, and felt like a little of his own urine in the colonel's drink would be a perfect payback for his confiscating the gold coin on the beach. "Goddammit, Radish. I'm not saying I agree with what you're doing, but step aside." He pushed Radish out of the way, and added a splash of his own to the ice.

"Not too much, Boone. You don't want to melt the goddammed ice." He grabbed the helmet off the countertop.

Franklin looked at the ice helmet, the contents of which were quickly becoming a steaming soup of melting ice cubes and yellow urine.

Radish spread his fingers over the helmet opening and drained the excess liquid into the sink, while keeping the ice cubes in the helmet. "There you go, Boone. I'll put a few fresh cubes on top, and no one will know the difference."

"Alright, Radish, just wash your damn hands before you leave." Franklin stepped out into the gravel yard, and after putting a few more cubes in the helmet, Radish followed him to the MP barracks. Before they entered, Radish and Franklin gave each other a trusty nod. Inside, the barracks were empty. Carp was gone, as were the other MPs, and the bottle of whiskey. Franklin felt deflated, but also relieved that the piss bucket plan would never actually happen. Radish, on the other hand, stood in the doorway with the lukewarm bucket of ice in his hands. He was noticeably downhearted.

Franklin said, "Probably we're better off." He looked at the ice bucket, then back up to Radish's face, and thought, Yeah, we're definitely better off.

RESEARCH

Franklin did not have much faith in anything Radish said.
The stories that he and Israel told were so far-fetched that he
found it difficult to stop his mind from mulling over the details. The day
after the drunk appearance of Colonel Carp, Franklin made it a point to
work predominantly in the lab on base. He was anxious and distracted,
and as soon as he was done for the day, he caught a cab into town. His
destination was the Rehoboth Beach Public Library, where he searched
the Sussex County newspapers for articles from 1923. He was not sure of
the exact date of the storied events, so he began reading headlines from
January first. Not halfway through that year, he found a curious headline:
Bodies Found Along the Dismal Swamp Road. The article described a
grizzly scene on the same road as Israel's:

> In front of the farmhouse owned by the late
> Rafael Mouzellas and his widow were found
> the bodies of brothers Jonathan and Ethan
> Stoccaccio, and the body of South Carolina
> businessman Samuel Shamft. Local authorities
> are conducting an investigation into the possible
> causes for such a scene.

It didn't go into too much detail, except for a few conjectures as to
motive and descriptions of the scene, but finished with a promise of more
information as it became available. Below the article were also printed

three photographs. Franklin could now put a face to the names of Jonathan and Ethan Stoccaccio, and Samuel Shamft. The picture of Shamft jumped out at him, as if they had previously met. He stared at the one photo as if searching for clues to a mystery, but eventually decided to move on.

After finishing with the main story pages, Franklin decided to look at the obituaries for the same week. The obituaries for Jonathan and Ethan Stoccaccio confirmed their dates of death were the same as mentioned in the article, but otherwise did not provide any clues or details about their relationship with Rafael Mouzellas. Little else was mentioned other than trivial bits of information about surviving family members and how the two men contributed to the city of Rehoboth Beach.

Franklin scanned the headlines for the days after the killings, but no stories announced any arrests for the murders, or even any suspects being questioned. He found nothing related until two months later. In the *Sussex County Daily* was a front-page story about Rehoboth Beach Mayor Thomas Whilliger, and his involvement in several felonies with the recently deceased Stoccaccio brothers. Apparently, when the Stoccaccios were posthumously investigated, their felonies and connections around Delaware and the bordering states piled up and a lot of evidence lead right to Mayor Whilliger. The story seemed bigger than any hurricane to hit the small coastal town of Rehoboth Beach, and it was on the front page for weeks.

Due to the Stoccaccios' crimes breaching the borders of multiple states, a federal investigation was opened on their family activities, bank accounts, and businesses that revealed a massive network of cronyism, nepotism, and murder from Charleston to Philadelphia. However, the killing of the three criminals did not seem to matter much to anyone in

Southern Delaware. The average folks of Rehoboth Beach didn't care that the biggest extortionists in town were gone. But the links and intrigue the Stoccaccio brothers shared with so many public figures were unable to escape the federal eye.

Franklin returned the old newspapers to the attendant, and left the library. He had a lot of information to synthesize, and his taste buds told him he wanted some of Israel's rum. Instead he headed to the Swordfish where he ordered a beer and called a cab to take him to the Georgetown Library, where the resources regarding local history were more expansive. Franklin wondered if there might be any information regarding the Cape Henlopen Lighthouse keeper that Israel had mentioned.

At the Georgetown Library, Franklin found a fresh network of information. In fact, there was an entire room devoted to the Sussex County Historical Society. He found tax records, daily journals, and obituaries for the operators of the Lewes Beacon and the Cape Henlopen Lighthouse. He found the entries of a beacon operator named Selig Roddig Smithsenschone, whose operation dates lined up with the years that Rafael Mouzellas would have been active. Franklin perused his journal entries, which looked like the scrawling of a drunken man with no thumbs. The journal entries stopped long before May 29, 1921. *This makes sense, since any journal Smitty would have been using that night was most likely lost with the beacon.*

Having gleaned enough to believe that Selig Roddig Smithsenschone was in fact Smitty Smithsenson, Franklin closed the record books on the Lewes Beacon. Next, he moved his attention to the huge collection of Cape Henlopen Lighthouse journals and resources. He found the journals for the year of 1921. They were written by a man named Jarvis Christian Meekers, whose career as lighthouse operator began in 1901. His last journal entry was around mid-summer of 1923—two years after the disappearance of the *Jacinta*, and not long after the time that Israel said he had overheard Jarvis' revealing conversation.

Franklin flipped through Jarvis Meekers' journals until he came to the year 1921. Jarvis seemed to be a good company man who kept great notes of his daily routines at the lighthouse. When Franklin came to the entries for late May he stopped. Jarvis' handwriting was much clearer than Smitty's drunken scratchings, and he seemed to have a penchant for rambling on and on about everything related to the lighthouse. The entry for the date of the twenty-ninth was as long-winded as all his others, but a particular section of it piqued Franklin's attention. It read;

> Despite having imbibed on the sweet mash and
> not so uncertain as to find myself again drunk
> and setting in this tower amongst a raging gale, I
> am certain that I see approximately a full league
> down the shore a broken-masted vessel lying in a
> most careened of fashions.

The journal entry went on to mention levels and movements of the storm, and ended with another curious section;

> It may also be the deprivation of sleep through
> which I have suffered at the hands of last night's
> weather, or the fog of terror through which I have
> fought all night to keep the light alive for any
> unfortunate sailor floundering off the shoals, but
> when I look to the dunes now for any sign of the
> broken vessel that I witnessed last night, I see no
> sign or trace of it, nor bits of mast or bow floating
> on the waves. It is as if the boat was swallowed
> by the sand.

Franklin closed Meekers' journal, and then moved to the obituary section of the resource center. Amongst the list of deaths from 1921 through 1923, nowhere did he find a Jarvis Meekers, or a Smitty Smithsenson. The two men either moved from Delaware, or met another fate that didn't lend itself to documentation in a newspaper.

On a curious whim, Franklin then searched for the more recent obituary of Ron Brotsky. Brotsky had died about six months before Franklin came to Fort Miles, but in the entire previous year's obituaries, he found no mention of the name. He considered the odd oversight, knowing that his friends in Barracks Five had mentioned reading about the death in the newspaper. *Maybe because Brotsky wasn't from Delaware, they didn't mention his death? Or maybe because he was in the Army?* The missing information only served to increase his curiosity, and he remembered the Georgetown Police Station.

Stepping out into the late-afternoon sun, Franklin stood on the sidewalk that ran along main street in downtown Georgetown. A few blocks east was the police station, where Franklin informed the attendant at the front desk that he wished to speak with a detective who knew something about the GI who was found floating in the Indian River Inlet the previous year. He was escorted into the main office, and told to sit in a chair that was placed at the end of a desk. Franklin noticed a fedora hat on the desk, and immediately had a strange feeling of deja vu as he tried to remember why he recognized it. The owner of the hat arrived at the desk.

Detective Ted Rutherford offered his hand to Franklin. When they made eye contact Franklin saw the detective's mustache and he finally remembered where he had seen him before. He was the strange man on the beach a few weeks back who had suddenly appeared in the dunes.

Franklin's surprise allowed no secrets. He said, "Hey, you're that fella from the dunes."

Detective Rutherford squinted and eyed Franklin up and down, then said, "Ah yes. You're the new beachcomber at Fort Miles. You're out working the dunes a lot, aren't you?"

"How do you know when I'm out on the beach?"

Rutherford smiled and said, "You know most of those beaches and dunes are public property, right? Just 'cause you have that uniform on doesn't mean you own the sand?"

"Yes, Detective. I understand all that."

Rutherford continued, "I grew up in these parts. I don't make it out there too often, but I fancy myself something of an amateur treasure hunter. Nothing like what you're doing. I mean, I don't have a fancy metal detector like you, but I'm sure you know that it doesn't take a metal detector to find shipwreck treasure around the Hen and Chickens Shoal, yes?"

Franklin relaxed, and again scolded himself for not being covert enough.

Rutherford said, "Anyway, I was wondering when we'd finally meet. What exactly brings you in to the station today?"

Franklin explained that he was hoping to talk with someone about the death of Ron Brotsky, to which the detective leaned back in his chair and pulled a single, thin file folder out from the middle of a pile of other folders and papers. Rutherford placed the folder in front of Franklin, then leaned over it, staring at Franklin. He held a pencil and rested his hand on a yellow pad of paper. Scribbled on the outside of the folder was a lot of data, the only part of which Franklin understood were the words "Ronald Brotsky." Detective Rutherford explained that he was one of the first officers who arrived at the inlet to find Brotsky, and was on the team that worked the case. He said, "But since you guys took over, no one here's really thought about it much. So any news you got, you ought'a just tell whoever handles this type of thing back at the fort."

Franklin asked, "You guys took over the case, what does that mean?"

"That means that since the Army van came and scooped up Brotsky's corpse, no one here has given a shit about the case. I'm not sure why you're poking around here, and not over at Fort Miles?"

"I'm just curious. I didn't know it was in the Army's jurisdiction."

"Mr. Boone, do you have something you want to tell me? Something about the death?"

"No," said Franklin. "I don't, other than the fact that I currently have the same assignment that Ron Brotsky had when he drowned."

Rutherford eyed Franklin, who didn't understand how his military occupational specialty had anything to do with the death. Rutherford asked, "Why do you keep saying that he drowned?"

"That's what I was told when I got to Fort Miles."

"Ya don't say?" He scribbled something on his pad of paper.

Franklin was too distracted to notice the intrigue in Rutherford's tone. He asked, "Since I'm here, would you mind if I asked you a few questions?"

Rutherford smiled at the irony of the conversation, and said, "You want to ask me some questions? Okay. Shoot."

Franklin asked, "Do you guys have any ideas as to what Brotsky was doing out there, before he died?"

"We have some ideas, but none any better than the last. The initial thoughts were that he was swimming and couldn't handle the currents. Which is the common go-to explanation for accidental deaths around here. But your guy was naked as a jaybird."

"It was early spring," Franklin said. "Wouldn't the water have been too cold for swimming?"

"I don't know, lieutenant. Unfortunately, I can't read the mind of a dead man any better than I can that of a living man. But I've seen surfers and fishermen tolerate the cold water of spring all the time."

Franklin continued, "Was there anything nearby, clothes, any kind of gear or tools?"

Rutherford took his time to answer, "I don't think—" he leaned forward and opened up the folder on the desk, and flipped through some of the papers inside it. "No, I don't recall him being found with anything at all. Which is why I believe he did not die in the Indian River Inlet."

Franklin asked, "I assume he drowned out in the surf and just floated to where you found him."

"Yeah," said Rutherford, "that could'a been what happened. There were just too many things that begged other questions."

"So you think he was killed and moved to the inlet?"

"I don't know. There were no signs of the body being moved... at least, not over land."

As Franklin pondered the detective's answers, he asked, "So you found nothing significant around his body?"

This time Detective Rutherford did not look through the file folder. He sat with his hand over it, staring curiously at Franklin, and said, "Apparently not. Nothing other than these photos. By the time we figured out that he was a GI, we had already conducted a preliminary forensic analysis, and taken these pictures. Your Army fellas didn't ask about them, so we didn't mention them." He looked up, and continued, "If you want, you can take a look, but I warn you, they are not pretty."

Franklin had not thought to look at the photos of the scene, and was unprepared for the detective's warnings. Rutherford slid the folder around

155

for Franklin to open it on his own, and again, stared at him. Franklin flipped open the file and was immediately met with the first photo. It took a few seconds to register what he was seeing. Brotsky's body was contorted and wedged unnaturally between the boulders of the inlet retaining wall. Franklin wrinkled his forehead in disgust and confusion. The rest of the photos were different angles of the same scene, different shots of Brotsky's various wounds, and then there was a stack of different shots of the corpse on the forensic table. Crabs had already had their way with Brotsky's eyes, and his cheeks had also been eaten through. Franklin regretted having looked at the pictures, but found Brotsky's mortal wound to be curious. He remembered being told that Brotsky's chest was smashed in by the impact against the retaining wall, but what he saw was a gaping hole clear through the man's thoracic cavity. The hole was about ten inches in diameter, and the inside of the cavity had been well worked by sea scavengers. Franklin noticed that there was no spine section in the wound, and knew that scavengers don't eat bone. He asked, "Where's his spine?"

Rutherford answered, "Yeah, his spine. That was an odd detail to the case. Looks like the crabs really did a number on him. My colleagues believe that the joints must have just loosened up as the crabs worked on him, and then the different vertebrae simply floated away."

Franklin looked at the next picture in the collection. It was a closer shot of the specifics of the wound. Again, he saw that the section of thoracic vertebrae that should have been in the wound were missing. And the ends of the lower ribs looked to be missing as well. He was about to accept that it had to have been Mother Nature that ate away at the sinews and tendons, but then noticed a series of black striations on the skin around the wound cavity. And the ends of what remained of Brotsky's ribs were also blackened. He asked, "What do you make of these markings?"

Rutherford stared at the picture. He answered, "I don't know what to make of those. They're signs of being burned, or charred, you might say, but I'm not so sure how they got there. An average firearm round does not burn the skin like that." He leaned over the close-up picture of Brotsky's chest. "Yeah, this is something that even the forensic doctor had a bit of trouble with." He pointed at the gaping wound in one of the photographs and said, "See here, these white markings? These are the ends of the spine."

Franklin leaned in for a closer look.

Rutherford said, "And you see how the bone is sheared clean through? That's the weird part. 'Cause, the vertebrae didn't separate at the joints. They were cut in half, as if Brotsky had a hole burned through him. But we haven't been able to determine what kind of round would make such a wound. We thought maybe one of those Army toys your guys play with, like a flamethrower. But we all know a flamethrower doesn't cause a wound like Brotsky had."

Franklin asked, "How would he have been burned in this way? What does that have to do with him drowning?"

Rutherford said, "I gotta tell you, you're the only person I've heard call this a drowning. No one here believes for a minute that Brotsky drowned. And frankly, other than the forensic analysis, we were never given any time to start an outside investigation before the Army took over the case."

Franklin asked, "They took the body?"

"Yes, which is standard procedure in matters that involve the military. They have jurisdiction when it comes to things that are their property—" he looked at Franklin, and realized he was speaking with military property. "So to speak."

Franklin had no more questions for Detective Rutherford, who shook Franklin's hand and closed the meeting with, "Well, Lieutenant Boone, it's a pleasure to have finally met you. I'm sure we'll see each other again. Maybe on the beach, and you can show off with that detector of yours?"

Franklin thanked the detective and stood up. He was about to walk away when he remembered another question. "Oh, sorry detective, but I do have one more question. Does the name Mouzellas mean anything to you?"

Rutherford shook his head. "Nothing comes to mind. Why? Who's this Mouzellas fella?"

"Not a single person, actually. It's the surname of a local family." Franklin chose not to delve any deeper into probing detective Rutherford. "No big deal. I was just curious." He thanked the detective again.

As he walked down the front steps of the station he wasn't sure if what he'd just learned was important. Brotsky was found dead, and the Army took over the case. And Rutherford thinks Brotsky was killed and dumped in the inlet. That was it. Franklin had no idea how to research the whereabouts of Brotsky's files back on Fort Miles, or any of the forensic details that the Army inspectors might have determined. He could ask Radish, but MPs were only involved in the front end of any accidental deaths. They didn't lead any investigations or do forensic research. So Radish probably wouldn't know much about the case.

Franklin looked up at the sky. It was the early evening and the sun would only be up for another hour. The scene on Main Street was bustling with people and cars going about their end-of-workday activities, and Franklin realized he had no idea where he was heading. He was lost in thought regarding the suspicious look of Brotsky's wounds, and how there might be a connection between his death and possibly Israel Mouzellas.

Connections? What with all the stories Radish has been telling, I wouldn't be surprised if he knew more about Brotsky than he's letting on. The newspaper picture of Samuel Shamft came back to him. Connections indeed.

He scanned the street for the closest pay phone and called a cab. He had one last stop to make before heading back to base: the North Lewes Harbor. He wanted to corroborate a minor detail. If Israel was telling the truth about how and when he left Delaware, his name might be on the manifest archives at the dock office. Franklin imagined the young Israel as a tall man-child, his hair thick and clumped in its own knots, despite his forehead being forever dented by the blow it sustained two years earlier.

•

The harbormaster was amenable to Franklin's request, and pointed to an old storage room in the back of the main office. In that room Franklin found shelves full of bulging, dusty manifests. Luckily, they were organized by year and it only took Franklin a few minutes to locate the manifest for 1923. He pulled out one for the summer of that year and was able to verify that a one Israel B. Mouzellas was on board as one of the deckhands of the USS *Peregrine*, a banana steamer bound for Honduras. The departure date was June 1, 1923.

GERMANS ON THE BEACH

The information Franklin learned made him wary of joining Israel's crew. There was an air about the farmhouse, and now Israel's reputation, that distracted him. Anxiety grew in his gut when his mind lit on the strange, untidy home and its odd inhabitants who lived like mice in a labyrinth of junk. In the minutes while he drifted off to sleep, Franklin stared at the ceiling and pondered his options. He flip-flopped between the pros and cons of working with Israel. Then, during the day, while he tested a new sensor or battery pack, his mind became less worried. The work calmed him. But a lot of his work was walking up and down the beach with a metal detector, and by the end of the week, he had found countless artifacts of all values. And right before quitting for the weekend—after a week of getting his mind back into his research—Franklin heard a familiar, low-end tone that made him stop dead in his tracks. It could have been lead, but to Franklin, the sound was the song of gold.

Sure enough, not a foot beneath the sand was his thirteenth gold coin. This coin was the breeze that blew his mind back to the issue of Israel, and the potential booty that would be on the *Jacinta*. Franklin didn't even consider the superstitious place that this new coin fell into in his collection, and with each day that passed, his worries were buried deeper beneath an imaginary yet glimmering pile of gold.

Franklin spent the weekend cleaning and cataloguing the treasures that he had found over the week while outside a nor'easter blew down the coast. It lasted half of Saturday, and all of Sunday, and by Monday morning he was anxious to get back out to the freshly churned beach. He wanted to search the beaches south of the shoals. There were currents in that small stretch that changed by the hour and they always left an interesting treasure trove after any storm.

With the 625G over his shoulder and a sandwich and canteen in his backpack, Franklin headed out to the beach. He carried his usual tools: a shovel, a sand sifter, and a bucket. He walked along the main road that ran directly through the South Field, making note of how the usual dump trucks and front-end loaders were absent. This was an official research assignment, so he was able to procure the key for the gate in the South Field fence, and from there he walked to the edge of the berm ridge and slid down into the dunes.

Franklin valued the Hen and Chickens Shoal not just for its mass of potential treasure, but also because of how the beaches in front of it were rarely busy with vacationers or beachcombers because nobody wanted to swim in the dangerous currents. He walked down to the frothy, wet sand near the water and stopped to take in the scene. The sun sat on the horizon like a glowing hot plate, and no clouds were in the sky. The early hour temperature was almost eighty degrees. Looking north Franklin saw the busy goings on of the cape and the entrance to the Delaware Bay. Armed transport boats escorted larger military vessels out of the bay, while huge commercial transport barges and tankers sat waiting on the edge of the Atlantic for their turn to head up to Wilmington.

Northward, moored to the mine wharf, was U-856. It floated, moored in the spot where it had been left on the day the Germans surrendered. It was covered in a steel-blue net camouflage in an attempt to

161

keep it out of view of any passing ship. From Franklin's perspective on the beach, it was easy to see that what was under the netting was a submarine, though the German symbols on the sides of the craft had been painted over, and the gun turret on the top was gone. Franklin squinted and put his hand over his eyes like a visor. He was impressed with any submarine crew. *No matter what side you're on, it takes guts to brave the entire Atlantic just to come over and spit out a few torpedoes.*

As he stared north, the sound of men's voices singing a military-style song came to his attention. The voices had an accent. Franklin turned to look down the beach and about fifty yards away, running towards him in a loose shoulder-to-shoulder formation, was the surrendered German U-boat crew. They were out for a morning jog, starting early enough that any civilians might not notice them. Franklin stared as the POWs ran past.

They seem chipper. I guess the beds in the stockade are more comfortable than the bunks on their U-boat. Nothing better than a good run on the beach to invigorate the soul. He was certain that American prisoners in Germany were not getting the same treatment as this U-boat crew.

Two jeeps followed the group of exercising Germans—each carried the driver and another rider who sat behind a .50 caliber machine gun that was mounted to the back of the vehicle. The grind of the sand under their wheels was loud and they were moving slower than the prisoners were running. The men behind the wheels looked bored, while the men behind the machine guns sat hunched and ominous. As the jeep closest to Franklin crept by, the gunner was already looking at him. It was Radish. He was shaking his head at Franklin, as if to scold him for not being more covert, then stuck up his middle finger. He held it there the entire time that the jeep passed, while his other arm was draped over his weapon.

When the joggers and their guards had passed, Franklin heard the sound of a horse neighing and turned to find the source. Lit by the low sun and riding along the dunes were two mounted MPs, and not a half a mile south of those were two more. Like most things here at the beach, the horses moved slowly in the heat as they fought off black flies that bit like syringes with wings.

The two mounted units came closer. It was Marteen and Wilkins. As their horses walked along the path between the dunes and the pine forest, Wilkins called out, "Hey Boone. We're on to you and your little metal detection operation."

Franklin felt a jolt of worry that these two might somehow stop him from being able to treasure hunt, but he relaxed as he remembered that he had done nothing wrong. The 625G was practically his, and he was allowed to use it any time he wanted. He thought, *perhaps they discovered Israel's dig*, but didn't pursue the thought. So far his hands were clear of any involvement in that operation. He shrugged his shoulders at Marteen and Wilkins, and noticed the splint and medical tape around Marteen's index and middle finger of his right hand. His injured fingers were almost completely healed, but still required support. Wilkins stuck his middle finger up.

That was the second time in less than five minutes that he was told to fuck off by an MP. Though he was sure Radish didn't mean him any harm, Wilkins and Marteen were not so brotherly. Marteen said nothing, but sat in the saddle with his left hand cradling the reins. His eyes locked on Franklin until he was passed, and the MPs continued on their patrol.

RE-INTRODUCTION

The day after Franklin bumped into the jogging Germans, he found himself at the tail end of his latest experiments with a new battery pack. The new device was supposed to have a longer charge than his previous battery, but, like a good scientist, Franklin believed that any conclusions regarding the battery's charge should be backed up with thorough field testing. Which meant a perfect opportunity to treasure hunt. It didn't matter where Franklin went to conduct his research, as long as he kept the power on.

The day was bright with a slight morning nip that would soon be blown inland by the crosswinds coming out of the bay and mixing with the open Atlantic. By noon, the temperature would reach ninety degrees. Franklin procured the key to the South Field gate. He could have just walked to Battery Herring and around the end of the fence, but that would take him straight down to the beach, and therefore a longer trek to the southern edge of the Hen and Chickens Shoal. Not to mention, that route made him more visible to passing MPs or beachcombers. The higher path that ran along the front edge of the pine forest was less traveled and a more direct route to his destination. Most of the path paralleled the front edge of the forest, but Franklin knew that at some points it wove inside the trees. He remembered his last foray into the woods. The obvious signs of gunfire in the tree bark. The strange sounds.

Keep it together. It's just a bunch of goddamned trees. At least in this daylight I'll be able to see the trailheads.

The path wound west, into the woods. Within twenty feet it became overgrown, and shaded from the low sun. Mosquitos were vicious as Franklin moved slowly through the thorny shrubs lining the trail. He swatted constantly around his head, and before he knew it, he found himself off the trail. To get his bearings, he checked over his shoulder. Behind him, things did not look any clearer. Luckily, he knew that not far to his left was the edge of the forest. The morning sunshine pierced through the short distance of trees, and Franklin knew, if he had to, he could trudge his way through the undergrowth, towards the light, and he would be out of the woods in no time.

As he swatted mosquitos and scratched at bug bites already growing on his face and neck, Franklin felt a strange chill up his spine. Then he heard a distant snap of a twig, or branch. He looked over his right shoulder, and there in the dark interior of the forest, where the sun had yet to brighten, he saw the dim shape of a man duck behind a thick tree trunk.

Franklin jumped behind the closest tree, and froze. Peering around the trunk, he struggled to find the location where he thought the figure had been. Even in full daylight, the mass of trees were all too similar for him to tell the difference between any of them. And in the low morning sun, he couldn't distinguish much. He stared hard into the dark, his breathing louder than the crashing waves. But nothing moved. A few birds flitted by, chirping.

Franklin turned and bolted towards the sunlight. Everything about him dragged through the dense undergrowth, slowing his speed. The thorny shrubs made him anxious, and with each step he fought harder to move, until he was finally out of the trees. His next step was on a loose edge of the forest berm. It crumbled under his foot and he toppled forward, face-first, down the hill.

Sand collected under his collar, grinding against his chest. He struggled to keep his chin up off the ground, as he braced his slide with his hands. The backpack flopped over his head, and the rest of his gear was thrown willy-nilly down the hill. He came to a quick stop at the bottom and clumsily fought his way back up to his feet. Brushing sand off his shirt, he gagged and spat the same out of his mouth. He looked back up at the forest for any signs of the mysterious stranger, but saw no one. He collected his gear as quickly as possible.

On the dunes in front of the Hen and Chickens Shoal, Franklin checked the 625G's sensitivity adjustment and turned it down, as the sand of the dunes was mineralized and often gave false readings, then started walking and sweeping. He had no real goals for this assignment other than wait for the battery to die.

About a hundred yards into the dunes, Franklin heard a voice. His nerves were still on edge from his recent forest experience, so he jumped at the sound. At first he thought it was Marteen or Wilkins out to harass him, but looking up he saw Israel standing on a hill about twenty feet away. Sand shook from his beard as it was blustered back and forth by the breezes. He smiled, leaning on the handle of a three-foot shovel stuck into the sand, and said, "You're doing it wrong."

Franklin was shocked to see him standing so nonchalant and out in the open. "Israel," he said, "what exactly am I doing wrong?"

Israel jumped down the front of his hill, and climbed up the next one to Franklin. He had streaks of a dark black soot across his skin and clothes, and wet sand in his mop of hair. His sandals revealed yellow-nailed toes rimmed in grime. Israel pointed towards the ocean and said, "You'll find more treasures down by the wet sand."

Franklin knew Israel was savvy with beach-combing, and looked towards the waves.

"You look for the low spots," continued Israel. He pointed towards the waterline, aiming his attention at a particular area between two sandy slopes. Waves washed in, over the higher ground, and as they receded they flowed into the shallow valley then returned back to the undertow. "That's where the best finds are. Everything that's pushed ashore at high tide washes back out via the low spots, and whatever doesn't make it back out to sea sits on shore. Right?"

Franklin couldn't help but agree, and kicked himself for not realizing this natural beach collection system on his own. Either way, he was happy for Israel's advice, and said, "Thanks Israel. I had not considered that."

"I told you, Franklin. I've been working these beaches my whole life. You stick with me, kid, and I'll show you how to make it rich off of these damned shores."

"So, you're rich then?"

"Never been richer, Franklin. Either way, you're here. I'm here. What's say I introduce you to the dig site?"

"Yes, well, I'm training right now. Kind of an easy day really, but—"

"That's good. I love it when you have an easy day. That means you can help me dig. I haven't seen our pal Jameson for a few days now, so I could use as much help as you want to give."

Israel's assumption that Franklin would stop his work and help him for the day caused Franklin's guts to twist. He scoured Israel's face for signs of untruths, and said, "He's not just my pal is he?"

Israel smiled. "What does that mean?"

"I think you know what I mean. Radish lives at your house."

"Is that news to you?"

167

"It was a bit of a shock when I discovered it."

"Well, it's not my place to make sure you boys are privy to each other's personal information."

"True. That being said, I'm working right now."

"Oh? What kind of work?"

"Well, today I'm running the detector until the battery dies."

"So, let me get this straight. You're getting paid to just walk around until your detector battery dies?"

Franklin understood the seeming absurdity of his assignment and tried to redeem it with a research and development angle. "This is important research—"

Israel stopped him in mid-sentence. "Franklin, I don't give a flying shit about your research. But I do know that you just told me you're getting paid today to walk around the dunes waiting for your metal detector battery to die. What this means to me is that you're free for the next few hours, since that battery pack of yours looks pretty fancy, and it really doesn't matter what you're doing with the detector as long as its power is on. Right? So you can join me. If you don't mind, I'd like to show you something."

"I don't know, Israel. Since dinner at your house, I've made a few discoveries that have nothing to do with this beach."

Israel looked curious, and said nothing. Like a skilled gambler, he waited, to let Franklin show his cards first.

The pause was uncomfortable and Franklin fell right in. "I've looked up a few things at the library."

"The library, huh? Impressive."

"Anyway, if I am going to be on your crew, I want to verify some rumors I heard."

"Oh rumors, huh? Just where did you hear these rumors? Actually, don't answer that, it had to have been Jameson." Israel sat down on the edge of the dune hill. He squinted up at Franklin, who was backlit by the morning sun.

"Well, I found just enough to make me more curious, but nothing about this boat you're looking for, and little about your family."

"No doubt," replied Israel. "I'd love to hear what you think you know."

"I know there was a big police investigation into something that happened at your house, and that you left the country on a banana steamer not long after that."

Israel shook his head. "Yes, the newspapers are a strange bunch. I can't vouch for anythin' that was written about the murders at my house. I was seventeen and could not have cared less about makin' any headlines. But, for the sake of efficiency, I'm going to be straight with you."

COMPULSION

Like so many previous afternoons or evenings, Israel was dropped off by Smitty Smithsenson at the top of the long gravel driveway that led to his farmhouse. This day he walked the drive like a beaten kid who had long forgotten why exactly he was spending so much time on the beach and dunes. Standing in the middle of his family property, surrounded by the vast openness of the Delaware countryside and distant forest, he felt small. He remembered his father, and his throat tightened because he felt like he was the only one who cared about the loss. Not a few months after the hurricane, his mother had seemed to lose interest in Israel and his sister. She stopped making meals and spent most evenings in town, at places where the darker side of Southern Delaware mingled, and waited for opportunities to walk through the door. The more he found himself alone, the more time Israel spent looking for the one person who used to keep his world under control. Even in death, Rafael Mouzellas gave Israel's life purpose.

He took a deep breath, then after a few steps, he looked up and noticed an automobile sitting at the end of the driveway, awkward and shadowed by the side of the house and porch. The hairs on the back of his neck stood up. His pace slowed as he approached the car. He stopped and stared in the windows. The seats were empty save a shotgun on the backseat. No visitor with a gun such as this had come to his house since before his father died.

Israel slipped his hands under the handle of the passenger door.

His mother's voice came from the house. At first Israel told himself she was screaming. But between the screams his mother was also laughing.

He opened the Cadillac door and pulled out the shotgun. Leaving the door open, he then continued towards his house. Ethan Stoccaccio pushed the screen door wide and stepped out onto the porch. Israel stopped at the bottom of the steps.

He raised the shotgun.

Ethan froze. He seemed to analyze his predicament, and then a smile grew across his face. "You get that gun from my Caddie, boy?"

Israel remained silent.

Ethan smirked, insulting Israel more with his facial expressions. "You sure you know how to use that?"

Israel replied, "I'm sure," as he moved up the first few steps.

Ethan stood his ground and raised his hands, giving Israel a clean view of his chest. "Well then I guess you ought'a do what you gotta do."

Israel pulled the trigger and the gun clicked the sound of an empty shotgun.

"Ha, boy," said Ethan. He grabbed the shotgun by the barrel and yanked it from Israel's hands. "Had you known better, you'd'a realized this gun is not loaded."

He flipped the long gun around so the butt was now between him and Israel, and raised it as if to strike. "I guess, though, this doesn't really surprise me. After all, you're the son of a man who liked to mess with other people's property. 'Course, your dad was also shit at that."

Ethan swung the gun down, attempting to knock the hilt over Israel's head. Israel dove out of the way and landed next to the pile of firewood

171

that sat to the left of his front door. As he jumped back up to his feet, he grabbed the long ax that had been lying on top of the wood pile.

Ethan tossed his unloaded shotgun to the ground and went for the pistol that hung from his belt. But Israel was quicker and shoved the blunt end of his ax across Ethan's face. Teeth and blood flew from his mouth as he stumbled backwards. His eyes were wide as he lost his footing and pressed his hand into his bludgeoned cheek.

Israel moved on Ethan before the he could make another attempt for his pistol. The small space of his front porch restricted him from swinging the ax too wide in any direction. So, Israel held the handle with two hands and slammed it forward into Ethan's chest. Ethan got his hands in front of him and resisted the ax handle. The two men pushed and pulled, but Israel stood planted like an ancient oak tree. His mind had never been so clear and his focus never so pinpointed. He got his right foot behind Ethan's left leg and gave the ax handle one last heave. They stumbled backwards, smashing through the feeble porch railing.

They landed hard, on top of railing wood and gravel. But the two men did not lose their grip on the ax handle. Israel fought with the strength of a man who had spent two years digging pits in the dunes, and with the determination of one who had swum countless times amongst the relentless currents of the Hen and Chickens Shoal. He looked down at Ethan struggling and locked his arms in place. Holding the ax motionless for a few seconds, while the man sputtered and choked on his teeth. Staring into the man's frenzied eyes, Israel knew he'd swum against stronger currents than him. Ethan fought with the strength of nothing more than desperation. The fall from the porch had knocked the wind out of him. Between that and his broken jaw, he couldn't call for help.

Israel had the advantage of time, gravity, and an absence of empathy.

He had little strategy other than using his weight, straddling Ethan as he pushed down on the ax handle. Locked in his first fight to the death, strange realizations came over Israel. One was the realization that he was suddenly in a situation that had to remain in his control. There was no going back, or getting help from anyone. However, it was also not long before he felt certain that he was winning. Suddenly, a strange silence washed through his mind, and he was looking down from the clouds. Indeed his perspective was looking from someplace distant at the very scene he was taking part in. As he watched himself fighting with Ethan, the seconds stretched long enough for him to be able to think, *maybe I'm actually in my bedroom window...* And then his vantage point shifted from high in the sky to twenty feet up, just inside the top floor of his house.

Israel's breath was calm as he pushed the ax down. While Ethan pushed back, losing his strength, his hands white-knuckled around the ax handle. As the ax got closer to Ethan's neck, the man panicked and tried pushing with his right elbow against the ax handle, while attempting with the same hand to find Israel's face and dig his thumb into the his eye. But Israel exploited the desperate move with a tilt of his head then a quick back-and-forth of the handle, and slammed it down onto Ethan's trachea.

Staring down at his first murder, Israel heard a repeating rap of metal on wood. It came from the top floor. His parents' bedroom window.

Israel stood, the ax still in both hands. His breath was catching up with his racing thoughts, while his heartbeat made his chest feel tight and small. Behind him lay scattered bits of porch railing in the dusty grass and gravel of his side yard. The wooden pieces led his eyes to the front of his house. He kicked a few balusters out of the way and stepped up on the now open porch end as if it was just one particularly high step.

As the sounds from inside continued, he found the front door unlocked but closed. He wanted to smash the door open, but had to check his haste against the fact that the door was his own property. No need to smash it when he can just turn the handle and move silently into the front room. But the door was well oiled and even Israel's attempt at subtly was too much. It swung wide open and bumped against a pile of firewood.

He stood in the doorway. The square family room was dark, save for whatever light shone through the back windows. In the dusty beams, Israel saw two sets of legs on the floor, behind the far end of the couch. The bottom set were shoeless and bare, while the top set still wore socks. The legs shuffled in a manner that meant Israel could not discern if they were having fun or struggling. A set of men's clothes and shoes lay on the floor in the dining room.

He hurried to end of the couch. Lulu-Pine's eyes met his.

"Lulu?"

Though somewhat choked, his question was loud enough that Samuel Shamft heard. Shamft flipped over and off of Lulu-Pine. He moved quick, like he had a lot of experience with people sneaking up on him. Wearing nothing but a sweat soaked undershirt and socks, Shamft's hands searched his hip for the place his pistol was always hung. His eyes left Israel and moved down to his pile of clothes. His shirt and vest were strewn among his pants, belt, and holster. Israel gave him no more time, and swung the axe blade into Shamft's neck.

The axe was lodged deep into Shamft's collarbone, and when his body flopped to the ground, Israel was caught off-guard and pulled forward. As he fumbled with his balance he was forced to let go of the axe. It fell away, tilting and making the final cut in what remained holding Shamft's head to his shoulders. Blood splattered across Lulu-Pine's face;

warm and running into her eyes and mouth. Israel had never seen so much blood. It poured from Shamft's neck, covering half of Lulu-Pine and soaking the floor around her. She turned to see Samuel Shamft's head, with eyes and gaping mouth, lying next to her.

She shuffled on her elbows away from Shamft, and bumped into the side of an end table. The lamp on the table tilted and fell directly onto her head. Dazed, she pressed her hands to her head, and writhed on the ground.

Israel recovered his balance, and got back to his feet. "Lulu-Pine," he began, but was interrupted by the sound of thumping noises. Above him, through the floorboards of his parents' bedroom, was a rhythmic sound of metal against wood. As he leaned down to retrieve his ax, Lulu-Pine pushed him aside and crawled past. "No," she said, low and almost to herself. She knelt above the pile of clothes, shuffling through it until she pulled out a leather holster and pistol. She turned and held the gun up for Israel. Her own blood ran from an unseen gash beneath clotted hair, and mixed with the rivulets of Samuel Shamft's.

Israel was shocked at the sight before him. Sitting the way Lulu-Pine was, with matted hair and bloodied, swollen face made her look ghoul-like. He had never seen so much white in a person's eyes. Her body shook as she tried to keep the gun up within his reach. He took the gun from his sister, and stood looking down at it. Many times he had shot a gun, but always in practice or while hunting. Behind the clarity of the pistol in his hands was the blurry image of his sister, panting and wiping more blood from her face. She struggled to stay up on her elbows.

More sounds from upstairs, and Israel turned towards the steps. He stepped up carefully, knowing which boards creaked louder than others. The bedroom sounds continued as he snuck his way up. At the top land-ing, Israel had a direct line of sight into his parents' bedroom. Through the few inches that the door was open, a silhouette of commotion moved with the thumping of the bedframe. Israel stepped to the door and kicked it open. Jonathan Stoccaccio turned and jumped off of his mother. Just like his criminal counterpart downstairs, he made a desperate move for his own firearm that he left in his pants. But Israel had a bullet in Jonathan before he could take a step. Flesh popped off the side of his neck. He screamed and slapped his hand against the steady flow of blood, then fell back on top of Sumi-Sun. She kicked under Jonathan's weight, but could not free herself from him before Israel put three more rounds into the man's chest. With the third shot, Sumi-Sun's shrieks turned from fear to pain, and blood ran from her right side.

·

Franklin could not believe his ears. He asked, "So you killed your mother?"

"That's one way of lookin' at it."

Franklin asked, "That was that? Her family didn't ask any questions?"

"Oh no, they asked a lot of questions. All of which I answered and when they started repeatin' themselves I showed 'em my shotgun. Never heard from 'em again."

Franklin tried to find a way to accept Israel's nature, a way to justify and make it okay for him to join his crew. Back in Baltimore, he had befriended some shady characters, but they hadn't been involved in anything more than a few home robberies, never murder.

Israel continued, "I am certain that not long after my father died, Smitty Smithsenson sold my family out to the Stoccaccios. That's how they knew where to go for their revenge. So the night before I left town

176

I paid him one last visit. Went to his shack and caught him sleepin' in, like he didn't have a care in the world. I promise you, I made sure he was wide awake before I cut his throat."

THE DEN

66 **Well, that's the truth about what happened at my house. I**
promise you, you won't find anythin' else about it in those old
newspapers. That bein' said, are you ready to do some work?"

"I suppose I am." Israel's story wore Franklin out, and all the standing around in the dunes made him worried that he might be spotted by
an MP or beach patrol. He decided to wait until he was alone to try and
rationalize all that he had been told. So, Franklin asked, "Alright, what is
it that you want me to see?"

"Good, follow me then. You can leave that detector on while I show
you where we'll be working."

The two men walked over the ridges of a few dunes. While they
walked Franklin kept his eye out for any beach patrols, civilians, or
prying detectives. They came to the top of a hill, and in the bottom of
the valley below them the ground was a contrast of black soil with the
white sands of the higher dunes. The dark piles reminded Franklin of the
mineral patches that showed up on the beaches. He knew these spots well
because they always caused a false reading in his metal detector, as they
were laden with iron and other metals from the breaking down of thousands of shipwrecks. Countless diggings and trainings on the beaches had
taught him that not far below the sandy upper layer of the beach was a
layer of a thick, oily tar-mat—a soil layer that was merciless in confusing
the 625G. Also lying on top of the black, patchy sand, organized in a neat

staging area, were two buckets and various garden tools.

Israel said, "Franklin, once you see this you will have to swear on your life to keep it secret. If you do so, you will be greatly rewarded. If you fail in this regard, I cannot make any promises as to your safety."

In light of the story he had just heard, Franklin's face flushed with heat at the audacity of Israel's comment. Any sane, self-respecting man would have turned and walked away at that point, but Franklin already knew too much, and was caught between fear and not wanting to seem like a coward. He answered, "I get it."

Israel smiled, knelt down, and dug his hand into the sand at the base of a slope. He lifted something out of the earth, and sand poured off a thin sheet of metal. It was buried and camouflaged underneath a pile of dune brush and grass. As Israel moved the metal door aside, Franklin saw the mouth of a narrow tunnel barely wider than his shoulders. "What the hell is that?"

"That's our job site."

"What do you mean?"

"Like I said, I've been workin' these dunes my whole life, and I've spent most of my time looking for one thing."

Franklin knew what that one thing was. He asked, "So you literally dig right in? No searching from the top of the dunes?"

"That's correct. I'm certain that somewhere around here is the *Jacinta*, and I am hopin' that your little gadget will point us in the right direction before I have to scoop out the entire damned dunes. But let's talk later. First I want to show you what we have here."

Before Israel dropped to the ground and crawled into the tunnel's mouth he looked down at the 625G and reminded Franklin, "Bring your little toy. Oh, and make sure you pull that door back over the hole once you're in." He knelt down, then added, "We've had a bit of a cave-in since the last storm, but don't worry, I've dug it all out. It's just a little wetter than usual." He squeezed into the mouth of the tunnel.

When all Franklin could see was the bottom of Israel's sandals, he pushed the 625G and the battery pouch into the opening. The machine was still on, and once in the tunnel the speaker sounded a continuous and high-pitched array of beeps and buzzes. The tones were absorbed by the wet earth but still unnerving in such close quarters, and Franklin was worried that it might be loud enough to alert a passerby. His hands fumbled in the dark, found the sensitivity knob on the control box, and turned it to stop the screaming pitch. Looking around, he consoled himself with the thought, *This is certainly more exciting than walking up and down the beach.* On his belly he squirmed down the tunnel, pushed the detector ahead of him as far as his arms would reach, then pulled himself forward. The tunnel was supported by a modest frame of wood beams and overhead planks. Franklin was impressed with how much Israel had accomplished.

Crawling through the tunnel was not as easy as Franklin would have liked. It was pitch dark and he began to feel claustrophobic. He gave the 625G another push and it fell out of his reach. He heard a close thunk. The tunnel was now awash in the dim glow of incandescent lights. Franklin wriggled forward another few feet and came to the end. He was peering into a small room.

"Welcome to my den," said a smiling Israel from the far corner of the space. With flask in hand he sat and leaned to one side so as not to bump his head on the low ceiling.

Franklin pulled himself out of the entrance tunnel. It was three feet above the floor, so he could easily avoid crushing the 625G and its battery pack as he crawled forward. The walls of the den were dark with thick veins of tar mat running through them.

The sides and ceiling of the den were supported with timbers framed and joined like the beams in the tunnel. Above the ceiling supports were boards of cedar to keep the dune from caving in. From left to right the den was about ten feet wide and approximately five feet across. The room was slightly curved. On the floor, tucked into the corner next to the tunnel, were four automobile batteries. They sat on crisscrossed wooden planks, daisy-chained together and attached to a homemade power inverter from which the cable for the light bulbs ran. Israel had also hooked up a small desk fan to the inverter, though its breeze hardly cut the stale air. Also sitting next to the array of batteries were several buckets. One had an old bilge pump in it with a rolled-up length of tubing, another bucket was filled with miscellaneous mechanical parts, and several others seemed to be filled with debris. Next to the buckets sat a red-rider winter sled with a long rope looped and tied off around the front edge of its frame. Also in the room were two medium length shovels, several small spades, two straight iron bars, a backpack, and a holster with two .44 caliber pistols dangling from one of the ceiling timbers. These looked like the pistols Jojo was cleaning and shooting back at the farmhouse. Franklin shuddered when he remembered how the crack of those rounds practically shook his teeth from their sockets. Israel looked at Franklin, waiting for him to situate himself and get used to the den.

"So, this is our headquarters. This will be our startin' point. I've braced the ceilin' and walls, but cave-ins and floods usually happen after a storm. I'm not too worried about them. I've been dealin' with them forever. I'm more concerned with bein' caught. It is imperative that all people privy to this site keep their mouths shut. I trust you, Franklin.

181

There's a felonious edge to you that I appreciate in a person, and your hands are calloused enough that I feel you will work out just fine on my crew. Unlike Jameson, he can't handle the physical labor that a hunt like this requires. I have no idea how he made it through his basic trainin'. Makes me wonder just how desperate the Army is these days. Present company excluded, of course."

"Of course," Franklin replied. *A felonious edge,* he thought. Franklin was reminded of Colonel Carp and how he seemed to find so much joy in bringing up his teenage misdemeanors. But he wasn't sure if Israel was just assuming he had broken the law, or had actually somehow learned of Franklin's youthful crimes.

Israel pulled his flask out of his backpack and handed it to Franklin, who declined. Israel shrugged and tucked the flask back into the pocket of his backpack. He pointed to the 625G and said, "Again, this den will be our startin' point. We'll use your detector to see if it gives us any reason to dig in any particular direction."

Franklin sat waiting for something more, some sort of instructions, not realizing that there was nothing left to instruct.

Israel said, "So you can get started anytime."

"Oh! So, pick a wall and start sweeping?"

"Yes. You can start anywhere, but if you asked me I'd say start over here on the south wall." He pointed to the wall behind him. "I believe this direction is the best location that would have been visible from where the old lighthouse used to sit."

Franklin slid over to the south wall of the den. He fumbled and shifted as he found the most comfortable position to operate the 625G in. He had to slouch and hold the unit at the middle of the pole, and keep it at an awkward angle due to the cramped quarters. It was already on, and he remembered the mineralized earth. They were sitting inside a big room made of soil rich in tar and iron. He turned the sensitivity knob back up, notch by notch until just before it began a steady squeal. With a slight twist back the noise stopped. Franklin looked up from the 625G, confident that the keel on a boat the size of the *Jacinta* would be large enough that the sensor would pick up a change in magnetic field despite the surrounding tar mat; that is, as long as the object was no more than ten feet away. Israel crawled out of his way, and sat back on one elbow as he watched Franklin work.

Franklin swept the 625G across the south wall, and the speaker emitted a scattered barrage of higher-pitched chirps. He was familiar with the sounds, but there were also new twists on old tones that made him uncertain if they suggested a good place to dig or not. There were no sharp, pin-point references that told him beyond any shadow of doubt that there was a sizable metal object somewhere close.

"Hmm," he said. "It seems that we are sitting in a huge metal room."

Israel replied, "Interesting, isn't it? So much of the soil below us is not far from just metallic dust."

Franklin was no geologist, so he let Israel talk and continued listening to the 625G like a doctor moving his stethoscope across a chest, listening for a heartbeat. Wanting to have some other sounds with which to compare what he heard on the south wall, he moved the sensor disc across the long east wall. The steady base tone was still there, but otherwise there were less distracting concentrations of metallic substances in that corner. He scanned the walls for about twenty minutes. After the entire den was swept, the 625G's beeping began to fade in volume, indicating that the battery pack was finally losing its power. Franklin was happy with how long the pack had retained its charge, and looked forward to documenting it when he returned to the lab. He pulled out a small pad of paper, checked his watch, then made note of the hour. Meanwhile, he had heard no sounds that raised any curiosity.

The two men sat back and assessed what they had heard. Israel had paid close attention, listening over the whir of the small desk fan for any changes or oddities in the detector's sounds. He was specific in his questioning.

"Franklin, in the corner where you first started—where the east wall meets the southern face—there was a strange low-tonal shift. Might that have meant anythin'?"

"Your guess is as good as mine. It certainly was the longest and deepest change in tone of all the areas I inspected. Any other changes were quicker, and sharper, indicating smaller deposits, and perhaps closer in distance. I can't be sure when everything that surrounds us is so iron-rich."

Israel was convinced, if just for the fact that he had no better options, and replied as if he was thinking out loud, "That's enough for me to go on right now. I'm goin' to start a new tunnel in that corner, and by the sound of it I'll move out in an easterly direction towards the waterline, but we shouldn't be diggin' much more than twenty to twenty-five feet, which is good because any closer to the beach and our flood risk increases exponentially." He crawled over to the pile of tools and shifted them around until he had a two-foot iron bar in his hands. Turning to Franklin, he said, "This is the shit part of the process. The diggin' is slow, and when we come up against an old tree, boulder, or piece of wood from some long-lost shipwreck, things get even slower. And that does not include the floods and cave ins. It's taken me no less than two years to excavate what you've seen so far, but it doesn't have to take that long to make progress. Remember, on my crew you get out what you put in. Not to mention, you can have whatever trinkets or coins we find as we dig. I don't care about that stuff. Unless it's from the *Jacinta*, of course."

Israel pointed towards the battery array and pile of tools that sat near the den's entrance tunnel. Franklin was not sure if he had heard Israel correctly, and shifted over to the buckets. He was shocked to see that one of them was almost full of clustered metal objects. He saw black rocks that he knew were ancient conglomerates of silver, long melded together by the corrosion of the salt water. Other items in the bucket were greenish clumps that he knew had to be copper. He looked at Israel and asked, "Did you say you don't want this stuff?"

"Franklin, what you see in that bucket is less than a day of diggin'. Besides the fact that I've been findin' that kind'a thing on these beaches my whole life, those type of treasures fall out of these tunnel walls so often that I no longer have the time to keep up with the maintenance required to clean 'em."

Franklin looked in the bucket again. *Less than a day?* The bucket had more silver in it than he had found in all his months of treasure hunting. He tilted the bucket as if it was his property and moved pieces back and forth, shifting them to get a closer look at all the contents. He asked, "You don't seem to have been very lucky with finding any gold?"

Israel crawled over and flipped open his backpack. Franklin looked in the main compartment and saw a small, dirty pile of gold coins and jewelry. "You know as well as I, only an idiot leaves his gold out in the open for the entire world to see."

Franklin's heart raced, and without thinking he reached in the sack. Israel smacked the backpack shut, saying, "Whoa there. Your signup bonus can be what's in the bucket, but you don't get any gold until you start pushin' those iron bars."

DIGGING

After his introduction to the den, all of Franklin's free time was spent in the tunnels. He hadn't seen Radish much while on base, and hardly noticed any sign of him at the dig site, and could not have cared less. If Radish wasn't helping with the digs, then Franklin would take home more of whatever treasure was found. In his first week of working with Israel, the amount of artifacts unearthed was more than he could conceal from the rest of his barracks. He was bringing in such large bucket loads of encrusted metal that he quickly ran out of space to keep it hidden from the prying eyes of the other soldiers in Barracks Five, or worse, Colonel Carp. Luckily, he had not had any run-ins with Carp in the past few weeks.

He had to start making difficult decisions about what treasure to take home and what to leave in the debris pile. Silver coins or jewelry always came before copper, but anything less than copper—like iron nails or ship parts—was discarded. However, if a silver conglomerate was too large, he would no longer take it home, and, likewise, if a copper piece was unique, he would make sure to keep it. When it came to gold, Israel would always take a look at the find, but would never claim it for himself. The two had a good working relationship, because Israel only seemed interested in keeping boat-related artifacts, like nautical instruments or sailing tools. And Franklin was only interested in the finer treasures, like gold and silver.

While working at the dig site, Franklin often crossed paths with Israel's son, Jojo. Jojo was one of the hardest workers Franklin had ever met. He never complained, and no matter the task, Jojo was always trusted by his father.

After watching the scrawny thirteen-year-old lift a laden bucket up into the exit tunnel, and hold it aloft in the precarious and cramped space while the debris slowly fell out onto the sled, Franklin couldn't help but ask, "You feel comfortable with your son handling that much weight?"

Israel never stopped to watch or assist his son with moving the buckets. He answered, "Jojo may be the smartest person I have ever met. What Jojo can't handle in strength, he will always manage in brains."

On several occasions, Franklin was pleased to find that neither Israel nor Radish were present and he was able to work alone. He felt that this meant Israel trusted him and therefore Franklin could relax a little more while working.

REMINISCENCE

Israel's knuckles were gnarled like knots on a piece of driftwood, and his hands gripped the iron bars like they were light as broom handles. Even while Israel was lying in the tunnels, Franklin could tell that he was tall, and more lanky than thick. During these digs, when it was just the two of them, Israel opened up the most. He recounted stories about his life that amazed Franklin; stories that involved blue Caribbean waters and finding stashes of gold, silver, and jewels on the bottom of the ocean floor. Israel spoke mostly about his ancestors and their relationship with the government of Rehoboth Beach and Sussex County. However, more than any other subject, Israel talked about his father, Rafael Mouzellas.

Israel's lineage was a mix of local Delaware Lenape Indian and Portuguese stock. Though he often spoke of Rafael, Israel didn't know much regarding his father's youth, only that Rafael had spent many years on the Atlantic working as a clammer, and then full-time in the Life Saving Service.

In the early years of the twentieth century, the Mouzellas family owned close to fifty acres of farm and swampland in Southern Delaware, but only a small portion of the land was tillable. The property bordered thousands of square miles of forest that grew over the dismal swamps. The land was close enough to the beaches for the Mouzellas men to easily access the ocean, yet far enough inland that the coastal police—most of whom were either old friends of the family, or tourist-season-imports who were not looking to get involved in any local dramas—stayed away. Between his ocean-based work and the farm he and his wife kept, Rafael was able to keep food in his family's collective belly.

As far as Sumi-Sun was concerned, Israel only spoke of her with a scowl or a derogatory remark. Her family was amongst the last remaining Lenape in Delaware since the removal policies of the nineteenth century. For decades, they had lived among the whites of Sussex County with hardly an eyebrow raised. So when it was learned that Sumi was pregnant with Rafael's baby, and then the white man and the brown-skinned woman took up residence together, the ripple effect of judgment throughout the countryside was not strong. It was not clear if Rafael and Sumi ever married, but not long after Sumi moved to the farm, Israel was born, and two years later came his sister, Lulu-Pine.

Israel chipped away at the tunnel wall and rambled. "My father was my number-one inspiration, and the strictest teacher. He was the toughest man I've ever known. He believed that I didn't need school as much as I just needed to watch what he did and I would learn everythin' I needed to know."

Rafael made it a point to teach Israel as much as he could about survival, from living off the land, to fighting, to mechanical understanding. One of Rafael's favorite lessons for his son was to toss him into the shallow surf in the middle of the winter. "I hated it when he would do that," said Israel. "And my mom would go nuts, but now I see why he did it. He was conditionin' me. My skin became thick, Franklin. I learned that I don't have to die if I don't want to."

By the age of eight, Israel had shot his first turkey, and by thirteen, he had killed his first boar. He recalled how his father, Smitty, and Buster

189

would go boar hunting every fall, so any kills would coincide with the county fair which came through Georgetown in October. He said, "That's right, the coldest months of the year we were eatin' better than ever, because the people took care of each other. Nobody went hungry when the weather turned cold. At least no one on the Mouzellas crew."

Israel stopped his prodding into the tar mat for a second, and said, "The old man always used to say, 'Israel, When you lose your nerve, you lose your advantage.'"

Having no real schooling, and plenty of help from his mother's family with working the farm, Israel spent his time exploring the local dunes and beaches, and shadowing his father on the clam crews as soon as he was able. By his teenage years, he knew every plant that grew near the shore and in the pine forest.

"The most important lessons in my life I learned from my father." Israel said while smashing his iron bar into the wall of sand. "How to tie knots properly, how to skin a buck, how to sharpen blades, and how to fix an engine. By the age of twelve, I could fix an engine better than any marina or port-mechanic in the state." He grabbed his spade and pushed the loose debris back to Franklin without so much as a pause in his story. "Perhaps the most important skill my dad taught me was how to sail a ship. You ever go sailin', Franklin?"

The difference in tone between his bragging and his question-asking was stark, almost loving. Franklin replied, "No. The closest I've been to a sailboat is walking past all the marinas in Baltimore."

Not acknowledging Franklin's answer, Israel continued talking, and his tone changed as he remembered the next part of his account.

•

"My father was as much a pirate as he was a clammer, and was not

190

too partial about any specific type of booty. His connections in Sussex County were vast, so there was profit to be made in anythin' from pig iron to booze. For this very reason, he had occasionally worked with shipments from Sam Shamft's Charleston operation." Israel paused, "You remember me tellin' you about Shamft?"

Franklin recalled the photograph of Samuel Shamft, and the story of how he died.

"Well, my father was definitely aware of the Shamfts' reputation and partnership with the local Stoccaccio brothers, and Mayor Whilliger, though he wasn't afraid of any of those men. In fact, as far as my dad was concerned, when any of those jokers left the Rehoboth Beach city limits, they were out of their element and in a world of trees, farms, and long-time partners and family friends. Remember, Franklin, my dad was here first, he worked the Life Savin' crew, and like most old time surfmen, he was let go when it ended.

"So, Smitty Smithsenson was the one who brought word of Sam Shamft's new boat, the *Jacinta*. He was the one who told my dad that the yacht was goin' to be makin' a pass outside Rehoboth within twenty-four hours, and the best part was that the captain was goin' to be Randal Shamft. That was the element that finally sold my father. He knew that Randal Shamft was green, as far as captainin' a sailin' vessel, and probably couldn't navigate his ass out of a pair of pants. Not to mention that a rookie like him would not be aware of the nature of the currents around here. The caper was too good to pass up. Since he'd left for the war, my family was starvin', and the *Jacinta* cargo—even if we got just a few of the crates of rum—would have set us up for the whole year." He paused. "And of course the gold."

"Up to that point, any Shamft deliveries had been chartered through

191

seasoned seafarers, while the younger Shamft was still in trainin'. Apparently, Sam Shamft felt his son was ready to start handlin' the deliveries. That was a mistake that my father believed he could exploit.

"The only thing my father questioned Smitty about was how they were goin' to successfully plunder the *Jacinta* if the Stoccaccios were also lookin' out for it. But Smitty told him the boat was ahead of schedule, and accordin' to his source, the Stoccaccios' pickup crew was nowhere near ready for the offloadin'. How Smitty knew that the Stoccaccio crew was not ready was somethin' my father should have asked about, but his mind had lost its edge, and he let himself believe that the job was so easy that he knew all he needed to know. Shamft had been makin' liquor runs up the coast for years, and they were always offloaded by the Stoccaccio crew, so that was not out of the ordinary. And any tolls my father required from the Shamft deals were paid to him through the Stoccaccios. But, again, my father only dealt with the Stoccaccios when it was time for a payment. He didn't care what they did with any contraband, as long as he got his cut. But when my father left for Europe, everybody else started acting stupid. The Stoccaccios and Shamft factions stopped respectin' my father's long-established requirements. He wasn't around, and I remember a few times those Stoccaccios comin' by the house. They were takin' advantage of his absence, and I couldn't do a thing about it. Of course, my mom didn't do anythin' about it either. My father was no longer around to threaten them, so their monthly payments all but stopped, and when he returned, he never re-established himself. This, Franklin, is why I believe my father never actually returned from Europe. I mean, his body came back, but what was in his head was not the same as when he left.

"So, my father felt confident that if we hurried and beat the Stoccaccios to the beach, we all might just be able to lure the ship a mile or two

192

north, and right into the shoals.

"Ya know, Franklin, any good mooncussin' job relies as much on luck as it does skill. The elements of the *Jacinta* caper were so vast and quickly changin' that my father chose expediency over consideration, and, well, here we are.

"My dad and Smitty were savvy surfmen, experienced pirates, and the moon was new. The darkness of that night's sky was too juicy of a morsel for them to ignore. Maybe it was so dark they did not see the clouds comin' in from Cape May. Shit, I know I didn't. For some reason, Delaware's two most successful mooncussers—a profession that demanded one be able to read the weather—didn't understand the true nature of the winds that were pickin' up as they made their plans."

Israel continued, "When there was going to be any kind of killin', my father preferred to plunder criminals' boats. He wasn't an animal. He didn't enjoy killin' civilians for nothin' more than their jewelry and billfolds. But Poppi had no problem endin' the lives of common thugs."

Poppi, huh. In the few conversations they'd had, Franklin had yet to hear Israel refer to his father by that word.

"My father used to tell me, 'Sometimes it's just easier. Put 'em out of their misery. Get that out of the way, then the heavy work begins.' Our initial feelin' about the caper was positive. Dad quickly mustered the crew, then we all readied the cart, lifeboat, Lyle gun, and other necessities for the job. Smitty's place was at the Lewes Beacon, so Buster Rolfe joined us for the beach work. Buster was another surfman who couldn't handle the merger of the coastal life-savin' corps into what became the Coast Guard. Buster could barely read, so passin' the new entrance exam was impossible, and served only to infuriate a man who was already suspicious of government meddlin'. But Buster could pull himself out to a flounderin' vessel in a winter ocean while sittin' in a breeches buoy and set up the distraught crew for the ride back to shore, none of which meant anythin' to the goddamned Coast Guard. And, of course, my mother and sister worked the lantern.

"At the Lewes Beacon, Smitty's job was to keep his eyes on the horizon for the *Jacinta*. When the craft was in view, he would turn the beacon's light off—a move that would confuse any seasoned sailor—as a signal to us, and my mother would then light the lantern that was hung in front of a reflectin' glass. On any typical mooncussin' expedition, the glow from the lantern was intended to confuse a captain into believin' that he was further away from land than he thought, or lead him to believe other ships were safely moored. Both scenarios would hopefully compel the captain to turn inland and begin movin' the vessel towards what he perceived as a safe anchorage. But we also knew that the *Jacinta* was ahead of schedule, and its novice captain would be eager to see the land signal from the Stoccaccios. We had a wide window of opportunity in which to confuse the hell out of Randal Shamft.

"I remember, as the first drops of rain fell on the beach, my father had just finished settin' up the Lyle gun. Buster was finished settin' up our cross posts, buryin' the anchor weight, and readyin' all the other lines and pulleys. My job was to set up the fakin' box, and soak the shot-line so it didn't ignite when fired.

"By the time we spotted the boat, the air was thick with mist. But for some reason my father was convinced that it was just the typical sea air that always had a bit more wet to it. The mist quickly turned to rain, and I could see some white froth in offshore breakers. But by that time my father wasn't about to let a little rain end the operation.

"One of the last memories I have of my father was him sittin' on the

194

cart with his binoculars up, waitin' and watchin' the *Jacinta* for signs that it was turnin'. When the blot on the horizon grew larger, he knew Shamft had taken the bait. The boat was headed directly towards the shoals. But the wind and water was gettin' choppier, and the boat began to struggle as it was pushed against its starboard side. And this is where I first saw a hint of doubt in my father. After he came back from Europe, he was mostly just angry, but up 'till that night I had never seen doubt on his face. That's when I got real worried. It was terrible.

"The ocean was rollin' waves up and under the cart by the time I heard the first crash. 'The sound of success,' my father yelled. I knew that was his cue to get ready. He gave me a nod, and let me light the fuse. The explosion sent the weight well over the deck of the *Jacinta*. You could see the hunk of metal glowin' red hot as it flew.

"My father trusted Smitty, and was certain that the *Jacinta* was only crewed by three men of questionable intelligence. He had no idea if they would even know what to do with the shot-line if they got their hands on it. But soon enough, he noticed through his binoculars, one of the crew found the line and began pullin'. The crew tried to save themselves by the book, and ironically did everythin' in their power to ultimately end their own lives. By way of the shot-line, they pulled out the more sturdy hawser line, and were smart enough to lash it to their mast. After that, we pushed the lifeboat into the waves. The lifeboat was then guided by Buster and my father, who pulled it via the hawser. I worked the oars to help them get over any threatenin' breakers, and was also in charge of the bailin' bucket.

"By the time we were less than ten feet away from the *Jacinta*, winds and waves threatened to either swamp the lifeboat or crash it against the side of the bigger ship. I recall seein' one of the *Jacinta* crew yellin' towards us with an outstretched arm, while I struggled at the oars to keep our course in a situation that was quickly movin' out of my control.

"There was nothin'," Israel said, repeating with a more assertive tone, "nothin' good about that job. And I knew it once I picked up those goddamned oars. If the storm wasn't enough, I remember seein' my father's face as he held onto the hawser, and I rowed. He was workin' hard, but his eyes were blank, and didn't seem to mind the rain that was hittin' them. Not like a determined man, but rather someone who has no more feelin' in his—" Israel thought for a moment. "In his mind."

"I rowed against a steady push of wind and rain. When our boat came within arm's length of the *Jacinta*, the man on board pulled his arm back and produced a long knife from somewhere unseen, and began choppin' at the hawser. Somethin' about our boat led him to believe that we were no lifesavin' crew. I guess they weren't as stupid as we originally believed. The hawser was no common rope; it was one-of-a-kind, and how my father made his money. I knew he would make the man pay for it with his life.

"The hawser snapped on its last few threads just as Buster finished lashin' another line around the *Jacinta's* rail. Buster waited for the next wave surge to lift our lifeboat, then leapt onto the deck, when another man appeared. Buster and this man's combat moved them out of sight, but my father was close behind.

"I saw my father leap on board and meet the first man who had cut the hawser. This stranger was hurryin' to help his crew mate, when my dad showed up. It looked to me like my father swung his left arm around to put his knife into the fella's gut, but when he did I heard a scream that was not a war cry as much as a pained beggin'. Then they disappeared below what I could see from my vantage point.

196

"Then I heard that boat's keel ground deep into the ocean bottom. A sound that sent shivers up my spine, even though it usually meant easy plunderin'. The *Jacinta* was completely stopped and heeled on its port side. Waves no longer pushed it as much as crashed over it. I saw riggin' snap in the wind, whippin' back and forth against the mast. I heard screams and shouts, which, if nothin' else, told me that those on board were still alive. That's when I grabbed the line that was lashed between the lifeboat and the *Jacinta*. I was desperate to get a look, or hear a word from my father, but the waves were not givin' me any time to stand up. The lifeboat slammed against the other boat's hull, and the lifeline slipped and seared like hot needles through my hands. And just as I was losin' my grip, I heard my father's voice. He was lyin' on the edge of the deck with his hand outstretched, callin' to me, tellin' me to let go and get back to shore. But his voice was drowned out by a banshee-like wind that ripped across the deck. The pitch of the wind through the *Jacinta* riggin' and the clankin' of the loose ends of cables was terrifyin'—somethin' I was unprepared for. I screamed and begged my father to jump into the lifeboat. But then two hands appeared behind him. They slipped somethin', a rope or wire, over his head and pulled him by his neck back and out of sight.

"I could see commotion over the deck rail. Though I couldn't tell who might have been winnin' the fight, it didn't matter because the goddamned mast broke and smashed the stern into splinters. I thought I heard a scream, but could not tell if it was my father. It seemed like it was miles away, but it was drowned out by the rain and waves. I have no idea if it was a man or the wind. But the sound of that mast breakin' was clear as day.

"By then the lifeboat was unmanageable. I fought to keep my legs under me. I tried to pull the lifeboat closer to the bigger vessel, but the

197

lifeline was strewn about in the gusts, and it had taken on too much water. Meanwhile, the wind pushed the *Jacinta* back and forth, at times diggin' it deeper into the debris under the waves, and other times loosenin' it and sendin' it closer to the shore. One last time, I grabbed at the twistin' rope, but it was hot like fire in my palms. A mixed blessin', ya know. That rope burned the flesh right off my hands. So I no longer have fingerprints. Which has come in handy on a few occasions, if you know what I mean." He returned to his tale. "After the rope was out of my hands, I was thrown back onto the floorboards of the lifeboat. I pushed myself up to my knees, looked back over my shoulder, and watched as what remained of the *Jacinta* floated up the coast. A huge portion of the stern deck had been smashed, and bits of hull littered the waves. Water filled the hull and the bow was tilted upwards. The last thing I remember was a wave pickin' up my boat so that I was again thrown down into the bottom. I knocked my head against one of the seats and lost consciousness. I woke up soaked, freezin', and contorted underneath that damned lifeboat. By my calculations, I had been layin' there for close to twelve hours."

Israel sat back and made a face of disgust, like a captain who realized one of his best men has just jumped ship. "That's why I have a slight limp to my step. My right leg has never been the same since. The entire right side of my face was swollen from a fractured cheekbone. And I had two broken ribs. Not to mention a blow to my forehead." His hand moved from pointing to his face, to down next to his right ribs. "I have never felt pain like that mornin', and I've been shot twice and stabbed six times.

"After wakin' up hardly able to breathe from the weight of a foot of wet silt on top of me, I pushed myself out of the mud. I crawled out from under the upturned boat. It was wedged between two trees on the top of the dune berm."

Franklin pictured this scene as best he could, and couldn't imagine how a storm could push any vessel up the dune berm and into the pine forest.

"Gettin' on my feet was the hardest part. I sat against the side of the boat for an hour before I tried walkin'. I remember movin' in and out of consciousness. My mind blanked at times, only to return with images of the *Jacinta's* mast crushin' my father's body. The pines and sky had that calm, clear feel that comes after a big storm, but my head felt heavy and clouded. I could not breathe through my nose. Soon enough, I made my way back towards shore. The edges of the dunes and shrubs wobbled and waved, like the space around a fire. When I reached the beach it was as flat and smooth as a sheet of glass. I saw nothin' but sand, and the waves were a low-tide wash. The strangest thing was when I looked up to where the beacon light should have been, there was nothin' but an empty, flat ridge in the distance. The hurricane had washed all signs of it right off the cliff."

•

When listening to Israel's stories, Franklin often felt compelled to question some of the details, but didn't want to be rude so he kept his mouth shut. He thought he was familiar with the nature of the walking dunes, but they were a surreal and mysterious thing, so Israel's claim that they swallowed an entire boat was something Franklin was willing to believe.

Israel stared at the floor and continued, "I was frantic, and after stumblin' up and down the beach for a few hours, I noticed an anchor sittin' half-buried in the sand. I assumed it was the *Jacinta's*. It was small, like a private yacht might use. The chain was still attached to the anchor and I pulled it up. I followed its course about twenty feet in a northern

199

direction before it ended. The broken chain in my hands." He looked back at Franklin. "So that was my first clue as to the boat's whereabouts." Then he looked up at the leaking planks in the ceiling, waved his hand at the corner above and behind him, and said, "It was about half a mile in that direction."

·

Progress in the new tunnel was slow but steady. In his first two months of digging, Franklin did not encounter any major obstacles blocking the forward direction of the dig. No sizable tree stumps, conglomerates, or shipwrecks lay in their path.

Franklin also got to know Israel and his family, and was often invited for dinner. Though better acquainted, he never felt completely comfortable around Israel's family members, and a large part of the reason he accepted the dinner invitations was simply to remain on Israel's good side. However, besides the few death threats should Franklin reveal the dig site to anyone, Israel never treated him poorly, and the food at his house was always better than the mess hall.

But the house never got better, and Franklin always found it strange how a man who treated himself with such high regard could live in such a messy abode. The inside was dusty and cluttered, the yards were piled high with junk, and everything outside was organized so that moving amongst the junk was like the aisles at a forgotten hardware store.

One particular Sunday, after a few hours of picking at the tunnel, Franklin rode with Israel out to his farmhouse. Israel pulled his truck around to the side of the house. This was the first time Franklin had been witness to Israel's backyard in daylight. All the other times he had been over for dinner were at night, and unless Israel was drunk and wanted to go out back for a bit of target shooting, they did not congregate outdoors.

The yard stretched back as far as the tree line. In the light of the late day the wall of trees was an entirely different sight than its nighttime version. The trees were lush green tops over a brown mass of trunks that were shadowed in the low sun.

They walked around to the back deck. From the corner of the house ran a line of workbenches. Franklin knew these as the ones on which he had displayed the 625G. On the other side of the house, across from the workbenches, was a small shed with two small, steamed-over windows and a trail of smoke running out of a tube on the roof. This shed was Israel's homemade rum distillery, the reason none of his bottles had labels.

The door to the distillery opened, and Franklin turned to see Jojo carrying in an armload of firewood. They did not hear a sound in the shed. Israel watched the distillery, his arms akimbo. Another minute passed and he called, *Jojo, você está aí há muito tempo.* Jojo did not appear in any hasty fashion. When the door finally opened and out stepped his son, Israel yelled at him in Portuguese. Jojo waved his arm in the air, and disappeared up onto the deck, then in the house.

Looking at the smoke that was coming out of the roof vent, Franklin couldn't help but ask, "Are you afraid of some sort of off-gassing from the still? Something that might hurt his lungs?"

Israel laughed. "Hell no Franklin. I don't want him drinking my rum."

They followed the young Mouzellas up the steps and into the house. Israel called after his son, "I better not smell rum on you, boy! And all those goddamned rounds better be loaded! Chop chop!"

When he entered the pantry, Franklin's nostrils were filled with exotic aromas that thankfully overpowered the musty odor that clung to all the furniture and floorboards. The smell of spices rode on a wave of roasted onions and garlic, and flicked a switch in Franklin's brain that made him fully prepared to strangle anyone who got between him and his plate.

In the kitchen, Sueli was doing battle with the pots and skillets on the stove, while Lulu-Pine was busy washing dishes. Franklin was surprised to see Radish, who moved around the table, placing silverware next to plates in a sluggish, drone-like fashion. He had a scowl on his face, and did not look up from his task when Franklin entered. An outsider would have thought Radish was in deep concentration, but Franklin could tell that he was angry.

From over the sink, Lulu-Pine was calling Radish out on some previously argued topic. "Well you certainly can do what I asked–" but when she saw Israel and Franklin in the room she stopped.

Israel could sense an odd current of energy between his sister and Radish. So, he greeted the room with a volume that tried to cut through any tensions, "Well if this isn't a pleasant surprise." Then said hello to his wife and sister. Lastly, he turned to Radish. He watched the young lodger who moved with an air that spoke of entitlement, and said, "I guess your shift ended early today?"

Radish remained silent.

Franklin would have liked to scold Radish, but this was not his house. He said hello to everyone, then excused himself so that he could rinse off in the outdoor shower and get into a change of clothes. After he cleaned up, Franklin returned to a table set with another colorful feast. In all his years of living in Baltimore, even the semi-flush years, he had not experienced a single meal like the ones Sueli prepared. Jojo came to the table and sat down. Both he and Radish leaned forward on their elbows and stared at Franklin as if he were holding them up. With his presence accounted for, the ladies sat down and began serving food.

As with any meal at Israel's, this one had some common dynamics. Israel rambled on and on about the current dig, or his time in Brazil, or his father, while everyone else put food in their mouths and spoke in quick, polite requests and Portuguese mumbles. But tonight the tension between Lulu-Pine and Radish interfered with Israel's stories. Their energy was palpable and caused Israel to stop twice, mid-sentence, and stare at them. He let the silent seconds ask the question, What might your problem be? Meanwhile, Jojo and Sueli ate.

Franklin felt the air between Radish and Lulu-Pine was a balloon that had been stretched too far, and could pop at any minute. He had had enough of Radish's behavior and could no longer contain his feelings. "Forgive me Israel, but I have to address Sergeant Radish." Franklin assumed his rank was enough leverage, and jabbed his thumb into Radish's ribs.

Radish jumped in his seat. "What the hell, Boone?"

"What the hell is right, Radish. How much rent are you paying here that you get to treat these people like they owe you this food?"

Radish glared at Franklin with a look that gave him pause. The two men were evenly sized, but Franklin did not expect they would get involved in any fisticuffs while at the farmhouse, and certainly not at the dinner table. Either way, he had scrapped with bigger people, and was prepared for whatever Radish might do. Radish growled, "How much rent am I paying? I don't give a damn about your rank, Boone. You city-born piece of shit."

Israel interrupted, "Excuse me, Jameson?"

Jojo froze, a forkful of string beans halfway to his open mouth. Sueli grabbed her plate, stood up, and moved to a chair at the kitchen countertops. She turned in her seat and said to Jojo, *Vamos, depressa!* " He

203

brought his plate to the seat next to his mother.

Before Israel could get an answer, Lulu-Pine shot to her feet and leaned towards Radish. Her fingers dug into the edge of the table, and her right hand moved to the handle of her steak knife. Israel and Franklin saw this at the same time and Franklin's interest in Radish ended. Israel put a hand up in Lulu-Pine's direction. No words were spoken. The room seemed to hold its collective breath as Lulu-Pine and Israel eyed each other before Lulu-Pine's shoulders relaxed and her hand left the knife. Franklin was not sure if Israel's eyes threatened her or promised her something, but she returned her glare to Radish and sat back in her chair.

Franklin moved his attention back and forth between the indifferent Radish and the furious Lulu-Pine. Meanwhile, a strange feeling or distant memory washed over him. He was pulled away from the table and into his own frantic world in which he tried to remember something that was quicker than his mental hands could catch.

Radish studied his navel and let out a hiss under his breath. Israel snapped his fingers. The sound cracked through the emotions at the table, and focused the entire room.

Israel spoke. "No, boy."

Franklin froze, caught between an outstretched finger aimed like a pistol at its target, Sergeant Radish.

Radish brought his eyes up to Israel, waiting for him to continue. His hands shook below the tablecloth.

"Jameson, tonight you will not receive the privilege of having a voice at my table. Especially if that voice is going to kill any pleasant mood already set."

Radish kept his sideways glance locked on Israel. He started, "Pleasant mood—"

Israel snapped his fingers again. "No!" he called. "I just told you to keep your mouth shut."

Radish did not reply.

Israel continued, "What is eating at you boy? What the hell makes you think you can act like this at my table?"

The ends of Radish's mouth moved up. He asked, "Your table?"

Lulu-Pine joined in. "You better watch that." But Israel lifted his hand again. He stared and waited, as if considering options in his head. Finally, he spoke up. "Yes, Jameson. This is my table. Just like everythin' on this farm is mine. Do you dispute that?"

Radish looked over his left shoulder, at the hutch that was filled with items that had *Property of the US Army* stamped on them. He turned back and said, "Oh yeah? Everything, huh?"

Israel knew what Radish meant, and replied, "And what, Jameson, is your part in all these things that are not mine? How many of those boxes have you had your hands on?"

Radish looked at Franklin, who was feeling overwhelmed with new information, then back to Israel. He considered his place on Israel's crew. He'd just been using Army gear to find random treasure, and never stealing anything more than the Army's time. But now he was certain that he was working with two people who were actively stealing from the fort.

Radish shifted in his seat, and gave a nervous, quick reply. "Okay, Israel. We don't need to go into what we get from the fort."

But Israel wasn't finished. "Oh. I don't think I've gotten everythin' I want from your little fort."

Radish asked, "What else do you want? I told you I'm done with–"

"Information," said Israel. "That's what I want more than anythin' else."

Radish turned to face Israel. He was hesitant to ask, "What information might you need?"

Israel wasted no time. "I'd love to know why you haven't mentioned anythin' to me about a certain German submarine that surrendered at your fort?"

The question was so out of context that it took Franklin a few seconds to understand what was said. How did things move so suddenly from the bickering at the table to the surrendered U-boat? Radish had not mentioned it to Israel. Surely he didn't think Israel would never find out about it? Radish looked at Franklin, his eyes like two soldiers who just realized they are surrounded and outgunned by enemies. Soldiers that Franklin wasn't sure were worth risking his own life to save. Although, he did have some pity on Radish, as he was only following orders, like every GI at Fort Miles who was told not to discuss the U-boat with anyone off base. Plus, it wasn't really any of Israel's business. Despite that, Franklin shrugged his shoulder, letting Radish know he was on his own.

Radish sat up and asked, "What good would telling you about that U-boat do me, Israel?"

"This has little to do with you, boy."

Radish sat quiet.

Israel continued, "Nothin' to say? Well, Jameson, you notice I said *surrendered*?"

"Yeah?"

"I assume that hunk of metal didn't do the surrenderin'?"

Israel's sarcasm thickened the already troubled air around the dining table. Franklin wasn't sure if Israel really cared about the U-boat, or if he was beginning some elaborate ruse just to agitate Radish. His lack of certainty distanced him and he felt like he was watching the scene from across the room. He looked at Lulu-Pine. She stared at Radish, but when Franklin's eyes set on her, as if she had a sense of his gaze, she looked up. He returned a nervous smile, then looked back to Radish. Lulu-Pine scoffed and bit off a piece of bread. Radish sat silent, perhaps just as confused as Franklin.

Finally, Radish said, "No, Israel. The U-boat didn't do the surrendering."

"So, what about the crew then?"

Radish pursed his lips, as if this was a moment he had predicted, and had worked hard to avoid. He exhaled and said, "The crew of the U-boat is being temporarily held at Fort Miles."

Israel leaned back in his chair, his glass resting on the end of the armrest. He waited for more information, but Radish revealed nothing else. Israel sipped then asked, "You watchin' them?"

Radish spoke quickly, well prepped for this question. "No, not me. That's not my assignment." His tone showed hints of desperation.

"That's it? We have Germans on the beach and you've got nothin' to tell me about it?"

Radish's discomfort was contagious. After all, Franklin had also not mentioned the U-boat to Israel. To some degree, he felt complicit. And he also felt like Israel was being a bully. The U-boat didn't concern him, or anyone off base, and orders were orders. He saw Israel's last question as an opportunity to help Radish, and said, "Well, in Radish's defense, we've all been instructed not to discuss the U-boat off the fort grounds."

Everyone at the table stared at Franklin. He immediately felt like he had overstepped his boundaries.

Israel broke the silence with a laugh and said, "Oh yeah. You've been instructed not to discuss it, huh? Well then, I guess the matter is closed."

He looked at Radish, and continued, "I can't apologize enough for puttin' you in such a compromised position, Jameson."

Radish's hands sat on his legs in tight, white-knuckled fists.

Israel did not look away, but shook his head, finished with his need to know more about the U-boat. But he didn't stay silent for long. Leaning forward, he pulled the cork out of his rum bottle, smiled, and dropped a dollop in Franklin's glass. "Finish up Franklin," he said, "I got somethin' I want to show you."

SHOOTING FIRE

A recurring subject—as if there were no other options for conversation—was Jojo's handling of the loading of some 12-gauge shotgun rounds. Franklin could not translate the discussion but Israel filled him in as he went and let him ask any questions.

"You see, Franklin, I've taught young Jojo over there how to load his own rounds." Franklin was impressed and a little worried at the same time, despite having already witnessed the skinny, twig-like kid handle two huge .44 caliber pistols. "And by load his own rounds I mean for any of our firearms."

The farmhouse was practically a makeshift armory, and in it Franklin had noticed at least ten pistols, five shotguns, and four rifles. His only response was, "Rum or rounds, you're a man who makes his own."

Israel replied, "You have no idea," then looked at Jojo and said, "Go get the fire rounds, and grab the Remington. Not the ten, but the twenty-nine." He stood up and said, "Let's go to the backyard. You like a bonfire, right?"

The sun was low but still provided a few last rays of light. The junk piles in Israel's yard were grey, detail-less heaps. The two walked out to the middle of the backyard, and in the dimming sunlight, Franklin noticed another pile sitting about thirty feet away. However, a few steps closer and he saw that the debris was the wooden cart he had bumped into on his first visit when he was showing off the 625G. On top of the cart was the upturned hull of a small wooden boat. *Is this the infamous lifeboat and cart?* Grass and weeds had long grown over it, and other piles of junk further obscured it.

Jojo soon stood next to the two men, shotgun in hand and ammunition pouch over his shoulder. He handed the Remington to Israel.

Isso está pronto?

Sim.

"Franklin, you ever see a shotgun shoot fire?"

Franklin asked, "What do you mean, like a flamethrower?"

"Nah, flamethrowers are a completely different beast."

"Different from what?"

Israel didn't respond. Instead, he turned and brought the shotgun up and aimed it towards the ramshackle old cart. "Different from this," he said and pulled the trigger. At first, when Franklin saw a cloud of fire engulf Israel's arms, Franklin thought the gun had exploded. The fist-sized ball of molten flame knocked into the overturned boat's hull and was followed by a two-foot smoldering trail of sulfur. A hole burned clear through both sides of the boat, and the shot ended in the field behind the pile.

Franklin screamed, "Goddammit! What the hell was that?"

Smoke rose from Israel's beard and shoulders, and residue from the fireball blackened Israel's face, creating a ghostly silhouette in the dusk's light. His teeth appeared to glow as he smiled.

"Israel! Are you alright? The fire! Your face! What the hell?" Franklin didn't know whether to help Israel or put out the fire growing around the wooden cart. He was amazed at how quickly the fire grew into a small inferno, fueled by the dried remnants of the rotten cart, lifeboat, and Israel's disregard for consequences.

"Jesus, Franklin," Israel replied, sounding none the worse. He handed the gun back to Jojo and said, *Não é suficiente. O disparo precisa ir mais longe. Você misturou muito magnésio e menos pólvora. Quantas vezes preciso te falar?* Jojo took the gun and turned back to the house. As he hurried, Israel yelled after him, *Para por agora e fala pra sua mãe trazer os baldes.* He took a quick look at the growing swath of fire and added, *Eu quero você encarregado da mangueira.*

A pillar of black smoke rose into the sky. Israel coughed a raspy hack and finally answered, "That, Franklin, was my very own incendiary round."

"What? Why would you make your own incendiary rounds?"

Israel tilted his head and shrugged, "Why wouldn't I? Your little Army buddies make theirs. I make mine."

The fire had efficiently engulfed the entire debris pile. Now, the surrounding grass and brambles fueled the fire further.

Franklin asked, "But why do you want to do that? What's your purpose?"

Israel answered, "My purpose, Franklin, is to make sure I have a tool for any job, and that I will never be outgunned."

"Yes, but why do you need incendiary rounds?"

"I don't know." Israel stood for several seconds, then finished with, "I've always figured I might use it to put a hole in a ship that needed to be sunk. I've met a lot of people in my time, Franklin. Lots who could have used this type of round, and others I would have liked to use it on." He looked at the ground fire that was growing, and shrugged. "I guess I make them because they're fun to shoot."

Because they're fun to shoot! Franklin's city-boy mentality could not understand Israel's passion for firearms. Before joining the Army, the big-

211

gest gun Franklin heard about was the standard .38 Specials used by the police. But his military training had taught him to tolerate being around such dangerous tools, and people. He wondered just what kind of people grew up in the inland fields, swamps, and shores of Delaware.

By this time, Jojo and the two ladies had arrived, each carrying a bucket full of water. They hurriedly tossed the contents over the fire, then ran back to an outstretched hose where they filled the buckets again. The entire time Israel explained his incendiary round recipe, seemingly uninterested in helping put out the fire that he started. Franklin, however, ignored his host, and joined the fire-line. After a frantic twenty minutes, they had the fire doused.

Franklin panted in the early-evening heat. His face was covered in sweat and soot, as were Sueli and Lulu-Pine's. They collected their buckets and headed back towards the house. As he caught his breath, he watched Jojo rounding up the hose, and above him, in the background, leaning over the railing of their deck, was Radish. He shook his head as he looked at Franklin.

While they walked back in the house, Radish waited and let each person pass by his condescending glare. Franklin was in no mood for any lip out of Radish, and was fully prepared to verbally shut him down when he noticed something odd. Maybe it was the smoke in Franklin's eyes, or maybe it was the lighting, but as he walked up the deck's steps he looked up at Radish and the details of his face practically slapped him in his own. Franklin was so surprised that he blurted out a confused, "What the—" and felt a flash of heat wash over his body. It was similar to the feeling he'd gotten whenever his father caught him lying. Only this time, Franklin was not the liar.

As Franklin gathered his gear, the living room was busy with activity.

Jojo loaded new rounds, Sueli sat across from her son, speaking in Portuguese with her feet up on the coffee table. Israel stoked the fireplace, and Radish waited behind the sofa. Franklin wanted desperately to be away from the farmhouse. After the incendiary display, and Radish's behavior, he was more than ready to go home.

For a few minutes, he entertained the notion of quitting his place on Israel's crew. Despite all the treasures he was finding, and the promise of gold, he thought again about Jarvis Meekers, the old lighthouse keeper who mysteriously vanished, the Stoccaccio brothers, and Samuel Shamft. Israel's words rang in his head, *I've met a lot of people in my time Franklin... others I would have liked to use it on,* and he suddenly thought of Brotsky. Sergeant Rutherford said they thought the wound was burned through his body, but they couldn't figure out what type of weapon would make such a wound. *Well, I now have a strong hunch as to what that weapon could have been.*

Franklin felt trapped. Standing across the living room, away from Israel and Radish, he pretended to take interest in a pile of logs that sat next to the hearth. Over his shoulder, Franklin glanced at Radish. He tried to get a good look at his jawline, forehead, and nose. The shadowed features reminded him of the picture of Samuel Shamft he had seen in the library newspaper. His eyes then moved to Lulu-Pine as she finished clearing the table. He watched as she moved in the dusty light. From dining room to kitchen, in and out of the chandelier's glare she passed. On one of her trips to the sink, she turned to place the dishes in her arms on the cabinet island and her eyes looked up and caught Franklin's. And in the split second it took her to lift her chin, the kitchen light caught her face and accented her high Lenape cheekbones. Franklin saw tired eyes that looked like they had sat by and waited for a long time. He saw the flat nose of a native genealogy that he would never understand. He saw the weathered skin of a woman who had spent too many hours on a farm. And as the kitchen light gathered all these elements and made them into the visage that glanced up at his own, he saw the unmistakable face of Sergeant Jameson Radish.

THE FIRST DISCOVERY

Franklin was grateful for the droning of the jeep's tires, and for Radish's silence. He stared out the window, uncomfortable for the thirty-minute ride back to Fort Miles, but it was either ride with Radish or take a cab. In the driver's seat sat a completely new person. Franklin's mind worked hard to see in the dark and put as many of Radish's features into the frame of Lulu-Pine's sandy-blonde nest of hair. He did not want to believe it, but the similarities were adding up too fast for him to ignore. Radish was no lodger at Israel's farmhouse. He was Israel's nephew.

Franklin knew Radish was twenty-two years old, and recalled that the rape of Lulu-Pine and Sumi Sun was in 1923—exactly twenty-two years ago. Then he remembered the picture of Samuel Shamft that he found in the old newspaper.

Clues, like puzzles pieces, were fitting together to create a picture that Franklin wasn't sure he wanted to see. But his investment of time on Israel's crew compelled him to not want to make any hasty decisions. The daily treasures were abundant. *Plus, what's wrong with being Lulu-Pine's son?* At least now he knew why Radish acted like a spoiled child at the farmhouse—because he was sitting across the table from his mother.

Franklin closed his eyes and leaned his head against the frame of the passenger door and pretended to be resting. He needed to process all that he had learned without interruption, and most of all, stop looking at

Radish. The weight of his recent discoveries kept him from being able to focus on anything else.

The entire next day, after a fitful night's sleep, Franklin's mind was still preoccupied with Radish and the Mouzellas family. He wasn't certain of anything, and thought back to the previous night. *All of our faces had smoky soot on them, the light was bad, and I was livid with Israel. Not to mention my nerves were stirred up by that damn fire. Who knows, maybe my shocked mind was playing tricks on me.*

He was so distracted while working in the lab that he barely managed to properly wind the 625G's copper coils. His mind was focused on one thing, and it wasn't electrical engineering. The only way to calm his head was to conduct more research about the Mouzellas family. *Why did Radish have that surname? He obviously wasn't going to be called a Shamft. But why not Mouzellas?* After his shift ended he called a cab and headed to the Rehoboth Beach Library.

At the periodical card-catalog, he looked up anything he could find regarding the "Radish" name. He found several headlines, but the stories concerned agriculture issues, and the fight for subsidies for farmers affected by the stock market crash, not Jameson Radish.

Franklin learned that a Cliven Edgar Radish was the patriarch of a prominent farming family. As far back as he could tell, that Radish family was in charge of most corn production in Sussex County. Cliven had three daughters and one son named Evan. Franklin could not find much information about the children, except for a few articles that mentioned Evan's name. The *Community* section of a small Sussex County newspaper had a gold nugget–an engagement announcement of the local corn mogul's son, Evan Radish, with another Sussex County native, Lu-lu-Pine Mouzellas. The article was dated May 7, 1925—two years after

Jameson Radish was born.

Franklin turned to the obituary catalog and flipped through the cards. In the "R" section he found Cliven Edgar Radish and his wife Emilia Radish. There was no record of the three daughters because they hadn't passed, or perhaps were no longer local residents. But Evan Radish was not so elusive. An obituary for him was dated 1933, and didn't have much to say about the deceased farmer other than that he was taken too early, and was survived by his wife, Lulu-Pine Mouzellas Radish and his adopted son Jameson.

Franklin's mind raced. Sergeant Jameson Radish was the bastard son of a common criminal, then adopted by a corn farmer who died when Radish was ten. After Evan died, Jameson became the "man" of the house until ten years later when Israel, his estranged uncle, returned from his two decades on the lamb. This explained a lot about Radish's behavior: why he lounged about so easily and kicked his feet up on the sofas and tables, why he sat at dinners like a spoiled child who didn't want to eat his vegetables, and why he so easily showed contempt for the rightful heir to the house and farm. Radish and his shiftless nature were most likely the reason so much trash had piled up at the house. Franklin knew that Israel's attention to detail didn't line up with such an accumulation of junk. As more puzzle pieces were added and more parts of the picture became clearer, other question arose. The biggest question of all was the extent of Radish and Israel's lies.

THE STORAGE ROOM

If Franklin tried just a little, he could avoid crossing paths with Radish. After what he learned, he needed a break from both Radish and Israel, two perpetrators of confusion. Franklin needed time to think. He decided that he would spend less time on the beach and more time in the lab, and cleaning and cataloging the treasures that he had accumulated since working with Israel. He had so many buckets of potential artifacts sitting next to his bunk that his barracks mates were no longer impressed, and rather anxious for him to remove the vessels that were beginning to stink worse than the dumpsters behind the Mess Hall.

Franklin stood at the foot of his bunk and stared at the two feet of space between it and the wall. The narrow pass was completely filled by the grimy buckets. He had been so busy digging and finding stuff that he lost track of how much he had accumulated.

I should rent a storage room. Or better yet, a place where I can store and work on the pieces.

He considered how a monthly rental fee might effect his bank account, but shrugged it off as he stared at his buckets. Even without all the gold he had found, there was enough treasure sitting in front of him that he could easily afford the added expense of a monthly rent. Then he remembered his gold collection, something that had grown right alongside the other treasures he discovered since working with Israel. The gold, however, was already stored in a safety deposit box at the Georgetown Savings and Trust. He was no fool when it came to his gold, and he had memorized exactly how many ounces of coins and other pieces he owned.

Actually, I believe I can afford any place around here that I want.

Finding a proper space to store and work on his treasures was not difficult. The rural roads of Southern Delaware had many farms with vacant barns, or unused sheds. Within a week of deciding to make the investment in a storage space, Franklin found an old, stand-alone garage on a local farmer's 500 acres. It was large enough that Franklin could store his artifacts, tools and instruments, and accomodate tables on which he could conduct his research. The garage was less than five miles from Fort Miles; close enough for him to walk to, but far enough away that he felt he would be safe from prying eyes. The owner of the building, an old widower farmer named Vernon Nutter, told Franklin that he would be the only one with the key, and he could put as many locks on the doors as he wanted—possibly Franklin's favorite selling point. Not to mention Vernon also charged Franklin a low rent simply because he was on active duty in the US Army.

Like most of the farms in Southern Delaware, the driveway to Franklin's garage was a long winding gravel path. It ran past Vernon's house at about fifty yards, wound around a small, ramshackled chicken coop, and ended at a gravel parking area right in front of the garage. The garage was barely visible from the road.

After a week of using the space, Franklin determined that his landlord was not a pesky snoop. If their paths crossed, the old farmer would wave and greet Franklin with pleasantries, commentaries on the weather, or stories about his deceased wife—but for the most part Vernon Nutter was a solitary man. Franklin felt comfortable he could leave the garage's drop-door open while he worked free from worry that Vernon's curiosity or conversation would interfere.

Franklin committed all his free time to the transferring of artifacts and setting up of his shop. Soon enough his storage and research area was fully functional. With each day that he cleaned a conglomeration of silver, or separated a cluster of copper coins, the stresses over the Mouzellas clan faded further to the back of his mind. In just a few weeks, he realized that he was more potentially wealthy than he had ever imagined. Besides the pounds of gold, his silver and jewel collection was worth enough to keep him alive for years. But Franklin didn't want to use his treasures for his everyday existence, he wanted to only use them in times of emergency should his savings not be sufficient.

It was not long before Franklin felt a strange pull at the back of his mind, like the world was spinning faster than he was allowed to keep up with; a hurried anxiety that perhaps his current job was too boring, and he might want to handle things at a faster speed than the easy sweeping of metal detection research. This was the same feeling he'd had back in Baltimore, when his belly would remind him that he was poor, when he was weak with hunger, and he knew that robbing someone would be the quickest route to feeding himself.

After two weeks of setting up his shop, and getting back into his research work, and avoiding any urges to reconnect with Israel, Franklin was unloading a bucket of blackened silver coins on one of his work tables when he heard a familiar voice.

"Well, well, well," said Israel.

Franklin spun around to see Israel leaning against the frame of the garage door. He was smiling and looked like he was returning from a long day of digging tunnels under the dunes.

Israel said, "Now I know what you've been up to."

"Israel?" Franklin stammered. "How did you—"

"Find you, Franklin? Come on kid. You know me better than that, don't you?"

Of course, Franklin knew that Israel had friends all around Southern Delaware. He looked past Israel and said, "What about Vernon?"

Israel laughed, "Who? Old Man Nutter? He and my father used to hunt boar in these woods before you were even a glimmer in your momma's eye. I knew you had this space rented the day after you signed your name on the line."

Franklin was speechless. He had no idea what Israel was going to do, only how much he was capable of.

Israel smiled and said, "It's okay, Franklin. Relax. You don't have to worry that I'm going to slit your throat. What good would that do me? And you can't really believe what you read in all those newspapers at the library." He walked to the table next to Franklin and sat on one of the stools.

Despite his morbid sense of humor, Israel's relaxed demeanor made Franklin feel more comfortable, and he remembered that Israel had never actually wronged him. He just withheld information about his relationship with Radish. But Franklin had never wronged Israel either, and was tired of being intimidated by the ruthless image Israel tried to portray. He decided to tell Israel what he had discovered.

"Well, I know the truth about Lulu-Pine and Radish."

Israel looked as if Franklin had moved one step too far into the quicksand that was his family. "Oh, you know the truth, huh? I'm listenin'."

"Lulu-Pine is Radish's mother. Which makes him your nephew."

"Wow. You needed to go to the library to figure that out? I had already told you that Shamft raped her."

"Yes, but, you never told me the other side of that. That she became pregnant, and was Radish's mother."

"Okay, well, sorry for my not tellin' you somethin' that is common knowledge. Seems to me that you're the only one around here who didn't know Jameson's family lineage."

Franklin began to feel like he had overstepped. He wasn't sure where exactly, because Israel had a way of intimidating him, and then making him feel like his worries were all in his head. But, he had invested a lot of time working with Israel, and often felt like he was something of a go-between for Israel and Radish. Whereas, those two men, being family, should have all their issues sorted out. Or, if nothing else, not kept their true relationship from him. Franklin felt like he couldn't trust Israel. It wasn't so much that Israel told lies, but rather that he didn't tell the whole truth. Franklin asked, "So, what about Lulu-Pine? I mean, you murdered Shamft right in front of her, then she had Radish, and was left holding the bag, so to speak."

"What about Lulu-Pine? She's my sister. She's a Mouzellas before she was ever a Radish. Remember, between all the killin' and then me leavin' town, it was only about three or four days. So I never really got a good sense of Lulu's condition. What the hell did I know when I was seventeen. I recall her seemin' tired, which is understandable, but none the worse. I left town. She stuck around the farm. Took care of things all by herself. Then married that corn farmer."

Franklin wasn't sure why Lulu-Pine's surname was important. He questioned why he had spent so much time looking into Israel's family history. He was certain something was off about the Mouzellas family, but when he thought of the reasons that compelled him to do the research, he

222

was not sure of their validity. He struggled to find his argument, and said, "Well, I feel like you haven't been truthful with me, and I can't be sure of anything you tell me. And Radish is such an oddball when he's around you. I don't want to be on any crew in which the head of the outfit isn't honest with me."

"Well, you've certainly got it all figured out. "

"Alright, I'm not saying you're a liar. I just feel like I don't know what to believe."

Israel pulled out his flask, took a sip, and shook his head. "Jameson," he said. "I had a lot of hope for that boy. Ya know, I did not learn of him for years after his birth, and it wasn't until I returned home that I learned the truth and actually met him. Like most people, whenever I corresponded with my sister, I was lead to believe Jameson was the result of her marriage to Evan Radish. But Lulu-Pine has since told me the truth. Sometimes I do blame myself for any damage to her mind. When I killed Shamft, she was right there, up close and personal. Of course, you and I both know the blame is on Shamft. Either way, she saw the whole thing, and now, after more than twenty years, and all she's been through, I don't think she's ever really moved too far past that day." Israel continued, "Before the incident, she was a happy-go-lucky kid. We were close. Of course, her downfall began the minute my father went to Europe. I couldn't control her after that. Stubborn as she was, she wouldn't listen to me or my mother."

Franklin tried a subject change. "So, is Radish the reason for the mess at the farmhouse?"

"Jameson is the very reason for the mess at my house."

"I should have known," Franklin replied. "So, his father is Samuel Shamft? Who would'a thought?"

"Nah, not exactly. Shamft is just the man who made Jameson." Israel shrugged. "Jameson is two years older than the day my sister hitched herself to the Radish wagon. You see, Franklin, I wasn't around, and was assumed gone forever. And, technically speaking, Jameson was the remaining man of the house. But when Lulu-Pine got married, ownership of my family farm–my rightful inheritance–was transferred to that corn farmer, and then, his untimely demise transferred again all my property to his bastard step-son, Jameson. I promise you, Franklin," Israel looked him dead in the eye, "if my sister's husband hadn't a-died from that scythe, I would have sorted out who owns what the minute I returned. My grand-father and father built that house. You think I'm goin' to just sit by while some jackass who can't even use his tools calls the shots under that roof? Jameson is just lucky he's got a few drops of Mouzellas in him. That's the only reason he's still breathin'.''

Franklin asked, "So that means Radish owns the farmhouse?"

"That is correct. I've even seen the title, complete with his scrawny signature signed on the line."

"And he owns the land?"

"That is also correct. My father's land."

Franklin could not help but wonder why, when Israel came back to Delaware, he hadn't just sorted things out with Radish.

Israel answered the question without having to be asked. "To be honest, when I came home I was more tired than I have ever been in my life. So much that even the disastrous situation at the house didn't bother me. The trip up from Brazil was six months of tryin' not to die on the open ocean, while keepin' an angry wife from slittin' my throat with promises of how much better things would be up here. I was not interested in breakin' Jameson down for the mess at the house. He had no control over the cards he was dealt, and to some degree I felt responsible for him… ya know, what with Lulu's mental state. I also thought I had a reliable, strong-backed, and ambitious young man at my disposal. Again, he does have Mouzellas blood in him. I told Jameson that I would buy the land back from him with the treasure from the *Jacinta*. But he's too much Shamft, and not enough Mouzellas. Laziest thing I've ever met."

Israel continued, "Indeed, not a few months into my new attempt at findin' the *Jacinta*, and Jameson started slackin'. The dullness of long hours with no reward did not appeal to him. Never mind the fact that I was willin' to bestow upon him as much of my own knowledge and experience as could fit in. He did not see it that way. We've argued and bickered since I returned, and you wanna know what he had the nerve to tell me?"

"I don't know, do I?"

"He told me that he's got a girlfriend in Dover, and that he's got half a mind to marry her and knock her up just so the land and house are never mine again."

Franklin could hardly keep up. He had a sudden strong desire to be back in the alleys and wharves of downtown Baltimore. He assumed Israel's next part of the story would be related to some sort of vengeance.

Israel continued, "I was so shocked and confused with anger, that I switched off. Literally, my head was so overwhelmed with Jameson's audacity, that my natural compulsions were stunned into inaction. This was a family member, you see, and so far he hadn't really crossed me, but his threat stopped me dead in my tracks. I was flabbergasted, to say the least."

Franklin was surprised that Radish had the guts to say such a thing to Israel, and he considered the validity of such a statement. *Did Radish really have a girlfriend?* That thought alone tickled him, but he was certain that, in the short time he had known Radish, he had never heard him mention a girlfriend. *Perhaps Radish is more aware of how much leverage he has over Israel, and is willing to use it?* No matter how impressed Franklin was, the thought of marrying and impregnating a girl just to spite Israel did not improve his opinions of Sergeant Radish.

Israel said, "Weird when you think about it."

"What's that?"

"On the boat we're looking for is Jameson's half-brother." He laughed and said, "You'd think he'd want to meet him." He took a sip and passed the flask. "I promise you Franklin, at this point, especially now that you're in on the dig, I'm not sure how much use I have for Jameson. Or tolerance. Believe me, I have tried to bring that runt into the fold. I have given Jameson every opportunity to join me in the dig, but he just doesn't want to be a part of it. He's stuck in the mire of confusion that comes as a result of not knowin' who he is." Israel was a walking contradiction of tight-knit family values, as long as the family member could pull his or her weight. He looked at Franklin and asked, "Franklin, do you know who you are?"

"Of course I know who—"

Israel cut in, "Because I know exactly who I am. And I know that the part of me that's supposed to give a damn about the fate of my mother, sister, and useless nephew has long ago jumped ship. And more often than not, I don't care about any way that I have treated them thus far in their miserable lives."

Franklin picked at the black chunk of corroded silver in front of him. He knew the only one who had to decide anything was himself. "Listen Israel, I'm still in with the crew, but I need to know I can trust you. I mean, trust that what you're telling me isn't a lie."

"No, Franklin, you need to remember that I never actually lied to you. You never asked me how I was related to Jameson."

The air in the garage thickened in the tension of Franklin's fight-or-flight response, and Israel's stubbornness. He stared at Israel like a house cat stares at the owner's Doberman, never sure if it's playtime or time to run. He hoped his status on the crew was enough to keep him safe, and said, "However you care to see it." Israel didn't react. Franklin was emboldened, feeling that if he was as important a member of the crew as Israel claimed, he ought to exert himself a bit more. He said, "Alright, but before we go forward, I've got to ask you a few more things."

"I'm listenin'."

"Does the name Ron Brotsky mean anything to you?" He had no idea what answer he wanted from Israel, and no clue what he would do should Israel have admitted to killing Brotsky.

"Not a thing. Should it?"

"Not necessarily. He had my assignment before I came along. Actually, before he was found floating in the Indian River Inlet."

Israel rolled his mouth down, and said, "Hmm. Lots of people end up floatin' in the inlet. The currents there are tricky, and swimmers die all the time."

"He was not swimming when he died."

"How do you know what he was doin' before he died?"

"All I know about Brotsky was that his body was found stuck on the rocks in the inlet, and that his chest had a hole clear through it. I saw pictures, and it looked like the chest cavity was charred, or burnt."

"I don't know what you want me to say, Franklin. I believe I have never met this Brotsky fellow. Let me guess. My hunch is he was some out-of-town city boy like you who thought his station in life guaranteed him a long and healthy one."

Franklin regretted opening up the subject of Ron Brotsky, but took note of Israel's dismissive answers. He moved on to his next topic, "I want to rearrange the score."

"What are you talking about?"

"I want a larger share than just a third. Radish isn't doing shit to help us. What with his new post he can't get away for too long, anyway."

Israel screwed the cap on his flask, and looked around Franklin's storage room. Shelves were filled with countless, sparkling treasures from their *Jacinta* search, and buckets sat on the floor, full of treasure that had yet to be cleaned. He joked, "Well, if all this isn't enough, I don't know what is."

Franklin was ready to defend his treasure, "Yes, but you said–"

Israel interrupted, "Okay Franklin. Relax. Like I've already told you, on my crew you will get out what you put in. Of course, if Radish isn't around then that means more for you." Israel's next question hit Franklin in his gut. "What, pray tell, is Jameson's new post?"

Franklin realized his mistake. He knew Israel was aware of the German POWs, but he also knew Israel was not happy about them being so close, yet so out of reach. Though Franklin didn't care much for Radish, it was not Radish's fault that he was assigned to watch the German POWs, and it was not Radish's fault that Israel had a life-long vendetta against all things German. Franklin thought fast. He watered down the truth and replied, "He's been given some new assignment at the stockade. Watching a bunch of prisoners who—well—all went AWOL."

This was not Franklin's first lie, and far from the most egregious tale he'd ever told. It was true in that Radish was assigned to watch a specific group of prisoners, was no longer on beach patrol, and was moved to the night shift at the Fort Miles stockade. But Israel put Franklin on edge, and he hoped Israel would mistake the blushing of his cheeks as sunburn and not signs of a face that was trying to hide an untruth. He said, "Plus, you know, he's always on the night detail, so he's usually sacked out during the day."

"I'm curious, Franklin, how do you watch someone who is AWOL?"

Franklin's eyes began to water, he was drowning in the embarrassment of being caught in a lie. "Well, not the ones who are AWOL, but the ones were brought back, or caught trying."

"Or caught trying," repeated Israel. "So, guarding all the AWOLs who just weren't savvy enough to actually succeed in escaping the confines of the great Fort Miles is Jameson's new assignment?"

"As far as I can tell, yes."

"You have a lot of deserters at Fort Miles, Franklin? Seems to me that if I had to be in the Army right now, Fort Miles is where I'd want to be. It's like a beach resort."

"There's always a few of them."

"I'm sure," said Israel. "You sure you got your story straight?"

"What do you mean?"

"You sure Jameson isn't watchin' those Germans?"

"Yes."

"Well, I would just hate for you to be tellin' stories. I know how much you hate liars." He put his flask in the back pocket of his pants, then took a last look around the garage space at all the ocean treasure Franklin was cleaning. He said, under his breath, "You city boys," then stood up and looked at Franklin. "I'm just glad we're all on the same page now. Right?"

Franklin stood as well, and answered, "No doubt."

As he walked towards the garage door, Israel stopped and said, "Oh, I interrupted you."

Franklin was on guard. "What do you mean?"

"When you were goin' to answer my question."

"What question was that?"

"Do you know who you are?"

Franklin stammered, "I believe so. As far as I can tell."

"Good. Now we both know who you are."

"What is that supposed to mean?"

"Nothin' more than a little advice for you."

Franklin hated it when Israel passive aggressively tried to make a point. He asked, "Alright, Israel, what advice are you giving me?"

"Just that the next time you go to that library and look up my family, or talk to the police, you ought to remember that I also have a brain in my head, a pair of workin' eyes, and enough wherewithal to find Baltimore on a map. Do you think it was hard for me to discover your past? I mean, we both know how easily a few chunks of gold will make anyone talk."

"What the hell are you talking about, Israel?"

"I just wanted to prove my point. Especially since both of us seem to have a penchant for violence, no?"

"I'm not so sure about that," said Franklin.

"Oh. I'm sure all those people you robbed would say somethin' different. When was it? In high school, or sometime thereabouts? Not too long ago. A lot of breakin' and enterin', and even a few assaults, huh?"

Israel waited for a response. Franklin couldn't think of any, so Israel continued, "But who cares, times were tough, right? And your own father was dead too, right? Jesus, Franklin. It must be harder than I thought, livin' in the city."

Franklin was frozen. He couldn't figure out if he was confused or angry, or both.

Israel continued, "Of course, our end point ought to be that we both focus more on the current moment and less on other people's pasts. You and I have lots of treasure to find, and well, from one criminal to another, we work pretty well together. I'd hate to have to dismantle the crew over a few past misdemeanors." He turned back towards the garage door, and as he departed said, "Tomorrow's Saturday. Can I expect you at some point, or are you goin' to keep avoidin' me?"

The thought of spending any time near Israel didn't appeal to Franklin, but the *Jacinta's* gold shoved its way right back to the front of his mind. He answered, "Yeah, I'll be there tomorrow."

CONTINUING THE SEARCH

Franklin wasted little time returning to the dig, and after about four weeks of working, he and Israel, with the occasional visit from Jojo, had dug a twenty-foot tunnel. Each time they removed five feet of material, Franklin brought the 625G back in to discern if there might be any new and informative beeping. So far, the metallic, tar-laced sand offered nothing to rekindle their hopes. After one particularly tough day, they paused to rethink their trajectory. Franklin could tell that Israel was not his usual enthusiastic self. He seemed tired and depressed at the notion of having to change direction, or start a new tunnel.

They rested in the den and refreshed themselves with Israel's rum. Every time Franklin took a sip, he felt like he could easily become addicted to its sweet honey-like smoothness. It reminded him of no other alcohol he had ever tasted.

Israel spoke and waved his hands around in large circles that represented the dunes above them. "I'll be damned if this isn't the area that we should be in. I feel like I've checked the entire beach."

As usual, Franklin's first thought was, *that may be the case, Israel, but we don't even know if the boat is under these dunes. It could be sunk somewhere out on the shoals, or halfway to Cape May.* These were realities that often crossed Franklin's mind, but the constant flow of new treasures paid so well that he wasn't as beleaguered as Israel. At times, like whenever he found a gold coin, Franklin didn't care if they ever found the *Jacinta*, as long as they just kept digging. However, instead of voicing such thoughts, he tried to keep the mood hopeful. "Yes, but you didn't have my detector when you were combing those other areas."

"True, but I had my homemade one. I feel that if the boat were there I would have bumped into it. This is the third tunnel network that I've dug in these dunes." He laughed. "Shit Franklin, you should'a seen the first tunnel. I was a rookie and rushed too much. I wanted to find the boat more than I wanted to live. So I didn't support the walls and ceiling like you see here, and the tunnel collapsed on me. I was trapped for hours before I broke the surface. I crawled out, black as night, covered in tar and sand. I must have looked like a deranged devil crawlin' out of the earth like that. Luckily, no one was around." He sipped. "Shit, some days I feel if the boat was at this end of the beach we'd have already found it."

Franklin agreed. "Maybe we should start digging at the other end of the den. Head off in a northern direction."

Israel sighed, "That is the next best step. We should start that process as soon as possible. However, I'm done for the day. If you want to start without me, feel free. As far as in which direction to head off, your guess is as good as mine. Don't forget to turn the fan off when you leave, and unhook the battery array." With that, Israel sipped again, then gathered up his backpack and pistols, and crawled up into the exit tunnel.

Franklin sat for a few minutes, trying to decide if he should start the new tunnel, or wait until later in the week. The stuffy den air and the previous hours of work did not entice him to want to stick around. Plus, there was not much more he could do, and the next day was Monday, when his schedule would be back to the usual research routine. He decided to quit.

At the end of the exit tunnel, Franklin stopped to listen for sounds of passersby. Hearing nothing, he popped his head out and listened again, this time accompanied by careful glances all around. With no one in sight, he hurried out of the tunnel and proceeded to cover the opening with the metal door, and then sand and brambles.

Franklin's mind was awhirl with fatigue and a desire to make his efforts worth the time. Sure, he had become a bit more wealthy, but the thought of the gold bars on the *Jacinta* was always on his mind. All his gold pieces were no more than an ounce or two, and he fell asleep many nights envisioning how fresh, clean, and well-pressed the *Jacinta's* gold would be. As he jumped down the last hill before the long stretch of open beach between the dunes and the South Field fence, he wondered if there might be a better way to determine how the storm would have moved the *Jacinta*.

Not a hundred yards away was Fort Miles; the huge American flag flying in the breeze, the low rooftops, and the entrenched batteries cemented into the dunes. The hustle and bustle of activity on the base reminded him of his research work.

Franklin stopped. He was working for the US Army! Maps of the dunes and the mouth of the bay were being drawn and updated all the time, and he shared a barracks with many of the cartographers and surveyors who made those guides. Lieutenant Thurber was a cartographer. Franklin's heart raced with the hope that the cartographers' technology might point him in a better direction. Where Israel had only the hunches of some drunken light keepers and a measuring stick, Franklin had access to the most advanced land navigation equipment that existed.

He was a frenzy of revived energy, and once back at the fort he immediately began putting together the necessary pieces for his new plan. At his next opportunity, he headed to the Georgetown City Hall to get a look at their coastal map archive. The Lewes Beacon had disappeared just a few decades previous, so the area maps of the time would still be advanced enough that he might be able to compare them to a modern-day map.

The research was easy. There were plenty of pre-1920s maps. However, only one map made reference to a Lewes Beacon. Franklin cross-referenced the Life-Saving map with a few other city and county maps. According to the dates, each one was drawn at similar times but for different reasons. The county drew a map so watermen would have an idea of how to navigate the mouth of the bay. Rehoboth Beach drew their own for land development and the tourist trade. And lastly, the US government drew up the most recent plans in preparation for breaking ground on Fort Miles. None of the maps were similar in scale or accuracy, but it was not difficult to determine where the beacon would have been. According to the Life-Saving map, the light tower and house would have been located behind the dunes and not far over the ridge that was on the outside edge of Fort Miles' perimeter fence and South Field. Franklin cross-referenced his findings with a current Army map and made a note at the corresponding area.

HIRING THURBER

It was early evening when he returned to Fort Miles, and he headed straight to Barracks Five. From a small collection of silver coins that he hid in his desk drawer, Franklin picked two well cleaned and detailed Spanish *reals*. He then stepped over to Lieutenant Thurber's bunk. Thurber was lounging on his mattress, reading a field manual.

"Hey Thurber, I need to speak with you."

"Yes Boone."

"Listen, I need to borrow you and your surveying gear. I have some nagging questions about the walking dunes."

"Okay, what are the questions?"

"Nah. I don't want to talk about it here. Too many eyes and ears. I just need you to bring whatever it is you use to survey the topography."

"I've already got maps drawn up of this base, Boone. What else do you need?"

"No, it's outside the base. On the ridge that's just on the other side of the fence, near the South Field."

Thurber was now suspicious. He wrinkled his brow, "Other side of the fence? What's going on out there?"

"I just want to take a look at the dunes from that elevation, and see if we can determine anything."

"Anything about what?"

Franklin was frustrated with Thurber's questions. "Can you please just meet me out there tomorrow morning?"

"I don't know Boone. I've got a busy schedule tomorrow."

"I'm talking about before you start your shift. I want to check things out before the entire base is up for the day."

Thurber grew more suspicious. "I don't know. I—"

Franklin interrupted him by tossing the two *reals* onto his mattress. They bounced off the tightly-made covers, then stopped against Thurber's leg. "Those are yours if you help me. I promise I'm not going to ask anything illegal of you."

Thurber picked up the coins and cupped them in his hands. "You'll give me these if I just accompany you to the ridge?"

"Yes. I just need you for a few minutes."

NEW DISCOVERY

The next morning, a thumbnail of pink sun crested the horizon. Franklin and Thurber walked across the South Field. Franklin noticed at the back edge of the field a tall mound of earth, with a few dump trucks sitting in front of the pile. In all of his wanderings around the fort, this was the first time he noticed the pile.

Somewhere on the other side of the perimeter fence was the area that Franklin assumed would have been the Lewes Beacon's yard. He carried the 625G, and Thurber brought his surveying transit—an extendable three-foot tripod with a theodolite attached to the top— and a backpack full of other gadgets. They opened the gate and moved towards the edge of the ridge, turned right, and walked out into the field that lay between Fort Miles and the pine forest. The field was an overgrown swath of dense dune grasses and low shrubs. The ground was more stable and harder packed than the lower sand of the beaches—a perfect terrain for building a structure. The topography spoke of a stretch of land that had been cleared long ago, and then, when deemed no longer useful (perhaps after the building for which it was clear-cut fell into the ocean) left to be overrun by nature. It offered a gradual transition between the closely-cropped fields of Fort Miles and the pine forest that surrounded the base.

Franklin and Thurber trudged over twisting shrubs and patches of thistle that crunched underfoot. A few saplings rose up, vying to be the first trees to dominate the space. After walking a few yards up a slope not steep enough to be considered a hill, they stopped to observe their surroundings. Thurber said, "Ya know, Boone, right here at this point, we are at the highest elevation within a mile of the shoreline for the entire Delaware coast."

Thurber's comment solidified Franklin's belief that he was on the right track. The first clue that he was in the right place was the elevation of the field. The entire stretch was at least forty feet above the highest dune, a perfect place to build a smaller version of a lighthouse. Everything around them sloped down and away from their location, including Fort Miles. Despite having often worked around the edges of the clearing on which he stood, Franklin had never wandered through this area.

While Thurber set up his transit station, Franklin noticed that the area around him had a scattering of grasses that seemed out of sync with the rest of the space that was covered in stalky shrubs. As he studied the stretch of earth, he noticed a large, gradual divot. It was a bowl with a diameter of about twenty feet, and scattered grass and brush growing down its sides. He thought it might be a natural sinkhole or dune element. But he was not in the dunes. The surface growth around the area told of an environment that had not shifted much in a long time.

Perhaps the pit is the old foundation of the beacon tower.

With that in mind, he assumed that the beacon house—the one that Smitty supposedly was trying to make his way to in the raging storm— was somewhere inland. They wouldn't have built the house between the tower and the shoreline. It would be somewhere between the divot and Fort Miles' guest parking lot. Franklin walked in a westward direction and scanned for signs of old foundations or construction. To his surprise, not fifty yards away was another small divot with the same type of new growth and young grasses as the pit behind him, only this new area was rectangular.

Thurber called over to Franklin. "So, Boone, what exactly are we doing here?"

Franklin stood on the edge of this new divot. Below him the earth sloped down into a shallow pit full of the younger growth. He turned on the 625G and swept the edge. Beeps and tones went off in a rapid pace. He could tell there were clumps of lead and steel, and assumed his detector was sensing the old nails and wiring that went into building the beacon house.

That was all he needed to feel confident that he had found what he was looking for. For lack of a better plan, he told Thurber to bring his equipment to a point halfway between the two divots. At that spot he stood and faced the southern stretch of beaches, and tried to put himself inside the brain of Smitty Smithsenson. He asked, "Thurber, what exactly are the currents along this stretch of coast doing? Do you have any idea of the general direction that the currents run?"

"As far as I can tell, the currents exiting the Delaware Bay flow out and hit the Gulf Stream, and then are pushed in a general northerly direction. However the coastal currents are different, and change more rapidly depending on the tide levels."

Franklin asked, "What about during strong weather? That would make the currents even more unpredictable, right?"

Thurber shrugged his shoulders. "I don't really know, Boone. I would imagine it would. If nothing else, the tides would be so high that most currents would probably be pushed right up and into the dunes." He pointed his hand and swooped it over the walking dunes that lay between them and the beach. "That's what they're there for, you know. Nature's own flood protection." Thurber smiled like he had just explained the hidden secrets of a shoreline.

"Okay, so what do you make of the dunes down in that direction?" Franklin pointed south at as much of the dunes as he could see from their vantage point. "Does anything look out of the ordinary to you? Any unnatural formations?"

Thurber adjusted his tripod and took a preliminary look through the scope on his theodolite, turning the knob on its side to adjust the focus. He said, "Hmmm. Yes. Of course you know that the entire 'walking' thing with the dunes is a circular pattern. Sand is blown by the winds in a southwest direction, and then pushed back North by the high tides."

"Translate that for me please?"

"What that means is," Thurber paused and motioned for Franklin to take a look through his scope, continuing, "right where you're now look-ing—where the ridge of this field meets the walking dunes—still on Fort Miles' property, the US Army cut one of the biggest circles in half. At the base of this ridge is the northernmost edge of the walking dunes. They move northeast for a bit—right through the fort's beach area—but at this point those sections have been totally ruined by construction. Anyway, right below us is the largest circular pattern, where ocean currents push in, then winds bounce off the rise in elevation and slowly move things south." His hands plotted an invisible route in the air.

They walked over to the edge of the field. The winds picked up as they neared the top of the rise. Below them were the walking dunes. This was still considered military property, and was just north of the usual areas where Franklin did most of his field work. From this elevation, he saw a massive swath of sand hills. Based on the different slopes of each one he thought that he could make out the circular pattern that Thurber described.

Franklin said, "I'm going to take a look down there," pointing to a random spot in the dunes. He tried to get ahead of any questions Thurber might ask, and slid down the hill. At the bottom he turned the 625G on.

Thurber followed close behind and asked, "What exactly are you looking for down here?"

Franklin had no desire to explain the Lewes Beacon, so he replied. "The same thing I'm always looking for, silver and gold."

Thurber shrugged his shoulders and climbed up the next hill. At the top, he stopped and opened up the legs of his tripod, and turned the theodolite around to face the southerly dunes. He looked through the eyepiece and turned the knob on the side, reminding Franklin of how they both were getting paid to play with some pretty advanced toys.

Franklin didn't care that Thurber was lost in his own world, and left him up on the hill. "Alright Thurber, I'll see you back at the barracks."

Thurber kept his eyes to his theodolite and gave Franklin the thumbs up.

Franklin had swept the particular stretch of dunes on which he was standing countless times. When first at Fort Miles, he'd been a nervous new recruit who didn't want to get in trouble so he'd kept his work close to the boundaries of the fort. However, as time went on, he'd ventured further out and away from the base to do his research, and eventually, his treasure hunting. The ground was dry and more manageable than the wet sand near the water so he didn't have to set his sensitivity levels low. He cleared one hill after another, and between each dune he swept the valleys, breaking every rule in *The Dune Preservation and Management Training Manual* by trampling patches of grass and beach brush that he came across. He strayed from the designated paths and swept his detector across the open spaces.

The tones Franklin received were few and far between. The area was rife with quick beeps that told him of insignificant pieces of metal, like wires, or steel nails washed up from the Rehoboth Beach boardwalk. No sounds waxed of the dense metals in which he was most interested. He wanted low steady beeps that were easily missed if he wasn't paying attention. But things were relatively quiet, save for the continuous surf sounds, which were often loud enough to cover what he was hoping to hear.

After an hour of sweeping, Franklin was tired. He moved up to the top of a hill and sat for a few minutes. On instinct, or newly formed habit, his taste buds craved Israel's rum, but he had none. From his vantage point, Franklin could see the entire sweep of the northern section of dunes. Less than a hundred yards away was the dig site. He studied the general area where he knew the dig site to be, then the distance between it and where he was sitting.

The dig site is based on where Israel assumed Smitty Smithsenson got his glimpse of the Jacinta the night of the storm. In other words, from that field above me. But at that vantage point—even on a clear day like today—one cannot see the entire northern edge of the walking dunes. The water currents move things north and inland, so it stands to reason that Smithsenson would only have had a good view of the beached ship if it was around here, or closer to the shore. Which makes sense. That would be a good location for the Cape Henlopen Lighthouse keeper to see the ship as well.

Franklin stood due north of the dig site. He clicked the power switch on the 625G. The battery was at fifty percent of its charge. Between him and the dig site was a stretch of some of the biggest dunes on the shore; a section of land that was considered within the Fort Miles' grounds. He

243

swept his way forward and came to the official edge of military property. Now the dig site was about fifty yards away. The hills here were steep, especially the one on which he stood. He brought his gaze down to his feet. There was the 625G, next to his sand and dirt-caked boots. The sounds of the ocean mixed with the calls of distant birds, blustering wind, and a low hum from his detector speaker.

He realized that while he had been looking at the sights around him, the 625G had been talking. It was a sound akin to a large stash of metal deep underneath him. It reminded him of the sound that the buried jeep had made in Israel's backyard—a tone that he didn't hear very often, as most of his finds were relatively small. No matter where Franklin swept the sensor disc, the hum did not stop, suggesting that the object was large. He scuttled down the side of the hill while keeping the 625G an inch off the ground. At the bottom the hum went dead. He moved a few feet back up the hill and it returned. It was practically inaudible, and was broken up in a few areas with quick, static-like crackles.

He was intrigued. Not only might he have found the resting place of the *Jacinta*, but it was directly northeast of the already-established dig site. In fact, the wall through which he had suggested he and Israel begin a new tunnel faced this very direction. With a revived sense of hope, he swept the hill for a few more minutes. No sides suggested a stronger or higher volume sound, but the perimeter of whatever was down there was definite.

Just as he turned the 625G off and collected what little gear he had, his attention was pulled up to the beach. There were the German POWs taking their morning run. The same jeeps with the .50 caliber mounts followed them, and there was Radish sitting behind one of the triggers. This was the first time Franklin had seen him since learning of his lineage, and the sight of Radish made him nervous. Master Sergeant Marteen was behind the wheel of the vehicle.

Franklin hurriedly secured his gear then slid down the hill below him, not sure if the MPs had seen him. He dropped to his belly. From his low vantage point, he heard the Jeep's wheels stop crunching over the sand. He assumed the silence was that the jeeps had passed, and he lifted his head just in time to see the jeeps were not only still directly between him and the surf, but the vehicle driven by Marteen was in the process of turning in his direction.

Dammit.

The jeep pulled up and swerved right so it was parallel to the dune wall. Marteen had to stand up on the running board to address him. He called over the dune, "Second Lieutenant Boone!"

Franklin stood up, hoping that the embarrassed red tint to his face would be mistaken for sunburn. There was Marteen and Radish, not ten feet away. From his gunner position, Radish shook his head like he was dying to teach Franklin a lesson.

"Second Lieutenant Boone," called Marteen. "What are you doing here in the dunes? Why were you attempting to hide when you saw us coming by?"

Franklin replied, "I wasn't trying to hide, I was just picking up my detector. It had slid down the hill here, and—"

Marteen interrupted, "Did you get clearance to be out here?"

Though his current "research" was not for the US Army, Franklin was dressed in the standard olive-drab t-shirt and fatigue pants. He wasn't worried that Marteen would ask too much about what he was doing so close to Fort Mile's perimeter fence, but he also didn't understand what Marteen meant by "clearance." He thought, *Since when does an engineer have to ask for clearance to do research?* Franklin had no sway or power over a disgruntled MP while on base, and didn't want to keep him around any longer than necessary. He called back, waving his hand, "Just conducting a little research here. Thanks." He held up the 625G.

"Exactly what kind of research are you doing?"

Radish sat in his seat with a smirk on his face.

Franklin had to think fast. Still holding up the 625G he said, "Working on a new sensor coil for the detector."

Marteen said, "Second Lieutenant Boone, right now you are on restricted grounds."

Franklin held up the 625G again. "I'm working for the same boss as you."

Radish shook his head with an accusatory look that made it clear he thought Franklin was a fool. Marteen tilted his head like he sensed Franklin was trying to pull a fast one. The two MPs mouthed a few quick words to each other. Their voices were low but Franklin heard his name. Finally, Marteen called out his last orders. "Second Lieutenant Boone, this will be your only warning. GET THE FUCK OFF THE DUNES."

He looked at the group of German prisoners standing in the surf, most of whom were looking his way. They seemed surprised by the volume of Marteen's orders.

"Alright, I'm leaving."

When Franklin started walking back to base, Marteen jumped back down into his seat. He spoke something into a walkie-talkie and waited until he was certain that Franklin was not coming back. Once Franklin was at the foot of the ridge, Marteen revved his engine into first gear. He made it a point to speed past and spin his wheels to kick sand up in Franklin's direction. Radish clutched his seat, and was whipped back and forth by the momentum of the vehicle. It rained sand and dirt all over Franklin's backside and head. He reached the top of the hill and cursed the MPs. While seething, he remembered the gold he was promised and that he had often been covered head to toe in sand and silt. A few grains of sand in his face was a small price to pay for the treasure that would some day give him a life far removed from the likes of Radish and Marteen. As Marteen sped off, Radish held his middle finger in the air, and kept the taunt there until his jeep caught up with the jogging prisoners.

Franklin didn't care about Radish, but he had to admit, besides the fact that Radish's fingers were inches away from a .50 caliber trigger, there was something else uncomfortable about this encounter. He was no longer certain why his heart was beating so fast—the new hope for the dig, or the behavior of the MPs.

Franklin locked the gate behind him and was back in the South Field. He stepped onto the gravel road that ran through the field when two mounted MPs surprised him. They were heading off for their beach patrol, and the MP closest to Franklin eyed him as they passed. He recognized the two men, but was not much of an acquaintance with them. One of them called from his mount, "Hey there. What's a matter, you couldn't leave the gate unlocked for us?"

Franklin replied, "Sorry about that, I hadn't noticed you there."

The MP continued, "Not just us." He pointed up towards the pine forest. His partner also looked off in the distance. There, on the path in front of the forest was another mounted MP unit assigned to trail the German POWs. Franklin walked away, scolding himself for forgetting about the mounted beach patrols. As he hurried down the road, he turned to see the four MPs stopped and chatting just on the inside of the gate. The two new guards carried on with their daily patrol, while the returning MPs walked their horses back and forth over the field. They were inspecting the area as if Franklin might have left something hidden amongst the cut grass.

•

Franklin showered and changed into fresh clothes, then hurried to the pay phone pavilion near the front gates and called a cab. He felt confident that his news would motivate Israel into immediate action and he might start digging a new tunnel the next day. While waiting he cursed the cab company and decided that soon he would buy his own vehicle.

As he stood at the front gates and pondered what he would say to Israel, Franklin heard a familiar voice behind him. He cringed at the sound, braced himself, and turned around to see Colonel Carp standing a few feet away. His arms were akimbo, and he looked at Franklin while shaking his head. Despite the colonel's condescending demeanor, Franklin was relieved. It was the usual attitude he came to expect from Carp, and an improvement over the drunken version that harassed him a few months earlier. Franklin snapped to attention.

"Damn, Boone. You in a hurry to get somewhere?"

"No sir. I'm just heading into town, to a friend's house."

Carp studied Franklin, and said, "Hmm. Into town, huh? You do look like you've just polished your balls. At least you have the decency take a shower before you meet whatever desperate woman has agreed to meet up with you. Or—wait a minute, Boone—" Carp tilted his head.

Franklin didn't let the joke rile up his emotions. "No sir, just a friend's house."

Carp shook his head. "Either way," he looked over both his shoulders, then fixed his eyes on Franklin, "Don't think I've forgotten the last time we saw each other. Any word of that gets out, and I'll have you digging latrines in the Philippines before anyone can pin any shit to me. I'm certain

248

you understand?"

"Of course, sir."

Carp relaxed, and continued, "Good, Boone. We all have our vices?"

"Yes sir."

Carp's demeanor changed as quickly as the subject. "So, by the looks of your shirts and shoes these days, I'd say the treasure hunting is going great for you?"

"Well, I haven't been out in a while. My research work has been pretty heavy."

"That's too bad, Boone. I'd join you again soon if I didn't have my own little hunt going on around here."

"Your own hunt, sir?"

Carp mumbled a quick word or two, then said, "It's these goddamned Germans. The brass says I need to keep them here until they can figure out the best way to use them, so Admiral Phillips has made them my problem. He figures I can dig up plenty of shit work for them to do. You know, there's always a ditch to dig somewhere. But I can't keep them busy for too much longer."

"All due respect, sir, but what are the Germans busy with, besides their morning jogs on the beach?"

Carp ignored the question, and as he walked off, said, "Use a rubber, Boone. We don't want any bastard Boones running around now do we?"

Franklin watched the colonel walk away, and turned to see if any other GI was within earshot. He relaxed his stance and rubbed his forehead, contemplating his exchange with Carp. It seemed to Franklin that almost every day he was coming up with ways to avoid running in to Colonel Carp, and this last interaction gave him his latest idea. If just calling a taxi put him at risk of being harassed by Carp, then Franklin

249

needed to end his reliance on taxi cabs.

I need to buy a car. Why not? I've got the money, and it would give me the freedom I need to go to my storage room, or Israel's, or even home to Baltimore. If nothing else, I won't have to stand around waiting for these goddamned cabs to pick me up so that assholes like Carp can harass me whenever they want.

He made note of how the colonel mentioned the look of his clothes. *Obviously, I've upgraded my wardrobe a bit too quickly. Made too many purchases that have the potential to raise unwanted eyebrows.* He concluded that he would put a halt on any more purchases, but then remembered the new vehicle. *Okay, I'll still buy the car. I definitely need the car. I'll make it a junker, that's enough to get me around town, and won't be so expensive. And if anyone has a problem with me buying it, well, they can just kiss my ass.*

Franklin's cab pulled up with a horn honk on the other side of the gates. He took one final look at Carp's back as the colonel hopped into a jeep and drove off, then got in his cab with an air of confidence that knew he would never again need to wait for another ride. *Yes, I am definitely getting a car.*

NAZIS

Jojo answered the door. Franklin was startled to see him standing across the threshold. Unless speaking with his father, the boy was quiet and never one for conversation. And though they often worked together, Jojo always kept a distant air about him. *Though, in the shadow of Israel's never-ending storytelling, anyone might seem quiet.*

"Hi Jojo," Franklin said, "How's it—"

Before he was finished with his greeting the boy turned and walked away from the door. "It's just you," he said, and sat down on the sofa.

No one else was on the first floor of the house. Franklin stood in the living room for a few seconds then asked, "Is your father—" Jojo poked his thumb over his shoulder, towards the pantry door.

Israel was in the backyard, working in the rum shed. He was lying on the dirt floor, both legs out the door, and tinkering with something underneath one of the vats. Franklin surprised him with his greeting. "I thought that was your son's job?"

Israel grumbled something in Portuguese and pushed himself up to sit on the dirt outside the door. "Well, well. If it isn't my good friend Franklin. What ever could be so important that you came out to my humble farmhouse on your own and uninvited?"

"I wanted to see what you thought about a new theory."

He told Israel everything he had discovered; that there seemed to be a large object in the north dunes, and that it was down the northern line from the dig site. Israel smiled, and looked either bleary from booze or just deep in thought. It was not like him to sit silent for so long, although Franklin understood Israel's apprehension to hasty excitement. His quest for the *Jacinta* had been rife with many hopeful false starts.

Israel tilted his head up. "You think it's not just a conglomeration of heavy metals in the sand or tar-mat?"

"I can't be certain of it, but it was a steady hum, not random bursts. It reminded me of the sounds when I discovered your buried jeep. And there seemed to be a definite edge to it. Only the hill was humming."

With a deep exhale, Israel asked, "What exactly does that mean to you?"

"The low tone tells me it's a dense metal, buried deep. And the long, steady sound tells me that it's big. I've never come across a tar mat deposit that has done that."

Israel shook his head and ran his fingers through his mustache. "This is good news, Franklin. You have done excellent work." He leaned to one side and tried pushing himself to his feet. Franklin saw his slight struggle for balance and moved to help him. Israel froze and looked from the outstretched hand to Franklin's face. Franklin removed his hand and said, "Sorry, Israel."

"It's okay." He propped himself up on the shed wall. "But I assure you, I do not need your help to stand up."

"Okay Israel, I just didn't want you to kill yourself before we find the boat."

Always an appreciator of audacity, Israel said, "Thanks, but despite me being nearly two decades older than you, I am confident that I will outlive you." He straightened up with a puff of his chest, and finished, "In fact, I plan on outlivin' all these Delaware assholes around here."

252

As Israel bragged, Franklin's excitement regarding his recent discoveries and theories waned, but he still had an important topic to discuss. "Israel, there's one thing that might be a problem."

"What's that?"

"When I was doing my research those MPs spotted me milling about in the dunes."

"So what? Were you on the base? Or—"

"Yes and no. It was the stretch of dunes right before the perimeter fence, in that no-man's-land that's not quite base property, but could be considered base property if you were an MP and wanted to be a jerk."

"What did you mean by 'those MPs'?"

"It was the two that you scuffled with back at the cantina, when we first met."

"You should be ashamed of yourself for lettin' those two lackeys see you in the dunes, but I'm not worried about them findin' the site. It's well hidden. Jameson's an MP too, he knows my policies regardin' MPs finding the site."

"Your policies?"

"Yeah. I don't mind them discoverin' the dig, but I do mind them notifyin' their superiors."

Franklin knew what Israel meant. Israel had made Radish the de facto guard of the site, and if any of his fellow MPs should discover it, he would be in charge of ensuring that they didn't say anything about it, using whatever means necessary. In actuality, Israel had no upper hand over Radish. Only through threats of violence and murder did he keep his grip tight. *And Radish is too stupid to realize just how much Israel is bluffing. If Radish were to disappear, it would be very difficult for Israel to get his name on the property deed for the farm. In fact, the longer it takes for*

Israel to find the Jacinta, the longer Radish stays alive.

Israel made his way to the deck steps and sat down. He lifted his chin and soaked in the day's remaining sunlight. With the sun washing his face, he pulled his flask out of his shirt pocket and sat it next to his hip, then started a new topic. "I ever tell you why I had to leave Brazil?"

"No Israel, of all your stories that was not—"

Israel interrupted, "For killin' Nazis."

Franklin did not believe him. Israel brushed some dirt off his pants, not making eye contact.

Franklin finally said, "In Brazil?"

Israel scoffed at the obvious question, and answered, "Yes. In Brazil."

Franklin had no idea what life in Brazil, or the people there, were like. He asked, "What the hell were Nazis doing in Brazil?"

"Not *were*, Franklin, *are*. These are the ones with enough foresight to get out of Germany while they could. Deserters, cowards, whatever you want to call them. It's the officers who showed up in South America, not the soldiers. And the Brazilians loved it. They welcomed the Nazis with open arms. Believe me, they didn't give two shits."

"Israel, that's crazy. Why would another country open their borders to the fascists?"

"Oh, don't confuse the players in this game. They're all fascists. The fascists are fascists. The commies are fascists—" he dared Franklin with a glare and finished, "—even goddamned Britain. And don't get me started on this country."

Israel tilted his head back and took a sip of rum. Franklin was having trouble discerning if Israel's tirade was because he was drunk or he actually believed what he was saying.

254

Israel continued, "I'd been livin' in Sao Luis for almost ten years. I'd even married one of their people, and not once did those Brazilian fuckers accept me. I even learned their language. I was a stranger in a strange land. And that's what I thought would happen when them Germans showed up. I was certain they'd be run out of town before their shoes were dry from climbin' off the boats they arrived on. But then I saw the boats they came in on, and these were no cargo vessels. No, these guys didn't have to stow away in any bilges or mop any decks to pay for their passage. They came in on luxury liners and sailin' yachts. They came in fat and glowin' with the delicious food that their chefs prepared for 'em. They came in with smiles on their faces, at a moment when they were more certain of their future then any other day of their lives. I promise you, Franklin, the minute I saw the first Nazi put his toe in Sao Luis I knew I was goin' to collect his soul. They were treated like natural citizens because they had money. They were given land and jobs. Meanwhile, I had to prove myself every day just to ensure I had work for the next. It was demeanin'."

Franklin could only reply, "I'm sorry to hear that." His gut reminded him that a person not concerned about murder is probably a bad business partner.

"Ah," grumbled Israel, "I don't care about your sorry, Franklin. And I don't give a damn how I was run out of town because of what I did. You know, I killed three of 'em. I thought I was doin' the town a favor, but three dead Nazis did nothin' but raise the eyebrows of the local governor. He was excited about all that Nazi money that was suddenly flowin' into his banks, and didn't need my Yankee ass gettin' in the way of it. So I had to leave." Israel smiled. "That was the second time in my life when I had to flee for doin' my hometown a favor."

255

Israel kicked his feet in the dirt below the steps and sat back against the riser of the step behind him. "Shit, I've killed more Nazis than any of your buddies at that damned fort. Where's my medal?"

"You want me to write up a recommendation for your service?"

Israel gave a tired smile and said, "Do you know why I killed those men?"

"Of course not."

"Because I'm sick of gettin' repeatedly fucked by all things German."

Franklin felt certain that Israel's tirade would end up about how, what, where, or why his father had been taken from him, and at the moment Franklin was not in the mood for more stories. "Okay Israel," he said, "Can you and I just work together and agree on focusing on the task at hand? I'm not sure I want to know why you chose to do what you did."

It took Israel a few seconds to understand that Franklin had finally asked him to stop talking about his past. Israel smiled and said, "I get it Franklin. I get it." After a deep breath he finished with, "We'll resume workin' at the site tomorrow. Get there when you can."

Franklin asked, "Do you want to start a new dig in the hill where I heard the sounds?"

"Nah, that's too close to the base, even for me. Especially if those MPs are already privy to you bein' there. And if you see our Jameson, tell him it would be in his best interests to put a little time in as well." He stood to go back in his house, then said, "Actually, scratch that. I don't care if I ever see that kid again."

Franklin stood in the dirt, and had to bother Israel with one last question. "Yes, but may I use your telephone?"

THE GUARDED SITE

Though anxious about his crewmate's murderous past, the thought of being so close to finding the *Jacinta* overwhelmed Franklin's rational thought and decision making. Every chance he got—be it during one of his assignments or when he was off duty and pretending to just be doing some minor treasure hunting—he made his way out to the dig site. For the first week after his discovery, the South Field had a mounted MP somewhere near it. Because of this, he could not access the dig site from the base grounds, and circling back from a southern location was tough as well because the site was easy to see from the South Field, if one were paying attention. He wondered if Israel would be able to get to the site.

The first time Franklin bumped into Radish that week was in the food line at the mess hall. He asked why there seemed to be a constant vigil of MPs in the South Field. Franklin had yet to ask Radish about his lineage, and he wasn't sure if he wanted to reveal how much he knew. He tried to control any accusatory tone in his voice, as Radish was a naturally paranoid person.

Radish replied, "I don't know. Probably because they saw you snooping around over there, Boone."

Franklin recalled what Israel said about his 'policies' and hoped to prick Radish's emotions with a question. "Well, what are you planning on doing about it?"

Radish stopped moving forward and turned abruptly to face Franklin.

Franklin was ready, and did not budge or show any signs of being intimidated. They stood chest to chest.

Radish said, "Do about what, Boone?"

"About your friends Marteen and Wilkins seeing me in the dunes."

"What do I have to do about that? Do you think that's the first time you've been seen in the dunes?"

Franklin's face blushed. Now he really wanted to punch Radish, but he knew his embarrassment was all his own fault.

"That's right, nobody's seen you near the dig site yet, but you bet your ass they've seen you everywhere else. You have no idea how many times I've already vouched for your greedy ass. So, remind me again why I'm the one who has to constantly clean up your messes?"

Franklin had no reply. His ego suffered and he kept his eyes locked on Radish.

Radish finished, "Or perhaps we should call Israel and ask him his opinion on all the times you've been seen in the dunes?"

Franklin was desperate for any way out of total accountability for Radish's threats. It was a long shot, but he said, "While we're at it, then, perhaps we should also inform Israel about the German prisoners you've been guarding for the past six months."

"Shit Boone. You know as well as I do that Israel already knows about the Germans."

"Yeah, but I'm not so sure he knows who's been guarding them. Especially since it's been you along with Marteen and Wilkins."

Radish smiled. "And what exactly do you think Israel will do when he finds out you've known all this time about my post?"

Franklin had no retort. He was beaten and stood down. Radish was right, Israel would probably not react well to the fact that Franklin had known all along who Radish had been spending so much time guarding.

He tried to change the subject. "So then when are you going to get back to helping us at the dig?"

Radish scowled and turned back to the food line. He pushed his tray along the countertop and said, "I could care less about digging in those goddamned dunes."

NEW DIRECTIONS

In a few days the vigil over the South Field slacked. The MPs soon had less of a presence, and the only time Franklin saw a mounted unit was on the typical beach patrol paths that paralleled the forest, and then disappeared into it, before making the southern turn down the shore. During this same time, the air of urgency around Fort Miles diminished. The threat of U-boats was less prevalent, as by early in the year it was clear that Germany was in its death throes. Hitler was consolidating his army, conscripting prisoners to fight for him, and making desperate decisions. The mounted beach patrol MPs joked that their job was getting more and more cake as the days went on. Franklin was told, however, that his research was still important—after all, the Pacific theater was still in full swing. He fancied the notion that his research might get him transferred to California or Hawaii, but wasn't sure if it was because he wanted dibs on West Coast beach treasure or as much distance between Israel and himself as possible.

In light of Radish's warnings, any time Franklin headed to the dig site, he proceeded with caution. He made it his practice to hike farther south, then turn inland and head towards the pine forest. From there, he doubled back north within the cover of the trees. It was three times the distance he had to travel, but in the long run, the extra steps meant less possibility that he would reveal the site location and lose his neck.

He dropped from the entrance tunnel into the den. To his left was a newly started tunnel, the depth of which was not five feet. Israel sat in front of the opening, hunched around the battery bank. He had moved it to the other side of the den so it would be closer to where they would be working.

As he collected himself, brushing soot off his arms and legs, Franklin said, "Sorry about the extra guards around here these days."

Israel replied, "Nothin' to worry about. The guards at this fort couldn't spot a U-boat if it sailed straight up their ass, much less a single man in these dunes."

Franklin changed the subject. "Looks like you've figured out a good starting direction."

"This is due north. Which I assume is the general direction of the hill you mentioned."

"Yes, I believe it is."

As far as Franklin could tell, the new tunnel was on a direct path to the north dunes—or, depending what side of the perimeter fence one stood on, the South Field.

•

In a month's time they had excavated about fifteen feet of tunnel, and by Franklin's calculations that meant that they had forty-five to go before reaching the hill with the mysterious humming. Franklin worked with a revived fervor, while Israel was as steady as ever, and on the occasion that Jojo helped, he dug with his usual detached intention. As the new tunnel grew, they moved the beams and framing from the first tunnel and set them up in the new one. They transferred any useless debris back in to the first tunnel, refilling it as they went. All the while, they continued to excavate buckets of tar mat, sand, rocks, rotten wood, and countless treasures.

A few months into the new tunnel, Franklin was taking his turn with the iron bar. He pushed the end of the bar into the wall in front of him and a tight-packed clump of sand fell off. It was a large enough pile that he decided it would be a good time to remove it, and as he shoveled debris into a bucket he heard his spade hit glass. This was not a foreign sound in the dig site. There was as much beach glass buried in the sand as there was any metal artifact. Franklin saw what looked like the tip of a bottle with a wax seal over the opening. He brushed sand away from the glass and noticed that the bottle was more than just the top. It was an intact, full bottle with the top still corked and waxed. He wiped the glass as clean as he could and saw that there was a slight crack in the side. From the crack dripped a liquid that was sharp and sour in odor. A dark stain grew around the bottle as liquid seeped out. Franklin dabbed his fingers in the liquid and sniffed. The strong sour smell carried a distinct wave of high-proof liquor. He tasted. It burned his tongue. Franklin was at a loss for words. In all their days of digging they had never found an intact bottle. He held the bottle in his hands as if it was a priceless vase.

"Whoa!" exclaimed Israel. He surprised Franklin, who had no idea that Israel was right behind him. Israel pushed past Franklin and stopped right above the glass. He dragged his index finger along the dripping edge, then slowly took the bottle out of Franklin's hands and brought it back to the den.

After securing the bottle in another bucket, they sat and talked. Israel's excitement was palpable, but he contained his enthusiasm when he said, "That's rum, Franklin. Perfectly kept, pure-cane rum."

Franklin had tasted the liquid in the bottle. Just the touch of it on his tongue sent a cold chill up his back, like when he was a child and would sneak tastes of his father's whiskey. Despite the significance of the find, he doubted that this particular treasure would bring much of a price. Yes, it was treasure, but it wasn't shiny and glimmering like the gold and silver that he was so used to finding.

By the end of that day they had a collection of five unbroken and unopened bottles of rum. There were no labels, and the glass was wide at the base.

Israel was aglow with a revived energy. He worked with a new focus, and no longer talked while digging, as if his mind was not in the tunnels with his body. Franklin didn't care. Israel smiled more with each bottle they found. He also dug more, and assigned Franklin with the tasks of cleaning, cataloging, and preparing the bottles for transportation.

Franklin usually learned of a new discovery whenever he heard Israel shouting down at the dark end of the tunnel. It would start with a loud "YAHOO," and a series of smaller victorious yells would follow as Israel finished unearthing his find. Then Franklin just had to wait. Soon he would see the whites of Israel's teeth in the glow of the tunnel bulbs as he crawled back to the den. He cradled the bottles in his hands like a nurse might carry a premature newborn to its incubator, and transferred them to Franklin with the same care. All the while, Israel was unable to stop smiling. The bottles were a good sign of progress; a much-needed salve for both men's weary psyches. Franklin finally felt like he and Israel were in sync and working like a fine-tuned machine.

•

No matter where he was, Franklin could not get his mind out of the tunnels. He was certain that he and Israel were close to reaching their goal. All the intact bottles of rum they found distracted him, and everything else in his life paled in comparison to his hopes of discovering the *Jacinta*.

Franklin was so excited about the dig that he had made it an active

263

part of his daily thoughts to ponder going AWOL. He told himself that once he and Israel found the gold and more bottles of rum he would have enough liquid assets to stay fluid for a long time. He knew he probably wouldn't find enough treasure to keep him alive forever, but perhaps it would be enough that he could buy some land.

Shit, Israel's lived twenty years on the lam, and he's doing okay.

Ultimately, he remembered that Hitler wasn't gaining any ground in Europe, so the idea of going AWOL never stuck with him too long. Despite Army life growing less and less palatable with each passing day, and the allure of treasure, he decided that he would stick out his term of service.

Better to be honorably discharged and rich than AWOL and on the lam.

That being said, in preparation for what he assumed was an impending huge payoff, he decided it was time to leave base for a different reason other than digging under the dunes.

He hung up with the local cab company, and stared at the phone receiver. He hadn't contacted his mother in over a week, and thought that while he waited he could pay a call and say hello. He reached into his pockets and rifled through the loose change, then pulled out what he thought was a dime. He put it in the coin slot, but the piece fell directly into the change return.

Picking up the dime, Franklin looked more closely at it. It was in fact a silver, three-cent piece from 1852. He stared at the coin for a few seconds, trying to determine how it got into his pocket, and was it found on the beach or in the tunnel? *Jeez, I never would have thought that I would have so much silver that I wouldn't be able to keep track of it all.* He put it back in his pocket and switched it for another, actual dime. This time the coin stayed in the phone bank, and the call went through.

Out of habit, as the phone rang, Franklin looked around to make sure Colonel Carp wasn't lurking nearby. His mother picked up the phone and they were able to chat for five minutes before the cab arrived. There wasn't much to report—at least as far as what Franklin was willing to tell his mother—so he made small talk and mentioned that he hoped to buy a vehicle.

"Okay Franky, but the little money you send me, I've been able to—"

Franklin interrupted, "It's okay Ma. I'm still going to send you that money."

Edith's voice calmed. She said with a slight laugh, "Well I guess they're paying you ok over there, if you can afford a new car."

"Well, you know I've been pretty fortunate these days."

"Oh, I know. Believe me, I'm not sure where I'm going to be able to put any more of the boxes that you've been sending home."

After cleaning and cataloging his finds, Franklin had made it a point to send his less valuable items home to his mother while, like a good pirate, he kept his high-end jewelry, silver, and gold closer and more secure. "Alright, just remember, that stuff isn't junk. It's actually quite the opposite."

"I know what you've told me, Franky. But can't we figure out some-where else to store all this stuff?"

"Don't worry about it. I've got a storage lab over here near the fort. I'm not going to be sending you any more boxes. And when I come home I'll sort everything out. Just keep them in my room."

"Okay, well, Franky. Your room is now the guest room. I haven't seen you in so long that I've done a bit of rearranging."

He felt a twinge of anger, as if an age-old safe place was being ripped

265

out from under him without permission. But he knew that whenever his stint in the Army was over, he wasn't going to move back in with his mother. He replied, "Jeez, Ma, then store the boxes in the basement. I don't care. Just don't let anyone else dig through my stuff. Please, this is how you and I are going to live comfortably once this war is over. Okay?"

"Okay, honey. I've been keeping the shipments in the basement, but even down there is getting tight now."

Franklin answered, "Okay. That's fine. Just keep this between you and me, and I'll come home soon to get the stuff. Like I said, I'm getting a car today, so, I'll be able to get home more often."

"Okay, Franky."

"Listen, my cab is here now, so I'm gonna let you go. Love you, and talk with you later."

He took the cab north to Dover, where the auto dealerships were more abundant. Old Man Nutter had recommended a few shops, and Franklin started with those. They were all in walking distance of each other, and before the day was half over, he had decided on a used Ford pickup truck. As he drove back to Fort Miles, Franklin was elated that he now had his own vehicle. However, his excitement was overshadowed by anxiety whenever he remembered the dig site and how much time he was wasting by not being there.

The next several days went by in their usual balmy and slow South-ern Delaware haze, and Franklin found himself with a few research proj-ects that demanded he stay in the laboratory. He found it difficult to focus on any task. His professional workload was larger than usual, and his personal work of cataloging and cleaning artifacts came to a temporary halt. Everything besides digging in the tunnels took a mental backseat.

NEW ENERGY

Israel took a stab at the working wall of the tunnel and dropped the bar onto the ground. He let his head rest on his arm and closed his eyes for a few minutes. He said, "We've got to be close to the fort, even closer to that hill you scanned, assumin' we're on the right trajectory, and we haven't found another bottle in weeks."

Franklin had nothing to say. His knee-jerk reaction was only to keep digging. He had no intention of giving up, and actually disagreed with Israel's assessment of where they were under the fort. He assumed Israel was tired and offered a restful compromise, "Why don't you take a break and I'll scan the tunnel for any interesting sounds?"

Israel agreed and crawled back to the den. Franklin turned the 625G on and dragged it back into the working tunnel. Though his goal was to scan the end wall, he wanted to let the detector pick up anything it might sense along the way. It was a slow crawl with the detector and battery pack ahead of him, made slower by no real significant sounds or warnings from the speaker. He inched his way forward, hearing only his pants dragging along the ground. Then he heard a faint humming coming from his speaker. He froze and held his breath, as if moving anything might lose whatever secret he had just stumbled upon. He pushed the 625G a few inches further. The hum grew louder. It was the pitch of what could only be a metal as dense as lead. *The keel? No conglomeration of tar mat makes the detector emit such a deep tone.* Pushing the detector further only made the sound louder.

"Franklin, why is that tone so loud?" Israel's voice was close, and it surprised Franklin. Though his voice was low and controlled, it shocked Franklin out of his focus and he nearly jumped up through the sand and back onto the dunes.

"Goddammit, Israel, it's loud because whatever it's sensing is closer than not."

Israel asked, "Do you have a sense of the direction?"

"It seems we're heading in the right direction. The volume increases as we reach the end."

Israel slapped Franklin on his shoulder and said, "Franklin, my boy, if we've found my goddamned ship, I am going to kiss your rotten tar-packed face."

"Okay Israel. Keep it for your wife."

They dug. Whenever they removed another five feet of tar mat, Franklin brought the 625G back in. They were still on the right track.

THE *JACINTA*

Franklin sat in the tunnel. He was tired and the rhythm of Israel's iron bar scraping earth made his eyelids feel like they weighed a hundred pounds. But his rest was cut short by a unique and alien sound. The bar hit soft wood—unlike the tree stumps and planks they usually dug up—creating a dull resonance with a hollow edge behind it. Franklin's eyes popped opened with an energized curiosity.

"Holy shit," exclaimed Israel. "I knew it!"

Franklin hurried to look at what Israel had discovered, leaving his detector behind. Like prisoners digging their way out of a jail cell and finally seeing a tiny ray of light shining through, Israel and Franklin scraped at the tar-mat until the entire diameter of the tunnel revealed the wooden boards of the side of a boat.

Amazed, they looked at each other. Before them was the side of an old abandoned vessel, and behind them the result of a painstakingly persistent excavation.

Franklin asked, "What do we do now?"

Israel didn't take his eyes off the wood planks and answered as if he'd been prepared for this moment for years. "We open up that hull is what we do now. Hold the light for me."

Israel rubbed his hand along the wood like a blind man reading Egyptian hieroglyphs. The light gave him a bearing on what was in front of him. He knocked on the wood. It returned a muffled sound that was absorbed by the tunnel walls.

Franklin asked, "How can the wood be in such good condition?"

"Not sure, Franklin. I assume that by bein' buried so deep, the boat has been in an oxygen-depleted zone, and so its decay has been slowed." He wobbled his eyebrows and said with a grin, "This is only good for us. It means the things inside will be well preserved. Of course, we haven't discovered anythin' yet, so quit askin' questions and hand me that crowbar." He found a soft spot in the planks and pushed the crowbar in. The wood was soft and the iron bar easily sunk through. With a slight pull of the end of the bar, the plank splintered.

After the first portion of plank was removed Israel stopped and put his hand up to the hole. "Air movement, Franklin. I feel a breeze." His voice was excited, and with the slight waft also came the musty smell of an old, damp room.

Franklin asked, "How could there be air movement in a buried boat?"

Israel didn't look back as he said, "Probably just decades of trapped air finally findin' its way out."

With another push of the iron bar, the next chunk of wood was removed. Soon Israel had a hole large enough for his head to fit through. He grabbed the light from Franklin and held it at an angle that would allow him to get a clear view of what was inside. He said, "Shit, Franklin, I can't see shit. Hand me the crowbar."

Franklin's heart raced at the thought of such a magnificent discovery. Even if the wood in front of him did not belong to the *Jacinta*, this was still a huge find.

Israel pushed the flashlight into the hole and looked inside. "Shit, Franklin. This is the goddamned *Jacinta*!"

They both crammed their heads into the breach and took in all that the light revealed. At first Franklin had no idea what he was looking at. They seemed to be in a large berth. According to Israel, the stern section of the boat had been crushed. To their right was a huge pile of tar mat and sand that had begun to digest the body of the boat. The pile sloped out of a large hole in the hull. Had they dug their tunnel ten feet to the right, they would not have had to break through the side.

Israel said, "It looks like the boat is upside down. That explains why it was so hard to find. If it was right-side-up, what remained of the mast would have protruded above the sand at some point. Some storm would have moved the dunes enough to reveal the location." He continued looking, and finally said the words that Franklin had been hoping to hear for months. "Let's go in."

Franklin held the light for Israel while he climbed through the hole, then passed it to him. He followed and landed on the ceiling of the berth. The old moist teak wood was soft and bowed under his weight. The structures of the berth and cabinets were upside down and the doors hung open. Franklin did not see any mattresses or any other accessory or artifact. In fact, the berth seemed to be completely cleaned out. He looked again at the hole in the side of the berth.

Israel sniffed the air, and scoped the room. On one side was the head. He inspected it and mumbled to himself. He moved to one of the dangling cabinet doors and clicked the old bronze latch a few times. "Interestin'," he whispered to himself.

"What's that?" asked Franklin.

"Look at the frame around these cabinets." Israel stroked his hand across a splintered section of cabinetry. "They've all got gashes where each door latch would have been."

The door to the galley was behind Franklin; almost directly below

271

their tunnel. Israel pointed at it and they cautiously walked along the ceiling. At this point the light's extension cable was at its full length. Franklin hooked it on the edge of a cabinet door in the galley and walked down the tight space. Israel was right behind him. At the end of the galley, Franklin turned and saw that Israel was staring at the floor, or what was originally the ceiling. There on the soft sheet of teak wood was the unmistakable, dusty outline of fresh boot prints.

•

Franklin stopped at the end of the galley. Israel raised his hand to signal that Franklin should halt his forward movement, then put his index finger up to his lips. Franklin held his breath, unsure of what was going on. He turned back and let his eyes acclimate to the boat's dark interior, while his ears strained to hear anything besides his breathing. There in front of them was the *Jacinta's* salon. This was the biggest section of the boat, and hanging above them were cabinets, bunks, and the navigation station. Franklin looked around, expecting to see piles of rum bottles and maybe—just maybe—some gold, but any halfway decent criminals would know not to keep such treasure out in the open. Nowhere did he see anything of value.

Israel squeezed Franklin's shoulder. He turned again and saw him pointing towards the other end of the salon. Looking in that direction, Franklin saw the doorway that lead into the forward section of the ship. The grip on his shoulder tightened, and Israel motioned again for him to stay quiet. Franklin listened. His heart raced. Their bodies blocked most of what little light they had as they crouched in a gray darkness. As his eyes acclimated, he noticed a slight contrast behind the door at the other end of the salon. Then he heard the voices.

"What the—" whispered Israel.

272

As quietly as possible, Israel made his way to the door. Franklin followed and they came to the v-berth, only this section of the boat was completely ripped apart. The wooden sides of the hull were splintered, revealing a wide, gaping hole as if the first twenty feet of the ship's bow had been shorn off. This would have been okay; the two men were ready for any damage that Mother Nature might have wrought upon the buried ship. They were not ready for the plastic tarpaulins that hung over the hole.

Their minds took a few moments to register what they saw. At first Franklin couldn't understand how a buried ship could have tarpaulins over it. The tarps swung gently in an unseen cross-draft, and when they puffed out for a few seconds Franklin heard low voices talking somewhere behind them.

His heart dropped. All the possibilities of what might be happening popped into his head, but none of them made sense. Israel crept his way forward and stopped in front of the tarpaulins. Franklin crouched next to him. The voices were strange, and he did not understand the language. In an instant it hit him, like the ceiling of a tunnel might collapse and crush the breath right out of his chest. He realized that whatever their emotional tone might have been, the songs and the accents he heard outside the tarps were German.

Israel moved the two pieces of plastic tarpaulin apart enough that they both had a slight view of what was happening. Franklin noticed the top of a ladder propped below the hole over which he was crouched. It seemed that the *Jacinta* had long been discovered. Indeed, the US Army had found what Israel had made his life's work. Following the ladder down Franklin saw that it was standing in a huge warehouse-sized room, made completely of cement floors and grey-blocked walls. The ceiling of

273

the room was rounded, and composed of the same material as the walls.

Franklin could not believe what he saw. He knew that underneath every battery at the fort was a bunker for ammunition storage and anything else the big guns might require. But, by his best calculations, this bunker was nowhere near any battery, and its sheer scope made it hard to imagine being underneath Fort Miles. But it did explain the fleet of loaders and dump trucks that moved about the South Field.

Franklin's focus moved to the collection of oddities on the floor of the bunker. Besides stacks of wooden crates all tagged with the typical black painted letters "Property of the US Army," there were all sorts of items that were obviously related to the *Jacinta*; rotten and ripped cushions, various eating utensils, navigation tools, hand tools, and other things he couldn't get a good look at. Every item was labeled and laid out categorically like an archeologist might organize his finds. Next to the nautical tools were stacks of other, half-decayed wooden crates. It was easy to see that these crates were not originally the property of the US Army, and inside them were neatly seated bottles—the same style of bottle that Israel and Franklin had already found in their recent excavations.

"The rum," Franklin said.

Israel was distracted and startled by his words. He replied with a one-word question. "Germans?"

Franklin said, "What—" and turned to look in the direction Israel was facing. There, almost directly below them, but off to the side, were the German prisoners from U-856. He looked from the prisoners then back to Israel. He seemed confused.

The Germans were all dressed in a rag-tag mix of pieces of their uniforms and other, lighter prison garments. All were busy with various tasks. Some were lazing around reading books and magazines. Another sat in a chair while his comrade trimmed his hair. One prisoner moved a clothes iron over a pair of pants. Still others stood around a small military camp stove and cooked what looked like sausages, while another was stirring a steaming pot of something else. No matter what their task, the verses of their song were passed around from prisoner to prisoner as if they were all in an a cappella group. The heavy-tongued sounds of the words hardly seemed able to fit into the melodies, but the song entertained the prisoners and each looked content.

Franklin's eyes moved back to the singing Germans. He was amazed at the audacity of what he saw. They were being treated better than any American prisoner in the brig, and most certainly better than any American prisoner in their country. They were exercising regularly, cooking their own food, and now excavating a ship that did not belong to them.

Then Franklin heard a single word that asked a question.

"Poppi?"

Franklin asked, "What was that?" But when he turned, Israel's face was soured by a dark anger.

Israel didn't answer. Franklin turned back to look at what Israel had seen, and had to lean a little in his direction. From that vantage point he saw the corpses. There on the floor, between the collection of artifacts and the group of prisoners, were three withered corpses. What skin was visible was brown and tight over bones. They were each still wearing the tattered and rotten clothes that they died in, and were as neatly laid out and labeled as the other items and the rum. A prisoner was squatting over the bodies. He zipped up a body bag over the head of one of the corpses, then moved to the next. These were the bodies of Randal Shamft, Buster Rolfe, and none other than Rafael Mouzellas. Even if Israel had not said the word, Franklin would have known by the odd placement of Rafael's

275

corpse's left arm. When the German got to Rafael, he tucked a loose and separated arm next to the body then zipped it all up into its bag.

The word "Poppi" rang in Franklin's ears. He stared in disbelief at the corpses; almost close enough to smell, but because of the circumstances, as far away as the moon. The sound of the tarpaulins rustled and he felt a slight movement behind him. He turned to see a blank space where Israel had been. Israel had made haste back into the boat's salon.

Franklin felt like he too was being cheated by the US Army. He had worked harder on the dig than on anything else in his life, and now his employers were pulling all his efforts out from under him. He remembered the gold, and forgot about following Israel.

He crept over to where Israel had been squatting and moved the tarpaulins apart again, scanning anything he could see. Unfortunately, he saw no piles of gold, or anything that looked like it might house a quantity of the precious metal. He remembered Israel's words, *Only an idiot leaves his gold out for the world to see.*

He searched as much of the space as possible, and in the back of the room, behind a wall that resembled the bars of a jail cell, with their M1 rifles over their shoulders, were three MPs. Two of them stood with their backs to Franklin. From his vantage point he thought they were Master Sergeant Marteen and Staff Sergeant Wilkins. But the third guard stood facing Franklin's direction. He stood alone like a recluse, shifting from leg to leg as the other two talked. And when he finally shifted to his right, out of the shadows and into the light, Franklin saw the scowling face of Sergeant Jameson Radish. This was bad, but what was worse was the fact that Radish's beady eyes were staring back up at him.

URGENCY

The shock of being noticed made Franklin negligent in handling the tarpaulin and he let go of it without thinking about the sound it would make. The rustling was loud and visible enough that the German singing stopped. As he scrambled backwards, the soft wood of the ceiling panels cracked under the hasty movement of his weight. Franklin knew his cover was blown, and his only thought was to get out of the *Jacinta*. He assumed that Radish was the only one to have seen him, and he wouldn't rat Franklin out because Radish also had his hands in the covert excavation. This hope, and Radish's unpredictability, did not make him feel better. He had to get back up to the dunes where, if noticed, he could feign that he was conducting research, and then—he had no idea.

His dream of plundering the *Jacinta* was over. Not caring how much sound he made, he trampled through the galley, into the captain's berth, and finally pulled himself back up into the tunnel. He was halfway into the mouth when he remembered the light. It was still hooked over the galley cabinet. From the mouth of his tunnel he gave the power cord a strong yank and the light clanked into the berth. Any last hopes of being conspicuous were over at that point.

Scurrying down the fifty feet of tunnel he dropped into the den. With little regard for anyone that might be around, he threw himself out onto the sand. There, the metal cover for the tunnel lay in plain sight, and the camouflage grasses and brush were scattered in every direction. The dunes were covered in the darkness of night, and Franklin had no idea what time it was. He stood up and scanned the area. No MPs or Israel were in sight. It felt counterintuitive, but Franklin ran over the dunes and back towards Fort Miles, ignoring the covert paths he'd used earlier to keep passersby unaware of the dig site. He didn't know what to do. Should he just go back to his barracks and act like nothing happened? Part of him was worried about Israel. He was the leader of his crew, and Franklin's instincts told him that Israel would know what the next step should be. He had to find Israel, and his best bet for doing that was to get in his truck and drive.

He scrambled up the dune berm. Now he was on the plateau outside the perimeter fence. He turned and broke into a hasty walk into the field where he and Thurber had found the old foundation divots for the Lewes Beacon, keeping his eyes out for any MPs. It wasn't a long walk through the field, but it was covered in dense thistles and brambly shrubs that made passage difficult. Then he continued around the perimeter fence, crouching and running over the rail tracks, then the front road, and finally he made it to the parking lot outside the fort.

With the light restriction still in place, the lot was dark. He walked across the front road as nonchalantly as possible, hoping that would be enough to keep him inconspicuous, and that no one would notice him, especially Colonel Carp.

Once at his vehicle he jerked the door open, and was in his seat in one fluid movement. The entrance to the parking lot was closer to the front gates of the fort, and as Franklin drove out he had a clear view of a portion of the grounds, particularly the brig. He slammed on the brakes. All the lights of the building were on, and it was flooded in the bright halogen searchlights that stood on all corners of the building. The brightness made it possible for him to discern the details of the people walking around the building, while dark silhouettes moved inside the barred frames of the brig windows. *The Germans? How'd they get in there without entering from the outside? There must be a secret entrance to the underground bunkers from the brig.* That was a perfect cover, as no one was too worried about any particular door other than the one that lead to the outside. Out of the brig stepped three MPs. Franklin could plainly see that they were Radish, Marteen and Wilkins. They each had their M1s over their shoulders, and disappeared into the darkness of the train switchyard.

Dammit, I've got to move fast. He pushed the gas pedal, and the back wheels spun for a second as they found their traction. The truck jerked onto the road. He couldn't drive fast enough. The seconds stretched longer than each tree or fence post along the country roads, while a sense of impending doom grew in his chest. He knew more than he was supposed to, and if he was picked up by one of those MPs he felt certain that things would not end well.

Having been to the farmhouse many times, he knew where Israel's driveway opened up on the road, and he made a hard turn onto the dirt. His wheels spun under the light weight of the truck bed as he bounced down the drive.

No one answered his hectic knocking at the front door. He ran around to the backyard. Once there he noticed how dark it was and looked up at the sky. No moon was visible, and his heart leapt into his throat. Israel's words echoed in his head: "A good night for doing some pirating." Indeed, this was a perfect night for a mooncusser, and Israel was more than experienced to know that.

No one was in the backyard. He ran back around to the front porch. A few inside lights were on and he pounded on the door again. After what seemed like an eternity, Lulu-Pine answered the door. She took one look at Franklin and said, "You gotta stop him."

"What do you mean? Where's Israel?"

She had no more emotion on her face than any other time, but her words were delivered with a sense of urgency. She said, "Israel's gone. He come home, collected some guns, then disappeared."

Lulu-Pine's information increased Franklin's racing thoughts. "Do you know where he went?"

"I got no idea. He don't tell me nothin', and that boy of his just scowls at me all the time. Not to mention his wife."

Franklin did not give a damn how Lulu-Pine was treated by her sister in-law or nephew, and turned to run back to his truck, but Lulu-Pine shouted after him.

"I kept them here so he could kill 'em!"

Franklin stopped short at the first porch step. He turned and asked, "What did you say?"

"It was the only way I could keep 'em here. I knew Israel would'a been home soon, and if they were still here, I knew he would'a killed 'em. Or maybe they would'a just killed us all. They killed my daddy too, ya know." She paused, under the weight of a heavy memory, and said, "I just wasn't ready for—"

Franklin wanted nothing more to do with the dysfunction of the Mouzellas family. He leapt down the steps. As he raced to his truck he decided that his best option was to get back to the fort and go to bed. He hoped Radish's involvement in the *Jacinta* dig would be enough to keep him from harassing him for knowing what he now knew. He was sure that

Marteen and Wilkins hadn't seen him in the bunker, so maybe, just maybe he could get back to Barracks Five and go to sleep.

KILLING

Franklin's truck could not move fast enough, and bounced uncontrollably whenever he hit the slightest bump. He turned into Fort Mile's guest parking lot and left the vehicle at the first open spot he could find. He turned the key in the ignition and suddenly realized, *My detector!* In his hasty retreat he had forgotten the 625G in the den. *Goddammit.*

He jumped from the seat. As he came to the realization he would have to go back to the dig site, an explosion sounded from somewhere around the front edge of the fort. In concert with the sound came a plume of fire that rose up into the night. Another explosion sounded, and another plume of fire. The beachside edge of the base glowed red with flames, and the fort's emergency sirens were raised. Due to the explosions' proximity, Franklin couldn't see what was happening.

As he ran to the front gates, another explosion burst. This time closer, near the train-yard.

In the distance, over the field outside the perimeter fence, a stream of fire like a miniature comet bursting through the Earth's atmosphere flew through the air. It came from the same brambly field which he and Thurber had inspected. Despite contending with the loud sirens, the blast had a unique and familiar sound, and when he saw the second arch of fire rise up above the fort's rooftops then come down and thud against the roof of the brig, he knew exactly what was happening.

Franklin ran towards the field, hoping that the fiery mayhem on base would cover him enough to get Israel away from Fort Miles. As he ran past the train-yard, he saw a streak of fire smack against the already burning brig. The side of the building that faced the perimeter fence was engulfed in flames. Incendiary rounds struck it and expanded like liquid fire against its side, and rolled through the windows that were open save for the few iron bars that were supposed to keep prisoners in their place. Fire grew from the inside of the building, merging with the flames that were busy on the exterior. Explosions caromed off the brig, nearby train cars, and the switchyard buildings. Molten rounds defied gravity like the fireworks at a Fourth of July display.

Franklin watched as one of the rounds hit the base of the brig and burned a hole through the cinder block foundation as if it was paper. When the incendiary rounds finally stopped, he could hear men's voices screaming from within.

He tried to get a glimpse of Israel's location. Another fireball rose from the corner edge of the pine forest. Franklin turned and sighted along its trail. On the top of the ridge, right in front of the trees, was a dark figure that had to be Israel. He stood out in the open, daring anyone to stop him, and fired another round. It flew over the brig and landed in the small patch of grass between the gravel road and the turn into the switchyard. When the round hit the ground, fire flowed forward and spilled across the road, catching hold of any tinder dry enough to burn. This created a fiery barrier for the GIs rushing to the scene.

Franklin, however, was on the other side of the fence, and ran through the clusters of grasses and shrubs.

Israel had set up his attack like a professional military tactician. He'd planted a few explosives, set with timers, on the ridge that overlooked the beach. Then he'd made haste to the pine forest, from where he shot his fireballs into the fort. As he shot the fire, the explosives would go off, causing confusion, so the GIs reacting would be unsure from what direction the attack was coming. Most of them seemed to think it was an attack by multiple perpetrators, while the others busied themselves with putting out the various fires. By the time Franklin was in the middle of the field, Israel was gone. Franklin took the chance to catch his breath. Behind him, the brig was engulfed in flames, as were several other rail yard buildings. The brig doors were wide open and men were running out, their shirts and pants burning as they dove to the ground. Other GIs dashed around them trying to put out and control the spread of the fire.

Israel's after the prisoners! He hates all things German so much that he is breaking onto US Army property to kill a few prisoners. Of course, where there were German prisoners, there would also be Radish. Franklin could only assume that Israel had noticed Radish down in the bunker guarding the prisoners. Neither the Germans' nor Radish's wellbeing would be of any concern for Israel.

For someone who prides himself on keeping under the cover of a moonless night, Israel sure chose a noisy method of getting at the prisoners. Then it hit him like a flood of light–all this time of digging, promising gold and rum, and the vast amounts of money they would each reap, had been a ruse just to coerce Franklin into helping with the digging. Israel didn't care about the rum or the gold on board the *Jacinta*, and he didn't have his sights on the German prisoners. He was going for his father's body. But since the *Jacinta* was now compromised, he was trying to create enough commotion so that he would have a better chance of retrieving it.

The one thing that gave his life purpose!

Franklin then realized that Israel was most likely unaware that his earlier egress had no doubt alerted the MPs in the bunker to his presence, and they had to be snooping around, or guarding the tunnels. He thought, *Israel's walking right into a trap,* and ran towards the ridge path. Not a few steps forward he heard the familiar voices of Marteen and Wilkins call out a warning. "You there," they yelled. "Freeze. Drop any weapons and get your hands up."

Franklin dove forward at the sound of their voices. He rolled down a slight slope into the beacon house divot, then crawled up the other side. From the other side of the perimeter fence, the two MPs rushed to the side gate. Franklin heard the first shot from their rifles. The rounds plucked into the earth next to his feet and knees, and he sprang up, sprinting towards the shadow of the pine forest. He never thought his training would have to be used to save himself from his fellow soldiers, but time was of the essence and he had to stop Israel before he got himself, or anyone else, killed.

Another round snipped through the trees next to him. He crouched and ran along the path that paralleled the forest and disappeared into the shadows. Marteen and Wilkins were opening the gate on the perimeter fence. They would be dangerously close in no time. Behind him searchlights flooded the base, and Marteen and Wilkins' silhouettes—rifles at the ready—raced towards him. With no regard for keeping to a specific path, he bolted into the trees. Instantly he tripped over the dense undergrowth, slamming down onto his torso, and knocking the wind out of his lungs. Gasping, he jumped up again. A shot from a nearby rifle sounded. The crack of the round sped past his head, clipping through the branches.

Franklin forced his way through the never-ending web of branches and fallen trees. Though disoriented, he knew the dunes were to his left, and after the next round zipped past his head, he made for the edge of the forest. Staying low, he stopped short at the top of the forest ridge. Marteen and Wilkins were somewhere behind him. They however, were still on the path, and hadn't yet seen his detour out of the woods. He jumped down the berm slope, sliding easily down, and stopped at the base. He dashed forward just in time to avoid being seen by his pursuers.

He made it to the dunes unharmed, and dove behind the first hill he came to. He crawled up the next hill and back down the other side. Trying to stay hidden and move fast was not easy, especially because Marteen and Wilkins had the high-ground advantage. Staying low and in the shadows, was his only hope. Near the top of the next hill, Franklin looked back over his shoulder, checking for the whereabouts of the MPs. They were sliding down the berm ridge and would now be at the same elevation he was. This was a minor relief, as he felt safe in the darkness of the dunes, but he knew it was no difficult task to track a man on the beach, even at night.

Another pop and a round puffed into the side of the hill in front of him. The MPs had spotted him. Franklin did his best to cover his tracks and kept heading towards the dig site. He had no idea what he would do once there, as it was very likely that the Army now knew about the tunnel network. He hoped that he would just find Israel there, and be able to coerce him into leaving immediately.

Franklin didn't want to run directly toward the site, so he circumvented it for about thirty yards then doubled back and approached it from the south. This was taking way too long, but he didn't want to reveal everything to the MPs. He was hoping to lead them on a different path, then shake them at the last minute, and give himself enough time to talk some sense into Israel.

When he arrived at the site, the door to the entrance was wide open, and Franklin could see a small dot of light at the far end of the tunnel. Franklin bent down to make his way into the hole, when he saw the light begin to flicker. Something was blocking the glow. Someone was crawling his way. He backed out and collapsed into the sand. Soon enough, the debris sled appeared at the mouth of the tunnel. On top of the sled was a dirty body bag, it was partially unzipped and revealed the mumified remains Rafael Mouzellas' head. Israel was right behind it. The sled and pile of bones fell out of the tunnel mouth and Israel appeared next. He noticed Franklin right away.

"Goddammit, Israel. What the hell do you think you're doing? We've got to get out of here."

Israel stood up and began to collect the remains of his father. He did not say a word. Franklin ran up to him, still trying to talk sense into him and hurry him along. Israel moved at his usual pace, as if daring anyone to tell him to do different. Franklin bent down and attempted to help pick up an end of Rafael's body bag, but Israel pulled both his .44s out. Franklin jumped back and fell onto the sand with his hands in the air, certain that Israel would not have a problem putting a round into him.

Israel's smoke-covered face was as black as the night—maybe Jojo had finally gotten the incendiary mixture right—and all Franklin could see was the devil in the whites of his eyes. Franklin begged, "Please Israel, we've got to get—" Israel ignored him and turned his aim up above the dunes. The two MPs were a few hills over. They shouted for Israel to freeze and drop his weapons. Israel simultaneously pulled both triggers. The MPs returned fire and grazed the side of Israel's head. Blood sprayed across a nearby hill, but the shot did not put him down.

Israel fired again. Each pull of his triggers came with a burst of fire,

287

like thunder accompanied by lightning. The .44s surprised Marteen and Wilkins. They thought they were just pursuing a rogue GI, and were not used to this type of activity around the beaches of Fort Miles. They ducked behind the closest hill, but Israel did not stop. He covered the distance between the MPs and himself, making sure to shoot whenever he saw one of their heads pop up. When he stood over them, Franklin realized Marteen and Wilkins were out of bullets. Marteen begged Israel not to shoot, only to be followed by Israel emptying the remaining rounds from both his pistols. After both guns were empty, Israel stood over the dead MPs and reloaded. He took his time, as if the business of murder required as much patience as digging a tunnel in the dunes. Smoke rose, like the ghosts of his kills, from the barrels and cylinders of his revolvers. When reloaded, Israel shot twice more, making sure each MP had a bullet in his head, then made his way back to the dig site.

With the murder of Marteen and Wilkins, Franklin decided beyond all shadow of a doubt that he was quitting Israel's crew. He was done trying to talk sense into Israel, and was not going to stick around to see if Israel was going to kill him as well. He rolled over and began crawling up the hill behind him, only to hear Radish's voice. He screamed Israel's name in a high-pitched squawk as he leapt through the air. Franklin froze and slid back down the sandy slope that he was trying to get over. At the bottom he found himself lying next to the corpse of Rafael Mouzellas. His eye sockets stared out of the body bag with a darkness that mirrored the moonless sky. Radish had yet to see Franklin. His focus was on his uncle who was just then jumping down the opposite hill into the valley of the dig site.

"Damn you, Israel." Radish crashed the butt end of his rifle against Israel's head before he could lift his pistols. Israel, unconscious, collapsed on top of Franklin. Radish cursed, and seemed to be crying as well. He was a frantic ball of emotion as he turned and aimed his rifle down at his uncle. That's when he noticed Franklin, and changed his aim a few inches in Franklin's direction.

He seemed surprised to see Franklin, and said, "Boone? You really fucked up this time. I knew I should'a never worked you onto the crew."

Franklin tried to push Israel off and scramble backwards, but with the sand and the dead weight of the unconscious body this felt impossible. He was free enough, however, to raise his hands in the air and beg Radish for mercy. He said, "Radish, come on now. We were both on the same crew. You know I don't give a damn about the guards, or the gold, or that fucking boat. And I promise I won't—"

Radish interrupted, "Shut the fuck up, Boone. I've been sick of your bullshit for a long time now. And now that Israel has gone crazy all over the base, I can kill you and him and be the goddamned hero of Fort Miles."

"Please Radish, this has nothing to do with me. We've gotta help Marteen and Wilkins. They might not be—"

"Fuck Marteen and Wilkins, Boone." In the fading light the evil in Radish's face was clear. There was a strange corruption to the Mouzellas blood that seemed to infect all the generations; perhaps the further away one got from the patriarch, the more demented the person became.

Radish lifted his M1 and Franklin closed his eyes in preparation for the shot. He heard the blast from the gun, but it took him a few seconds to realize he wasn't shot. But he did feel something splash against his face.

He wiped his hand across his eyes. The sand stuck to his palm scratched his cheeks and lids, and added to the confusion of what he saw next: Radish's headless body.

In a single second Franklin saw the human frame cut out like a stencil against the backdrop of a moonless, star-peppered sky. The stars were crystal clear and provided enough light to see everything around him. Franklin thought he might be dead, and Radish's body was some sort of ghoul coming to take his soul down to hell.

He wiped his face again. The texture made him look at his sleeve, and the sight brought him back to the reality of his situation. The slop all over Franklin's face was Radish's blood, brains, and bits of skull.

The body stood upright for a second, which was more than enough time for Franklin to collect his thoughts and realize that he was, in fact, still alive. Radish's headless body fell forward onto Israel. Now Franklin was stuck under two Mouzellas men, and was being doused in blood draining from both of their bodies.

Franklin pushed with all his might, and when finally out from under the two men, he was again halted by the familiar clicking sound of a 12-gauge shotgun. Up on the same hill where Radish had just been was Jojo. He held a shotgun that was almost as long as he was tall. Franklin froze with his hands up, and had a hunch that he would be less lucky with Jojo than he'd been with the older two Mouzellas. He closed his eyes and hoped that his death would be painless.

A voice. Franklin opened his eyes. Sueli stood behind her son as if trying to acclimate to the sight below her, and for the first time he heard her speak English. "Jojo, don't waste another shot on the white boy. Move your father–" shaking her head, she finished, "–and the cursed one." She grabbed the gun out of her son's hands. Jojo hesitated then mumbled something in Portuguese and climbed down. Franklin watched as Jojo pushed his cousin's body out of his way with less deference than a butcher flipping over the carcass of a pig. He then dragged Israel over to the sled and rolled him on top of Rafael's body. Sueli slung the shotgun over a shoulder and bent down to help her son. They both disappeared over the dune.

Fort Miles' sirens blared, but the noise was somewhere far away. It sunk into the distance as Franklin relaxed. And as his body softened into the sand, his mind stopped caring about Israel, or the Army, or gold. Ocean breezes pulsed over the dunes and puffed a light sand in his face. Soon, the stars dimmed, leaving the sky a solid black, and a strange slowness enveloped him as he lost consciousness.

CHECKING OUT
OF FORT MILES

Franklin's eyes blinked open to a glowing white radiance and he assumed that he was dead and viewing for the first time the pearly clouds of heaven. Then the visage of Colonel Carp appeared at the foot of his bed. He was as far from heaven as he possibly could be.

"Well, if it isn't Sleeping Beauty all woke up," said Carp. "You've had quite a nice little snooze, Boone."

"Wha—"

"It's okay, Boone. Don't worry about sorting anything out quite yet."

A nurse milled about the room. She stood behind Carp and scribbled something on a clipboard, and then hung it on a hook at the foot of his bed and left the room. Despite being alone, Carp leaned in closer to Franklin's face and whispered, "You're a goddamned hero around here, Boone."

Franklin struggled to understand what was happening. He looked at the open window in his room. Daylight spilled through the glass like a massive celestial interrogation light. He asked, "What's going on? Where am I?"

"Relax, Boone. You're at the infirmary. The doctor said you've got no visible wounds, and probably just passed out—which is not surprising when I consider who I'm talking to—but now that you're awake they're going to run a few more tests."

As the events of the previous night flooded back into his head, Franklin tried to determine if he was in the brig infirmary or the fort infirmary. His immediate fate would be easily determined with the answer to that question. If he was in the brig, he was under arrest and would be subjected to an interrogation in which he would be forced to admit what he'd been up to for the past year. Then he remembered that the brig most likely no longer had an infirmary, thanks to Israel. Carp's words finally sunk in. *A hero.*

He asked, "Colonel Carp, sir, what are you talking about?"

"I'm talking about you stopping those Germans from escaping." Carp looked at Franklin with a proud-father gleam in his eyes. Franklin began to suspect he was not in trouble. Carp continued, "Those Krauts had dug a tunnel network under the brig that ran all the way out to where you were found, and, of course, the bodies of those MPs. Not to mention all those Germans that were found shot to hell around the same area."

The odd details in Carp's description of the site made Franklin hold his tongue.

Carp continued, "You guys put up a good fight, just like you've been trained. Luckily most of those Krauts died in the brig fire. Which they obviously started as a decoy so they could slip out the tunnel while everyone was busy with putting out the flames, but being Krauts, I guess they don't know how to start a fire without killing themselves." Carp poked his head out the door, then closed it and turned back to Franklin. "Ya know Boone, your heroics have really helped me. I still have to look into it, but I think I can write you up for a Bronze Star. The fucking Bronze Star, Boone. Who would'a thought you'd receive such an award? And because I handled this situation in a quiet, non-public manner, Admiral Phillips is loving me right now. The brass in Washington didn't know what they wanted to do with our prisoners, so this incident was perfect.

"Shit, Boone, after last night, the brass no longer has to worry about the prisoners. They didn't even have to scratch a pencil across paper. You know how the citizens of this country react to any killing of our boys. That only strengthens the Army's mission. Shit, Boone, as far as the brass is concerned your friends out there died for the cause. They gave their lives to prove just how sneaky and deadly those Germans are. And you, you'll be the hero—" Carp spread his hands apart, miming an imaginary marquee across which read his taunt "—and lone survivor." He continued, "You're double lucky too, 'cause, believe it or not, the brass doesn't seem to give a damn about my disposal plans."

"Disposal plans, sir?"

"Yeah, we're gonna load all those dead Krauts onto their U-boat, then tug that puppy out to sea for some live-fire drills. Washington is sending out a film crew to record the sinking, for posterity, I guess. If you hurry up and get out of here, you might even catch the event before you leave in a couple days."

Franklin was confused into silence. His mind raced to understand where the colonel was sending him.

Carp, however, seemed to be able to read his mind. "I've put orders in for your transfer to California. They've got a lot of work over there that's right up your alley. You don't really think I'm going to let you run around my fort any longer than you have to, do you? So, once you're cleared by the doc you're going to pack up your shit and get the hell out of my hair. Your plane leaves in two days, after which time you and I will hopefully never see each other again."

Franklin could barely keep up with what the colonel told him. For the moment, he ignored his new transfer orders as he tried to sort out all the strange aspects to Carp's story. He pondered the amount of energy it must have taken to conceive of the plan, then plant the corpses of the dead Germans around the dig site (assuming he even went to that length), and then sell the story to Admiral Phillips.

Carp leaned over the bed. "Something you need to ask, Boone?"

"Sorry, sir. I'm just still trying to piece together everything that happened."

"I thought I just told you everything that happened."

The two men tried to read each other's face.

"Listen, Boone. Before you do anything stupid, allow me to remind you of how any different account on your part will affect your life. My story gets you a Bronze Star, most likely a promotion—which means you can send more money home to your mommy—and a transfer to the Pacific. You've had more than enough leisure time here at Fort Miles, and the Pacific theater will be a good place to use your metal detector for the actual job it was designed. Now, of course, if you want to tell another story—any other story—I cannot vouch for your future." Carp paused, then continued. "Scratch that, Boone, since I've already floated my line, I can't let you tell any other story. If you open your mouth at all, I foresee a vastly different MOS for you. Instead of running out the batteries of your metal detectors and sweeping the beaches of Hawaii or San Diego, you'll be securing beachheads for the Armor units in the goddamned Philippines."

Carp leaned in and whispered, "Boone, I do not give a shit about how much you know about the underground bunkers. If you think that is something unique to Fort Miles, you are obviously not as smart as I was originally led to believe. And I promise you that I will do everything in my power to ensure you keep your mouth shut. I've got full command of the construction of this base. Admiral Phillips doesn't ask me any questions, and I am certainly not going to let your loud mouth change that. I know that you and those idiot MPs dug those tunnels, and were most likely looking for that piece-of-shit boat that I found first. Again, I do not care what you know, because I know for certain that before I leave this room you and I will have come to an agreement. Believe me, Boone, you are only alive because your unconscious ass was found by someone other than me. And you're lucky, because Washington is always looking for the next poster boy for their hero brigade. Something that if you play your cards right you might be able to parlay into a USO tour and perhaps even avoid the chance of seeing any action. Which I know makes you feel better, you being a coward and all. It's your choice, either you tow my line, or I put you on that U-boat with all the Germans you killed and inform the brass that you died in your sleep. Which isn't a bad life plan, Boone. You'll be one of four amongst the KIA of Fort Miles. Always remembered for being a hero. Your name will be on some memorial plaque somewhere, and your mommy will receive your medals so she can set them up on her mantel for all her crone friends to stare at. You gotta admit, being remembered sure beats fading into dust in some geriatric hospital bed, which is how I foresee your natural demise."

Franklin understood Carp's motives and realized that his best bet for survival was to go along with the story. He found it amazing how, despite being guilty of several crimes against the US Army, Carp still worked hard to give Franklin an opportunity to not only walk away with a clean slate, but to actually use the story to potentially create a new image of himself. Franklin knew Carp was a company man, a patriot to the highest extent, so he assumed that somewhere in his scheme was something juicy—some reward to his personal or military life—that allowed his conscience the balance it needed to live with the lies.

"I can see in your face, Boone, that you're coming to your senses. I know you're smart, but I also know that you're a sneaky bastard, and I feel confident that you and I will agree on the best plan for each of us."

"Yessir."

"You're lucky, Boone. You wanna know why?"

"Yessir."

"By joining me in this plan, you've made the best choice for your future. But you're even luckier that you didn't kill those Krauts before they finished with that boat. Yeah, that would'a pissed me off. They had just finished sorting out all the booty on board before you came along and killed them. They were my secret weapon. Nobody asked where they were, and if I fed them enough, they would'a dug me a tunnel right up to Hitler's own asshole. Jesus, those bastards were hard workers. I had the best excavation crew at my disposal, and all I had to worry about was the loose lips of a few MPs. Shit, Boone, you did the dirty work for me, and made it so I didn't have to disappear anybody."

Franklin was now back to being confused. Apparently the colonel still believed Franklin, and possibly the MPs, had something to do with the deaths of the prisoners, but he also seemed to have been ready to end the lives of Radish, Marteen, and Wilkins once the excavation of the *Jacinta* was complete.

"Remember, Boone," continued Carp, "Part of the reason I haven't disappeared you is because you're just the kind of sick fuck that this Army needs. Not the fighting type, I understand that, but, I swear I don't know how you did it, or what you used, but the holes found in those Kraut corpses looked like you blasted them with a direct line from the sun itself." Carp smiled, and shook his shoulders with an affected shudder then finished with a look that froze Franklin. "Indeed, you're smart, but

297

you're a sick motherfucker alright, and that's why I like you. You keep your mouth shut now, and you'll be sailing through the rest of this war."

Franklin eked out a nervous, "Yessir."

Carp turned to leave, but right before he did he remembered, "Oh yeah, Boone, I forgot to give you your prize."

"My prize sir?"

"Yeah. Your reward for towing the line." He reached into his pocket while again making sure no nurses or doctors were anywhere near the doorway. "This was found in the pockets of one of those dead Krauts. That fucker was trying to get away with my loot, but thanks to you he did not make it. I assume you know that this was a part of a larger cache, but I expect you'll be happy with just this one. Take this token of my appreciation, and all the other treasure you've got tucked away in that safety-deposit box, and get your ass to California before I change my mind."

Franklin watched Carp pull something out of his pocket. At first he couldn't tell what it was, but when the colonel put the object on the bedside table it thunked against the wooden top with a familiar sound. Franklin's eyes widened. It was a thin, perfectly cleaned, three-inch-long bar of solid twenty-four-karat gold.

Before departing Colonel Carp said, "Remember Boone, if you decide to blow any whistles, things will be quite different for you. As you lay here starin' at the ceiling for the rest of the day—the length of your future is in your hands."

EPILOGUE

Colonel Carp wrote up his final report of the incident in the dunes. He massaged the truth into a harrowing tale in which Franklin had led a small band of soldiers against the armed, escaping Germans. The prisoners were blamed for the burning of the brig and the deaths of the three MPs.

Carp's story was filed away amongst all the other Army reports full of heroic actions made by countless men in the service of their nation. No one asked why or how the prisoners killed the GIs after sneaking through what was supposed to have been a secret tunnel. And the Washington brass didn't bother to ask how the prisoners had been able to dig a tunnel that ran from the fort grounds under the South Field and then close to sixty feet into the dunes.

When the story about who set the fire rumored its way around the fort, many GIs claimed to have heard explosions coming from different directions. However, being the experienced leader that he was, Colonel Carp knew that in just a few days, especially after the U-boat spectacle, no one would be thinking about how the brig fire had started. Any claims about explosions were simply brushed off as delirium resulting from the fog of war. In his report, Carp even went so far as to include his opinions on how the moonless night played a large factor in any reports that contradicted his own.

With the sinking of U-856, anyone on the beach from Assateague to

Cape May was witness to the plume of black smoke that rose from the Atlantic. Newspapers were told it was a controlled sinking over a spot a few miles offshore in which the Army chose to sink its old vessels and ordinance. A small group of photojournalists were brought out to a comfortable distance from the U-boat to observe and take pictures. Carp assured the reporters that anything sunk was no longer armed, and the wreckage on the ocean bottom was actually creating a man-made reef. He called it, "A last bit of practice for the boys in the batteries before the work in Europe is finished."

Ultimately, no one, civilian or soldier, cared much about the loss of a few German sailors, and life on the base and around Rehoboth Beach went on as usual.

Franklin received his Bronze Star, not forgetting to appreciate the irony in receiving an award made out of such a boring metal. Like Colonel Carp said, he was on a plane to the Pacific within two days.

Franklin did not attempt to get back in touch with Israel before leaving. For all he knew Israel was dead from either the shot to his head or from the blow he'd sustained from Radish. With little time to sort out his possessions, he collected anything that would fit in a safety-deposit box from his storage garage and paid Vernon Nutter a two-year, up-front rent to continue housing the rest.

In hindsight, Franklin realized that the gold had hardly been the reason he teamed up with Israel. Like Israel, a man who could have done anything with his own two hands, Franklin found a certain excitement in sneaking around. He wanted to use the US Army against itself. He wanted to be fed and paid by them, while at the same time see how close he could come to stealing directly from them, for no other reason than to satisfy his curiosity. He also realized that Colonel Carp was doing the same thing. Whether out of bitterness or boredom, the colonel raced right along Franklin's own ambitions. Carp's rank had been the advantage over Franklin that got him to the *Jacinta* first.

•

Within a month of his transfer to California the war in the Pacific came to its fiery end, and Franklin found himself at another crossroad in his life. He had a good military record, and enough experience from his time served, plus a college degree, that it wasn't difficult to find a civilian job. But Franklin did not fare well during his post-military life. The violence and tension that he experienced was enough to trigger an instability in his mind that made it difficult for him to function in his work and personal life. His doctors claimed that he was suffering from a tenuous mental state, which they attributed to his time in the Army. Franklin agreed with the diagnosis, although he knew that his anxiety was not the result of any frontline action.

Often he could not sleep, and many nights he woke in a cold sweat, with his heart racing. But he did not wake up from visions of bombs, landmines, or the din of war. Instead, Franklin's visions were of Sergeant Radish standing on the dunes with no head above his shoulders. Sometimes the decapitated specter stood exactly as it had when Franklin saw it. Other nights the body stood in front of a moon that was so big and bright it made the body feature-less. And some nights, Radish's body rode up and down the beach in military jeeps or on horseback. But the worst nightmares were the ones that began with a calm nighttime beach. In these scenes, the waves were small and lapped at the sand as if they were the edge of a lake, and out on the horizon, against the moonless sky, floated a distant ship; a sailboat. The boat did not move or make any headway, and as it floated, dark against the pitch-black backdrop, a sadistic wind

301

howled into every corner of his mind. And just when Franklin thought it couldn't get any worse, the screeching morphed into the pained, bellowing call of Sergeant Jameson Radish.

Franklin's nightmares resulted in such a lack of sleep that his ability to focus was diminished. He remedied his insomnia with a nightly ritual of drinking rum until he passed out. The rum turned off his mind enough that while he was unconscious he was not burdened with dreams. But this was not quality sleep, and soon he found himself so tired throughout his days that he could not stay awake at his desk. And even though his naps were not long, ominous visions crept in. So, he carried a flask of rum with him wherever he went. And soon enough, he found himself unemployed.

Luckily for Franklin, not having a full-time job seemed to do him some good. He was able to schedule his life any way he wanted, and didn't have to explain to anyone why he was late, or why he looked so tired, or why he smelled of alcohol. After a decade of civilian life, his nightmares tapered off, and as his sleep improved, his mental health released the grip it had over his nerves. He never wanted for food again; whether or not he was employed, he always had a stash of gold and silver that kept him able to afford any necessities. And he always tried to pay closer attention to the simpler things; grass blowing in the breezes, the distant smells of the ocean, and of course, the stage of the moon.

•

It wasn't long after Franklin left the Army that he renewed his treasure hunting along the beaches of Southern California. He bought himself a high-end commercial metal detector, and learned where all the best spots were supposed to be. But the bounty there was much less than his experience along the Delaware coast. And soon enough, he moved back east. He made a quick, and anxious, trip back to Vernon Nutter's and to the Georgetown Savings & Trust, to collect his treasures. He could not bring himself to stay long in Delaware. Too much baggage waited along those shores for him to handle. So, he sold his parents' Baltimore row-home and moved his mother and himself to the east coast of Florida. Through a bit of research he learned that the shipwrecks off the Florida coast were as vast as the area around the Hen & Chickens Shoal, and to his relief, his research was not wrong. The coast of Florida was ripe with so much Spanish gold that he never had to work for anyone again.

Despite his leisurely new lifestyle, Franklin often thought about his time at Fort Miles. He had taken as much from Israel Mouzellas as he had from his experience in the Army. *Possibly more,* he thought, as he swept his metal detector over the sand. He made it a point to only treasure hunt in the morning hours, when the sun was barely above the horizon. The Florida temperatures were cooler during that time, and he also wanted to be covert, but still up during the light of day, as the moon at night set off an anxiety in him that he found difficult to manage.

TREASURE

The speaker on his detector popped out a low buzz, and Franklin froze the sensor disc over the spot. After a few scoops into the sand he had another gold coin. Though he had long ago lost count of how many pieces of gold he owned, Franklin's heart still sped up a little bit every time he found one. He knelt above the hole and brushed the wet sand off of his palm. It was a beautiful Spanish ounce coin, turned to a matte amber in the light of the rising sun. As Franklin stared at his new treasure he heard a whistle that reminded him of someone he used to know. He sprang to his feet and aimed his .44 up the beach in a single movement, ready to put a round in whoever was foolish enough to spy on him. He scanned the low berm of dunes that stretched to pinpoints in both directions, squeezing the coin in his left hand until its ancient imprint pressed its pattern in his skin.

Other than a few screeching seagulls, he was the only living soul on the beach.

CPSIA information can be obtained
at www.ICGtesting.com
Printed in the USA
BVHW042302291121
622764BV00013B/596